LOON RANGERS

Loon Rangers

James McVey

Saddle Road Press

Loon Rangers © 2021 James McVey

Saddle Road Press
Ithaca, New York
saddleroadpress.com

Cover art "Loons Call Here" © David Grath

Book design by Don Mitchell

ISBN 9781736525845
Library of Congress Control Number: 2021940502

Books by James McVey
The Wild Upriver and Other Stories
The Way Home: Essays on the Outside West

v1.3

And in your lonely flight,
haven't you heard the music in the night,
faint as a will 'o the wisp,
crazy as a loon,
sad as a gypsy
serenading the moon

Johnny Mercer, "Skylark"

THERE, SHE SAYS, *pointing to the restless clouds swirling above the high peaks. Do you see?*

A flock of Canada geese flies north along the mountains, vanishing in a shroud of mist, as ghost fingers wrap around the rain-soaked peaks. The geese break free of the clouds, moving up-valley in formation until a white plume collapses upon them again. Back and forth like this, in and out of tattered clouds snagging on the granite peaks ... glimpses of something nearly there but never quite. And then a rent from deep inside the maelstrom ... a crag of Adirondack black rock etched in a patch of blue. And the geese again: cutting a V through the breaking sky like an arrow shot straight into the north ...

"Do you see?" she says, tapping a finger on the windshield, bending her lithe frame around the steering wheel to get a better look, cranking the window down to hear the distant harangue of big birds calling ....

With three days of rain taking leave and those big honkers on the wing, I could feel the rumblings of spring stirring under my skin. Be it the angle of sunlight, the scattering clouds, or just some inner beast preened and ready for another turn of season, I felt it as sure as a warm wind fanning the glow of dormant coals. I felt it all right, swirling inside with all that god-rendered fury going on in the high country.

The rain had been bad enough, the rain and two days penned up in a stuffy conference room in Albany, poring over government protocol. About as much as a wildlife initiate could stand. But we were gone now, free from agency headquarters, heading north into the mountains.

From here on out, it's all official business. We're field techs, Annie and I, duly commissioned to conduct a common loon survey under the auspices of the non-game unit of the New York State Department of Environmental Conservation, thrown together by some quirky roll of the dice to spend the summer canoeing the lakes and waterways of the northern Adirondacks. Annie: wildlife biologist, dedicated to the protection of wildlands and endangered species. Me: recidivist drifter, serving a sentence of community service under the state's alternative rehabilitation program. Everything happens for a reason, people say. This may or may not be the case, though I don't know how anyone could know for sure. And even if they could know, there's no guarantee that it's going to be a reason they like. I've also heard there's a place for everything in this world. A place for everything, everything in its place. This one I know to be a lie. A cruel joke, plain and simple.

"Mind if we stop?" I say, pointing to a roadside store just off the highway.

Annie shoots me a sideways glance before guiding the state vehicle down the exit ramp and onto the parking lot. The car splashes through potholes to the hiss of muddy water on hot pipes.

When she cuts the ignition, I hear the ticking of the engine and I know she's watching as I step around the puddles on my way to the store. But it's more than just watching, it's like she's reading my thoughts. I noticed it first in the conference room during one of our long afternoon sessions. With all those guidelines and directives and memoranda piling up in front of us, it was all I could do to keep from leaping across the table and throttling Frank, our boss. Kinky black hair, pale city skin, the tinted lenses of his glasses smudged with finger grease, he brandished the state shield like a seal of approval—droning on about regulations and conduct and public relations. Meanwhile, I'm staring at the flowering rhododendron outside the big picture window through the runnels of rain flowing down the glass, when I notice Annie looking at me, eyes riveted, and I swear I hear her thinking to herself ... *what a strange bird, every nerve on edge, staring out the window like some wild animal in a cage.*

It's dark and dingy inside the store, east-coast old. Aisles of ho-hos and cheezos, beer nuts and candy bars. I find what I'm looking for and start for the counter. Standing beneath a rack of stacked cigarette packs, the clerk slides the box of beer across faded formica, punching numbers on the register. A bell rings and the drawer pops open. Big white numbers in the window.

"Six seventy-five," he says.

I pull out the requisite forms and begin to process the transaction, exactly as I was shown in Albany.

"You work for the DEC," the clerk says, studying the voucher. "Maybe you can answer something for me." A greasy STP hat keeps the long hair out of his face. "What's going on with the striped bass in the Hudson? Am I gonna be able to fish for them again?"

I'm filling out the blue voucher, when Annie walks up beside me.

"Actually, this is the person you need to talk to," I say. "I was just telling this gentleman here that you, I mean, *we* work for the DEC, and he had a question about the, uh ..."

"Stripers."

"Yeah, the stripers. Maybe you can fill him in about that while I square up. Which reminds me," I say, perusing the selection of rolling tobacco on the shelf next to the tins of chew. "Why dontcha throw in a pouch of that Dutch leaf there. Yeah, that's the one."

The man rings it up. "Total of seven-ninety."

Annie peeks around my shoulder as I complete the form, then turns to the man behind the counter. "Numbers are way down," she explains. "No one knows why, but it's probably due to a combination of things: over-fishing, decimation of spawning beds, pollution. You're not going to want to eat them, anyway."

"Why's that?"

"They're contaminated with PCBs. General Electric has been polluting the river for decades, and, honestly, there's no telling when the fishery will recover, if it ever does."

"And there you go, sir," I say, pushing the blue slip across the counter. Picking up the tobacco and beer in one fell swoop, I nod to the man in the STP hat.

On our way to the car, I can feel Annie's eyes upon me.

"Research materials," I explain, holding up the box of beer.

"You realize those vouchers are only supposed to be used for gasoline and emergencies."

"Believe me," I say, walking in the pale sunlight, noticing for the first time the bright green color of her eyes. "This classifies."

Back on the highway, Annie guns the state-issue six-cylinder until all 250 horses are wound tight. And with a stream of R & B pouring over the FM waves, the red Impala pings and haws its way up the long hills (*Fly, oh mighty chariot! Up the Northway! Over Leatherstocking vale to the Great Adirondack Park!*) before racing downhill in a jackhammer shimmy like it might fly apart at any moment. Bad alignment, or maybe the wheels need balanced. Either way, it's not my concern. The old coupe is state property, like everything else here ... including the beer in the back seat.

I pop the caps on two bottles with my pocketknife, handing one to Annie. Back in my element now, I ask her about the business of wildlife.

"It's what I do," she replies. "Non-game, I mean. Endangered species."

She looks out the car window at the forest passing by.

"Actually, I started off in the game unit," she says. "I went to work in the fall during deer season, and they put me at a highway rest area at one of the checkpoints for hunters. After a week of checking teeth, the job started to get to me. Maybe it was seeing all those carcasses, I don't know. Maybe the higher-ups thought it'd be good P.R. to have a woman out there with all the hunters. If they weren't thinking about public relations then, they certainly were later."

She takes a swig of beer when a change comes over her. I see it in her eyes, a faraway look, and for a moment she's somewhere else.

"What happened?" I ask.

"I saw hundreds of deer, strapped on the roofs of cars or stiff in the back of pickups. And I couldn't help notice after a while how each of them had been killed. I started paying attention to the wounds—who did it right and who bungled the job. I'd ask the hunters how each buck was taken, but I didn't really need to. I could tell already. If I knew they were lying, I let them know about it.

"Word got out I was hassling the hunters, so they transferred me to non-game. One day I'm up to my elbows in gore, the next I'm digging scat holes for captive bald eagles. Which was fine by me, it's what I wanted all along," she says. "Non-game, I mean. It's where I belong."

Maybe Annie isn't the company drone I pegged her for back in Albany. She has spirit, that much is certain, and her rough-hewn beauty makes for pleasant company, especially when the wind musses her hair. Hers is a natural beauty from the inside out. Thin but not slight, a body that requires little maintenance. Flaxen hair down to her shoulders. And those clear hazel eyes.

"How did you get interested in wildlife in the first place?" I continue.

She looks at me before turning her attention back to the road. "And why do you want to know?"

"Just curious, I guess." I keep my eyes straight ahead, listening to the whine of tires on the highway. "We're partners, after all."

She checks me out again but now it's more serious, like I'm getting close to something important and she wants to know if I'm up to the task.

"Let's just say I'm in the business of helping animals. Mobile freelance work, responding to emergencies at a moment's notice."

"No kidding," I reply. "Sounds like you've been out saving the world."

I mean it to be funny, but it doesn't come across that way. And now I'm feeling on edge though I can't exactly put my finger on it, like when you know you should be having a good time but you're not. Some kind of undertow pulling me in a different direction. It doesn't make any sense. I mean, here I was: a second-hand canoe lashed to the roof, a Chevy block humming under my feet, drinking beer with a fine-looking woman while blazing a trail through Leatherstocking country under a springtime sun all set to roll back winter's grip. Life made simple ... and yet the pangs persisted. The funk festered. I knew the beast well. I also knew that if I ran fast enough, I could outrun it.

"And what about you?"

I could outrun *anything*.

"Tell me about you now," she says. "I read in the report you're doing this as some kind of work program, parole or something."

"Suspended sentence ...." I start, ready with the canned retort. The well-rehearsed cover.

But that's as far as I go. Maybe I just don't care enough to explain myself. Or maybe it's Annie, the way she looks at me. Easy to lose your bearings, looking into eyes like that. Like the calm at the center of a hurricane.

But where have the last six years gone, anyway?

All just a rat's nest of twisted and tangled memories. Surely, I could undo the mess, go back in reverse order and unravel the snags one by one to arrive at some facsimile of the past according to a sequence of events that might, in the end, add up to some pattern or purpose.

But there were gaps. Serious gaps. I'd lived in too many places, bunked under too many roofs, for anything to take hold. I had phone numbers and street names in my address book for places where I'd lived that, try as I might, rang no bell whatsoever—not even a mental picture of a house or room or neighborhood. And of the places and scenes that I could recall, they refused to line up in any logical order that might indicate some semblance of method, let alone progress. Sure, there was a job here, a woman there, but, overall, it added up to nothing more than happenstance. It's as if all the years weren't made of time at all, but rather a thick fog of confused feelings and jumbled thoughts all stirred and blurred somewhere deep inside the nether regions of my interstitials. Life as a funhouse, with no way out. A silent movie I was forced to watch again and again, the black-and-white scenes flowing one into the next ....

"I've seen your file," she says. "I believe the magistrate wrote something about 'a general disregard for authority, demonstrated in repeated acts of social deviance'."

But it hardly matters, Annie, don't you see?

"Of course, he concludes by calling you a 'good-hearted roustabout who means no harm'."

The Impala drones on.

"Your record is impressive: Disorderly Conduct, Trespass, Possession of a Controlled Substance ...."

"Wrong place, wrong time," I reply.

"I did have a question about one of the charges," she says. "'Walking to Endanger'?"

A gust of wind blows through the open window, pushing a lock of hair across her face.

"I was walking home one night after closing the bar, having a time of it with the cobblestone sidewalk and rose bushes. A cop happened by and noticed the blood on my shirt. I don't think he knew what to do exactly, but he figured he ought to do something. 'Walking to Endanger' was the best he could come up with."

She looks at me, a hint of mischief in those green eyes. "Let me guess, endangering yourself," she says.

Either she knows where I'm coming from, or she sees right through me. Maybe both.

"Besides," I say, turning the tables, "why take a chance on a derelict like me?"

She looks out her window at the land rolling by. "You do have some redeeming qualities," she replies. "You're at the Forestry School and, physically, you should be up to the demands of the job. Plus, Frank saves money on you. The truth is, we're badly under-funded and under-staffed. And with your record, you come cheap."

I reach back for another beer and look outside at the confused sky. Suddenly, the loon project has lost some of its luster. Joke's on me, I guess. But what defense is there against a past that lies in wait, ready to pounce when you least expect it? All the ghosts in the closet ready to come back and bite your ass, until one day you wake to find yourself a spectator to your own life as you go through the motions in the cheesy B Western you've created for yourself? One foot in, one foot out.

No, the plan is still on. Get through the summer, stay out of trouble, put in my time and move on. Worry about the details later. If things get squirrelly, I just fall back on my wits—those razor-sharp instincts honed over the years in the company of dubious miscreants. In fact, seen in the right light, this summer job is testament to my time-honored code. It's a cover, as good as any. Keep a low profile, fly under the radar, stay out of the crosshairs. Slip around unseen in the spaces in-between. And whatever happens, *just keep moving.*

"Have you ever seen a loon in the wild?"

Don't ever stop moving.

"Loons," she says. "Ever seen one?"

I study the label on my Ballantine: Purity, Body, Flavor. The three rings of success, right there on the bottle. Drinking and driving—it's the one thing I can do as well as anyone.

"I just spent three days with one back in Albany."

Annie exits the highway, following the signs for Keene, passing white clapboard houses with red geraniums in the flowerboxes. In town, Old Glory flies from nearly every front stoop. Funny thing, all those flags. And now there's a cop in the middle of the road, signaling for us to stop, his white glove fluttering in the air like a dove.

I stash the empties and hide my beer beneath the seat for good measure. I'm trying to figure out what the cop wants, when I see a second policeman farther up the road, halting oncoming traffic. Meanwhile, the tattered remnants of storm clouds swirl through the village, like ghosts running from door to door. It seems the cops have stopped traffic to give them one last chance to get out of town.

I'm still trying to make sense of everything when I see a group of old-timers in military regalia, marching up a side-street, coming our way. One carries a flagpole fixed on his hip. The war veterans are flanked by a drummer and a guy blowing the flute. Only it's not a flute, it's a *fife*. And that's when it hits me. In all the commotion back in Albany, all the instruction and talk and sorting of gear, I lost track of the days.

"Memorial Day," I say.

As the veterans turn onto Main Street, passing in front of us, I can guess which wars they were in. The oldest man marches alone in front, a soldier from the Great War, no doubt. The next four are from the Big War, that's fairly obvious, looking dapper in berets and green coats with chevrons. The three bringing up the rear are veterans of Korea.

A couple dozen spectators line the street and applaud when the veterans pass by. Just then the mist gathers thick along the pavement, and it makes for quite a sight, what with the fife and drum, colorful flags, and a band of old warriors marching knee-deep in fog. Looming in the background, the granite flank of Mount Marcy glistens in broken sunlight.

The parade concludes without fanfare. The cop waves his white glove, and we continue on our way past manicured lawns, quaint homes, and a green sign at the edge of town informing us that it's ten miles to Lake Placid, fifteen to Saranac Lake (*out across the rolling landscape through hills and dales of farms and forests and rivers*) when I get to wondering about the other guys, the ones from the last war, and where they might be. It's possible that a town so small didn't send anyone, but if all these other vets are here, chances are there's a few who spent time in Indochina (*through the Keene Valley past John Brown Farm and the Nordic complex, crossing the river by Olympic ski jumps, skirting the condo villas near Lake Placid, passing the regional office at Ray Brook, and down into the valley).*

Stars in the windows. The friend down the road whose brother came back in a box. The tally of dead flashed every night on the screen of a black-and-white RCA, for those keeping score at home. The war that never was. The defeat that never took place. And where was everyone now? Where did they go? Faded away like nothing ever happened.

(... coming into Saranac from the east, the road winding between boat houses and ice cream stands along the banks of Lake Flower, where an impressionistic tableau flashes across the water—a clock tower rising above the village, the bright neon of a gas station, clapboard houses crouching beneath billowing spruce where an old man rocks in his chair in the fading light of a screenedin porch ... turning west at the light into the village proper and a narrow canyon of windowed alcoves and wooden storefronts. Gone is the spit and polish of Lake Placid. This is the rough-and-tumble Adirondacks, tamed a bit compared to the olden days when a man could by gawd do anything he felt was in him to do. Tamed some, maybe, but not all the way. A town like this can make a fellow as comfortable as the next, if'n he wants it that way. But that's not always how he wants it, not if he's got a little hell to burn ...)

We drive in silence, sizing up the town that's to be our home for the next three months. A half dozen motorcycles are parked in front of a bar where a crowd of people pack the outside porch. Across the street, beneath the brick clock tower, a courthouse stands between a market on one side and a deli on the other. A boy wheels down the street on a stingray bicycle, one hand hooked in the gills of a twenty-inch northern.

The road forks at an old hotel, winding past a post office and firehouse and more taverns than I can count. Crossing railroad tracks at the edge of town, we pass the last of the houses on our approach to Lake Colby. A narrow drive turns left off the highway and follows the lake around to a large compound situated between the grassy bank and a steep, wooded hill. The lane curls past lone evergreens before looping around a flowerbed in front of an old house where we park the car. The cobblestone structure is impressive if a bit ostentatious. Must have been quite the chalet back in its day, but now it looks like a glorified nut house. A fancy one, but a nut house just the same. It stands two stories high with big picture windows facing the lake and a cupola perched on top. The roof is copper, steeply pitched. Adjacent to the house is a dining hall, tucked among the trees. And beyond that, a circle of cabins.

I grab my rucksack and start for the house. Inside the door, I drop my pack at the foot of the staircase and make a quick tour of the lower level. A spacious living and dining room take up the east wing, with a large fireplace along the far wall. A chandelier hangs above a long, polished table with high-back chairs. The kitchen in back, with high cupboards and a wooden table. A porter's chute in one of the walls.

On the other side of the staircase, a hallway leads to the west wing. I follow it through two crooked turns, all the way to the end where I come upon three closed doors. Curiosity gets the better of me, as I turn the faceted glass knob of the door on the left. It opens with a *whoosh* of cold air, black as pitch. I reach inside for a light switch along the stone wall, finding only cobwebs that cling to my hand.

From the other end of the hallway, Annie calls my name. Just as well, I think. Best to leave these three doors for daylight.

When I return to the living room, she's reading a piece of paper.

"It's from the caretaker," she explains. "Says he'll drop by day after tomorrow to check on us. The bedrooms are upstairs. I took the one in front overlooking the lake."

I climb the stairs and unload my gear in the back bedroom, stuffing my clothes in a small dresser next to an old bed with metal springs and iron frame. At least the mattress is decent. A window looks out to the slope of a steep hill. I'll check this out later, too. Right now, it's best if I slip outside and get some air.

I bound down the stairs on my way to the front door, pausing at the entrance, aching to get outside into the gathering twilight where I can find a little space.

"Just be ready early," Annie says, walking toward the dining room table with two hiking boots in her hand.

I take another look down the crooked hallway, reminded of the long road of twists and turns that has landed me here in *this place now*. Funny how time sneaks up on you, until you find yourself someplace you could never have imagined. It's like we're all puppets on a stage, pulled by strings we can't see for reasons we'll never know. Maybe it was something we did in a previous life, and we're only now paying the price for it.

Damn ....

I charge out of the house, taking the outside steps in one leap as the screen door slams behind me—the sound ricocheting down the back alleys of memory to my childhood cabin, flushing a bevy of Kodachrome images, haunting and terrific. At the edge of the asphalt, I start down a footpath leading into the dark forest ...

Damn but a guy sometimes gets driven to the shadows.

... quick and quiet through the trees, around bulging roots and granite, like a catamount on the prowl under a rising moon, flecks of quicksilver scattered across the water ...

It may be nothing he's done, but he gets pushed and pushed some more until there's no place left to go—so he hides in the shadows where the black gathers thick, to forget himself for a while. To envision coming out again. To wonder what it was that drove him there in the first place.

Inside a dense pocket of spruce, I take a seat on the trunk of a felled tree—tilting my head toward the deepest darkness I can find, blowing the urgency from my lungs, taking my place among the nocturnal sounds that resume now after a brief interlude: the bark of bullfrogs from a nearby slough, the shrill of crickets, the sigh of a wanton breeze in the boughs overhead. All is formless, with only the cadence of sound in the air.

"Damn."

(The word appears of its own volition, like a gasp out of black and murky water. No moral appeal, for those bittersweet days are long gone. No, it stands alone as a simple, across-the-board soliloquy. Let loose to wander the night to alight on the bough of a spruce, slip through its silver needles to settle on a frond of arching fern, slide to the ground to seep into soft and spongy earth ...)

And that's when I hear it. Coming off the lake, piercing the night air. The wail of a loon.

I turn to listen. A faint trace of moonlight shines on the branch above me. A star snaps in the night sky. The outlines of trees and mountains.

Standing up to leave, I brush the moss off the seat of my pants. Picking my way through the forest, I find the trail and start back for the house, walking along the lake until I stop and try to make sense of everything. Looking up at the tilted cup of moon, I sigh. The loon wails again, high and lonesome in the spooky half-light over the lake: let *gooooo!* let *gooooo!*

THIS OUGHT TO BE SIMPLE ENOUGH: canoe a hundred lakes, look for loons, and write down what we see. In all these miles of backwoods, I'd have to go pretty far out of my way to find any real trouble. Get lost in a place like this, and I might never find the way back.

As wildlife techs, our job is to repeat a survey that was conducted three years earlier on the same lakes. The earlier group spent an entire summer searching for loons in the northern Adirondacks—recording all sightings, describing behavioral tendencies, noting what calls were made under what circumstances. They examined the territorial limits of each pair they found and monitored the movements of single birds. Most important, they tracked the reproductive success of breeding pairs, recording the location of each nest, counting the number of eggs, measuring the adjacent water depth at five-foot intervals. They monitored nesting behavior, entered hatch dates, and kept tabs on the chicks throughout the summer. And they made entomological entries, going so far as to gut a Brook Trout to determine the contents of its last meal.

Covering the same rivers and lakes, Annie and I will record the same type of data on the same forms that were used in the earlier study. Our results—along with those collected by two other crews in different parts of the state— will then be compared to the results from the first survey in order to establish statistical data on the reproductive success and population trends of loons in New York State.

With this data, the DEC will then make a determination regarding the viability of the species in New York. Presently, the state classifies the common loon as a "species of special concern," which compels the DEC to monitor its population numbers and trends. If numbers are down from the earlier study, or if there is a decline in reproductive success, state wildlife officials have the option to downgrade the loon's status to "threatened" thereby granting it more protection. If the situation looks really dire, the loon could be listed as "endangered," which would trigger even more protection. In addition to collecting loon data, we've been instructed to expand our field notes to include all other wildlife that we might encounter. The Audubon Society, in cooperation with the state, is conducting a general bird survey for the greater Adirondack region, and we've been told to assist them by recording any and all bird identifications.

Like I say, it all seems simple enough. And except for a few minor glitches—not the least of which is the fact that due to some disagreement between our predecessors and Frank, half of the data collected in the earlier study was withheld and remains at large—all systems are go. We have our assignment and now it's just a matter of execution. We are foot soldiers in the war to protect the common loon, charged to defend its viable and lasting presence in New York waters.

We rise early on our first day and drive to Lower Saranac Lake. By eight o'clock we have the aluminum canoe in the lake, and by nine we're taking on water. I trace the leak to a neat row of rivets under the bow seat. We're able to stay on the lake for just over an hour, before we have to drag the battered craft ashore and drain it.

At 2,285 acres, Lower Saranac is an enormous lake with a number of small islands. A dense fog covers the calm water for most of the morning, and sometimes all we see beyond the canoe is our wake trailing behind. Occasionally, the fog clears enough for us to glimpse the forested shoreline and a nearby island.

By midmorning the fog burns off altogether, as a steady breeze picks up and the islands appear one by one across the blue lake, rising above the water like the peaks of underwater mountains. If nothing else this first day, we find a rhythm and routine to our work as well as a few tricks to save us time. If, from a distance, we determine a segment of shoreline to be nothing more than a wave-battered rock wall, we circumvent the area and head straight for the far point, confident that no loon would nest in such a place. Annie scans the shoreline with her binoculars while I paddle and keep us on course. It's a mutually satisfactory arrangement. She provides the brains, I provide the brawn. Periodically, she'll do a 360 with the binoculars to see if there's a loon behind us—a loon that may have abandoned its nest and retreated to open water, without us noticing.

We spend the day combing the shoreline from Kelly Slough to Crescent Bay. Late in the afternoon, just as the sun slips behind a bank of clouds over Shingle Bay, we come upon a marshy point, surrounded by tamarack with all its silver needles waving in the wind. We paddle along the hummocks, looking for any sign of loons—a nest, an egg, a telltale feather. Finding nothing, we drag ashore and empty the canoe of gear (daypack, binocs, topo map, clipboard, cushions and paddles), drain the water, and get ready for the long paddle back.

It's a good mile across the lake to where the car is, and we'll be battling a cross wind. At first it's not so bad, but when we paddle out beyond the point, the waves begin to hammer the hull. Water splashes into the canoe, as the wind pushes us sideways in stiff gusts. I spread my feet wide on the floor, keeping an eye on Annie for any sudden shift in weight. But she keeps it steady, even when we roll over high waves.

Water leaking at the seam, waves splashing over the gunwale, we paddle portside into the teeth of the wind. The take-out comes into view as the sun breaks free of the clouds, scattering shards of glittering light across the water. The distant peninsulas turn blue as the lake catches fire with sun diamonds. Awash in liquid light, Annie turns around to look at me, her green eyes shining.

There are times in life when you think you have it all figured out. The moment sneaks up on you unawares, and it doesn't last long. But for a while, anyway, you swear you have it down cold. The feeling might linger for a bit, but eventually it slips away, and all you're left with is an empty shell of a thought. You turn the thought over in your head, trying to recapture the magic, only to whittle it down into some worthless platitude. And then you're back to square one, no wiser for the experience. That's why I put my faith in the close at hand. Seems to me the only thing a person can hang their hat on in this world. But even that is not foolproof.

It was Annie's idea that I keep the journal. Frank told us back in Albany to keep a running log of things as a way of supplementing the field notes. Feel free, he said, to record additional observations about loons or anything else related to the survey. Write it all down in a notebook and turn it in with the data at the end of summer. The way he looked at me when he said it made me think there was some other reason for the journal that he wasn't letting on to, like the State of New York had other ideas for what we'd write down.

I thought Annie should be in charge of the journal, since she was the professional. But she didn't think that would be fair to me, so we flipped a coin. Loser keeps the journal. I gave her a week to change her mind, but she wouldn't have any part of it. A bet's a bet, she said. One way to look at this story, then, is on account of a blown wager. But it hardly seems the first time. Sometimes I get the feeling that most things can be explained by a lost bet made long ago in some faraway place by long-forgotten people playing with house money.

Eventually, I got around to purchasing a 10" x 8" composition book at the local market and sat down one night in the cupola to hatch a plan of attack. On the outside cover, I wrote, "STATE OF NEW YORK — 1984," since, technically, the journal belongs to Albany. At least according to Frank. Which is fine by me. This way I'm not accountable, since I can hardly take responsibility for something that's not mine. Annie couldn't totally disagree with this line of reasoning when I explained it to her, although she did say to be sure to include what she would want to see in the journal. So I've done that, too. I've made sure to tell her side of the story, just so long as it doesn't disrupt the overall flow. It's not easy to keep an objective record of scientific work, but I've set out to do the best job I can.

"The world is going to hell, you know."

I wake to two bulging eyes behind thick lenses and large rectangular frames, three feet from my face. This after a fitful night of sleep. Dreams galore. Nasty nightmares.

"To hell in a hand basket, you can bet your bottom dollar."

The eyes blink, only something's not right. They're not lined up properly. They're like cockeyed headlights on a car, where one beam shines on the road and the other veers somewhere into space. Not only that, one of the eyeballs moves around while the other one stays steady.

Now he's pacing the floor, waving his arms with a folded newspaper in his hand, a ring of keys swinging from his hip. "Nobody wants to face facts, but the signs are everywhere. Everything is out of whack, turned upside down. You have birds and animals all over the world in places where they don't belong, strange diseases set loose, the sky raining poisons. *Don't you see?* The four horsemen are upon us. Overpopulation, pollution, extinction, and now this!" he says, slapping the folded newspaper with the back of his hand. "*Global warming!* Can you believe it? We are actually changing the climate. The Great Tribulation is at hand, I tell you. Three-quarters of all life on Earth will be wiped out!"

I pull on my jeans and slowly make my way into the hall. "Annie?"

"She's gone to town," he says.

From the hallway I get a better look at him: slight build, thin hair, pocked complexion. Jumpy as all get out, like he just put his finger in a wall socket.

"I'm the caretaker here," he says. "Fillmore's my name, but most people just call me 'Flashlight' on account of my eye. Let me show you around."

He leads me downstairs to the living room. "You'll notice the phonograph in the corner over there. Feel free to use it when you want, the fireplace too. Telephone is in the hallway at the top of the stairs."

In front of the fireplace is a red love seat. A large oriental rug covers most of the floor. Against the wall is a tall grandfather clock, next to a number of painted portraits with gilded frames.

"I should tell you about the history of this place," he says. "It was built in the twenties by a prominent theater mogul from New York City. The house was used to entertain distinguished members of the New York theater community. The parties were said to be legendary. The paintings you see here are of important patrons."

I look closer, noting some of the names inscribed in the brass plates along the bottom of the frames: Crandall, Buckminster, Griffith, Taylor, etc.

Flashlight leads me through a swinging door into the kitchen. "When the house was a private residence, every effort was made to keep the servants separate from the main living area. You may have noticed the peculiar layout—stairways that dead-end, doors that open onto walls, different floor levels. The house was remodeled a number of times to suit the whims of its owner. Don't expect it to make any sense."

All the while I'm waiting for Annie to arrive and bail me out. This isn't exactly what I bargained for, first thing in the morning—a tour of the funhouse with some half-baked walleye.

He leads me across the living room and into the west hallway where I was last night. We walk through the crooked turns to the three doors at the end. He opens the door on the right, but there's only a stone wall. "See what I mean?"

"In here," he says, opening the middle door, "is the study."

A cozy room, the study has two reading chairs, a lamp and coffee table. The walls are lined with wooden shelves stuffed with books and magazines in no particular order. A large picture window overlooks the lake where the morning sun sparkles on the water.

"Guess I can add this to the collection," he says, placing the folded newspaper in a cardboard box. "Anyway, feel free to browse at your leisure."

He returns to the hallway, pausing in front of the third door. When he opens it, a draft of cold air forces its way into the hall like the icy breath of a monster locked in the basement.

"No l-light here," Flashlight stammers. "You'll have to find your way the best you can."

I've seen my share of freaks along the way. In my many forays into the nation's underbelly, I'd learned not to judge on appearances. There was the mock gunfighter in Cripple Creek who could extract his glass eye and plop it into a glass of beer; the hobo in Rapid City with wax ears who regaled me with tales from a life on the rails; the one-armed truck driver who gave me a ride across the Everglades, talking all the while about gators and crocs insofar as I could negotiate his thick Bajou accent. So, why not a pop-eyed doomsayer? No big deal. As I had with Annie, after a little give and take, Flashlight and I work out a suitable halfway point from which to relate. A happy middle ground. At least this is what my instincts tell me. Besides, I'm not about to let some dark cold basement get the better of me.

"There's a light switch at the bottom."

I walk down two or three stairs into the dark when I realize that I'm barefoot. No shirt either. Down into the dank stairwell I go, cobwebs twisting around my outstretched arm like cotton-candy at a country fair. The air is cold and black, and I know I'm dead meat for any fanged arachnid lying in wait.

At the bottom of the stairs, feeling the hard dirt underfoot, I grope for the wall and find two insulated electric wires running vertically along a stud. I trace them to a switch plate and snap on the light.

"I've been meaning to fix it up a little," says Flashlight, coming down the stairs.

Together we scan the semblance of a workshop—cobblestone walls, a workbench with shelves full of old tools, a garage door at the far end with two small windows packed with insulation, an old ten-speed bicycle in the corner. "I haven't been down here in quite some time," he says. "Feel free to use this bike, I believe it still works."

The caretaker crosses the dirt floor, rips away the insulation, fumbles with the ring of jangling keys on his belt, before unlocking the aluminum garage door and rolling it open to the sunny day. We spend a few minutes tidying up, yanking spider webs down, pulling power tools out of hiding, making an overall inventory of things. Before we leave, I convince him to keep the garage door unlocked. "So Annie and I can get to the bike," I explain.

As we're ready to return upstairs, he pauses in front of a low doorway leading into what looks to be a storage room for old furniture. I take it there's something he wants me to see, so I peer around him to get a better look.

"On the back wall there is the breaker panel," he says, "in case you blow a fuse."

Just then a voice from the top of the stairs.

"Miles, is that you?" It's Annie, calling me from above. "Let's get at it, we have work to do."

I start up the stairs before pausing to look at Flashlight. "Don't forget about the door," I say.

We spend the day finishing off Lower Saranac. As it did yesterday, a thick fog covers the lake in the morning. We set out for Little Fox Island even though we can't see it from shore. After a few minutes on the lake, water begins to swell in the riveted seam along the aluminum floor of the canoe. The fog grows thicker as the morning turns progressively darker, just as I remember it years earlier in Seattle under the shadow of a solar eclipse.

Annie stops paddling and peers into the fog ahead, beads of water dripping from her paddle onto the calm surface. I see the wake first, ripples spreading across the water. A shadow in the mist. Then the russet neck of a bird, twisted in some weird contortion. Bill pointed to the sky, the creature gulps at the bulge in its neck as we drift past. Merganser, Annie says. Swallowing a fish, I add. As suddenly as it appears, the bird fades into the fog behind us, vanishing in the gray oblivion.

Tooth and claw of nature, up close and personal.

Little Fox materializes before us like a ghost ship, adrift on a calm sea, nary a wave to lap against its rocky shore. We paddle around back and pull the canoe onto a grassy bank, then flip it on edge to let the water drain. I right the canoe, straighten up the gear, and join Annie on a patch of moss under a pine tree. The rocks are covered with lichen, wild blueberry grows along the bank. She offers me her bag of granola and I take a handful.

"Would you nest here?"

"No," she replies, staring at the dirty stone grill along the ground, crushed soda cans in the ash. "It's good habitat, everything you could want—an island, plenty of access along the leeward shore, deep water all the way around …. There's just one problem."

All the islands on Lower Saranac tell the same story. Nearly all have a camping grill cemented in place. Some even have a picnic table. Prime habitat, for sure, but not a snowball's chance for nesting loons. We make a thorough check anyway, paddling around each island, going about our official business in this weird wrinkle of history between pushing the bird out of its habitat and wishing it back … between the eons it has occupied these islands and the god-knows-how-many years before it will again. If it ever does.

Everything gets it in the end, that's a fact. And that includes the whole sorry lot of humanity. All-out nuclear war, some rogue virus, a black hole or big fireball from space. Take your pick. Any way you slice it, it's a losing proposition.

And yet, it's funny how Annie reacts. When I asked if she'd nest here, she just gazed at the crushed soda cans in the ash like she was staring into a live fire. And then she giggled, so softly that I barely heard. Mind you, there was nothing cynical about it. It was more like she was getting a kick out of everything. All the world conspiring to crush any sense of hope, and she finds it amusing.

Later that evening, we set up a makeshift office in the cupola. Located down the hall from the bedrooms, the cupola offers a nice, second-story view of the lake. So nice, in fact, we decide to make it the nerve center of our operations. The room is just large enough to fit two wooden chairs and an old, ramshackle desk where we pile our assorted materials—maps, graphs, forms, loon articles. We pin a 30 X 60 Minute topo of the northern Adirondack region on the wall, so as to keep the big picture in mind. There's a candle on the desk with a brass holder that sets a mood conducive to rumination. A handy 7-quart cooler fits perfectly in the far corner, and, if positioned properly, can be accessed from the chair closest to the window. Situated on the desk is an old wooden toolbox with three small drawers that, as it turns out, serve nicely as compartments for substances best kept under wraps. I move the toolbox over to the end of the desk, so that with a little effort, I'm able to reach both the cooler and box from the window chair, even as I lean back and put my feet up on the desk.

When night falls, I clear a space in the corner and start in on a rack of Genesee. Six sweaty cans of sweet mercy. Leaning back in the chair, I gaze through the window to the big oak tree outside, roll a cigarette, and consider the sequence of events that have led up to this current exile in the Adirondacks, wondering what surprises this latest chapter might bring. Someday I'll stop this nonsense of circling back over the years, looking for a pattern in all the random encounters, searching for a clear-cut cause-and-effect that can explain everything—as if a person could actually stop time and line up all the pieces in a neat row.

Someday, but not tonight.

On about the second or third Cream Ale, I figure I'll kill two birds with one stone and start writing in the journal. Since I'm backtracking on the past anyway, might as well be writing it down. Just as soon fill the pages with whatever comes to mind.

So, I open the notebook and begin to describe the first day as best as I remember it. It's been over a week now, so I shouldn't expect to remember everything *exactly* as it happened. The candlelight doesn't help either, making it difficult to see. But I start in with gusto all the same, describing the events more or less as they happened, embellishing a few things to jazz it up a little. It's not long though before I run into a few problems, beginning with verb tense. Should I describe things as if they're happening now, or should I describe them like they've already happened and I'm just now writing it down? People say all we can ever really know is the present moment, and the past and future are only what we think they are *now*. And what we think they are now (that is, the story we tell ourselves they are) changes from moment to moment. This makes sense, I suppose, but even the "moment" seems to be something of a fabrication—just another story. By the time we're done "experiencing" the moment (that is, after we've ignored all that we *could* see in favor of what we *want* to see, then sift it through the filters of mood and memory and send it on ahead to central command which, like any good source of authority, is going to twist it to serve its own purposes) ... well, by then the "moment" we think we're in has surely passed. The moment we're really in at that point (that is, the moment *after* the one we think we're in) keeps happening under our noses without us ever really knowing it. "The moment," then, remains forever elusive. It is never truly known, only imagined from a distant point in time through the smoky spyglass of memory ... and only then do we say we're "living in the moment."

Because the journal is fast becoming a major pain in the ass, I crack open another beer and look for relief in Door #2 of the toolbox. Before I know it, I'm writing along lickety-split, trying to figure out what's involved in writing a journal, when I realize that I'm pretty much making it up as I go and that I should just keep writing and not think about it too much.

But it doesn't take long before I run into another problem: what to call myself. I'm supposed to be scientific here, which means I need to be objective, so maybe I shouldn't use "I" when referring to myself. On the other hand, it sounds strange calling me "he" or "Miles." It's bad enough to have to write about yourself and describe how things looked yesterday or a week ago compared to how they look now, but not knowing what to call yourself makes it doubly intolerable.

This little pickle gets me all tied up, so I turn to Door #3 for courage. Not too much, mind you. Just enough to free the logjam and get things flowing again. And dang if #3 doesn't prove just as fruitful as #2. Feeling the bravado kick in, I resolve to push ahead and call myself any damn thing I please. And as I chug along, I remind myself: whatever you do, don't think about it too much because that's when you (me, I mean) get into trouble. That's when things get knotted up and don't come out right. The words don't square with what they're trying to say. They're just sounds without meaning. Everybody knows words are no good, anyway. Dust motes on the wind. Scattered flotsam on a murky sea of desires and fears, all churned up and mixed together. Words hide the truth, as much as they reveal it.

Anyway, I can always come back later and clean the story up—make things clear that maybe weren't before—even if it means the story becomes less true. Or less *real*, I should say, since it's all true.

So there you have it. What a mess. And to think I didn't even get through describing the first day. Nothing to do, I suppose, but forge ahead. Full-bore, come what may.

We get a late start today, leaving the compound sometime around noon. Driving north out of town, it occurs to me there's something wrong with the car. The engine seems to be running fine, but something doesn't feel right. I believe it has to do with the color—candy apple red. I resolve to get to the bottom of the matter one of these nights in the sanctum of the cupola.

We cover three small ponds on the other side of Upper Saranac without seeing a loon. We find a merganser on Polliwog Pond, but otherwise not much activity to report. Polliwog is a beautiful lake. The high-water signs, however, indicate that it's probably unfit for loon nesting.

Middle Pond sits just west of Polliwog. This is another small pond that we are able to cover quickly. Middle has many snags along the shoreline, as well as big trees that have fallen into the water and lie submerged along the bottom. Floating above these trees is like flying over a shipwreck, looking down into an underwater grave.

A beaver dam at the edge of the pond has raised the water level a foot higher than it would otherwise be. At one end of the lake, along the woody shore, we paddle into a small lagoon surrounded by tamarack and big logs. In this quiet sanctuary, sunlight streams through the forest like shafts of light pouring through the stained-glass windows of a cathedral. We stay long enough to feel the tranquility of the place, before we're accosted by a swarm of black flies— my first encounter with these infernal creatures.

Near the take-out we see a ruby-throated hummingbird, perched in a small tree along the shore. As we study its finer markings, a red-tailed hawk bursts from the shrub directly behind the hummingbird. We watch it flap away, rising for the woods beyond, a small rodent tucked in its hooked bill. Strange that a hawk and hummingbird should share the same bush. On our way out, we hear the *whack* of a beaver tail on the water, somewhere near the dam.

Driving back to town, we pass a young woman roller-skating on the road with ski poles, only they're not your run-of-the-mill roller skates. And this is not your average workout. She's pushing hard in her high-tech gear, digging with her poles on every stride, making her way up a hill with the same movements as a Nordic skier. Dressed in tight, synthetic shorts and shirt, her long blond hair pulled back in a ponytail, she cuts quite a figure on the country road.

Another night in the cupola, another six-pack, another stab at the business at hand: adding up the past to get to the present. Trying to figure out how I got from there to here.

With a little help from Door #1, I start at the beginning and work my way forward, picking up the story where a young boy comes of age in a small mountain town on the downwind side of the Great Divide. Granite and sandstone, spruce and fir, chinook winds and six-foot snows. Fishing for cutthroat, hunting rabbit and deer, panning for gold in the sandy washes of tumbling creeks. Home-schooled on Thoreau and Paine, Woolf and Proust, Twain and Vonnegut. Trudging to the outhouse (running water would come later) in waist-high snow during whiteouts, tethered to a long line of climbing rope knotted to the cabin's brass doorknocker. Peeking under the batwing doors of the local saloon at grizzled miners and tattooed bikers gambling in a blue haze of cigarette smoke.

His dog Billy—an old bulldog chained to a railroad spike hammered into the hardpan out back, who barked and frothed at strangers and once shredded a neighbor's cat that wandered too close. Bringing Billy into his bed at night in the room he shared with his little sister—the labored breathing and mud-flap jowls flecked with spittle, the short wiry hair shed on his flannel sheets. And on those rare occasions when he was let off the chain, Billy knew better than to stray too close to the edge of the forest and the shadowy threat of mountain lion and bear. It was his job to keep Billy fed. Drop a dollop of Alpo into the tin bowl and be done with it.

And on warm summer nights: riding his dirt bike up an old mining road to the high mountain lookout they called Crow's Nest, sitting at the edge of an outcrop, watching the big light-shows down on the Plains—lightning coursing through the heart of towering stratocumuli gathered fifty miles away on the horizon, the dark sky split open in fractured jags of electricity—imagining one day stepping off the mountain and following the lightning eastward, walking through the door of opportunity straight into the heart of the American Dream.

But any charm there might have been to his funky birthplace along the Divide begins to wear thin. Fighting winter winds, day in and day out. Watching his parents (hippies of the sixties, still bearing the torch) scratch out a living, year after year—his mom a librarian, his dad a postman. The futility and boredom of high school. The resentment and creeping despair. And finally the corrosive desire to once and for all escape his hardscrabble hometown and its washed-out freaks, sleazy coke dealers, and New Age dreamers.

And then one Christmas—a present in the mail from the uncle everyone called Hotfoot for his propensity to always pick up and move on. Wrapped in a Hoboken newspaper, a 3-D Automatic Slide Viewer of important American landmarks: the Statue of Liberty rising above the New York Harbor, the Lincoln Memorial surrounded by cherry blossoms, the Liberty Bell at Independence Hall, Monticello and Mount Vernon (was it true George Washington grew hemp?), the Pentagon and New York Stock Exchange. Iconic pillars of the Dream, seared into the soft pink flesh of his imagination, courtesy of Uncle Hotfoot. And the words on the card, written with a shaky hand: *Go East, young man, for there is where your fortune awaits!* In a bold baritone voice, as best as he could remember it from the one and only time they met: *Go East, young man!*

And on the day of his high school graduation—out the door with his rucksack and down to the interstate. Never to return.

It's AN ODD FEELING to know something so well without ever actually seeing it in real life. With the exception of that first night on Colby, my experience with the loon has been purely vicarious. In fact, the only time I can recall seeing a loon in flight was on a television commercial for an off-road truck. And yet, thanks to all the scientific articles Annie brought from Albany, I feel I've gotten to know the bird well.

The common loon (*Gavia immer*) is one of four species in its genus—the others being the yellow-billed, arctic, and red-throated. The loon lineage dates back sixty million years, making it one of the oldest bird species on earth. As a fish-eater, the common loon lives almost exclusively on or near the water, nesting along lakes in North America before flying south in winter to warmer climes along the Atlantic and Pacific coasts. Its summer range extends from Iceland and Greenland, west through Canada and Alaska, all the way to the tip of the Aleutian Islands. *G. immer* is the only loon species to nest in the continental United States. Due to loss of habitat and other manmade factors, the loon's breeding range in the lower forty-eight has been reduced to the northern parts of Minnesota, Michigan, New York State, and New England.

Loons have torpedo-shaped bodies, thick necks, long pointed bills, narrow wings, and short tails. Wingspans can reach up to four feet in length. Their short legs and webbed feet are set back on the body, rendering them virtually immobile on land. A loon's bones are solid, allowing for perfect buoyancy and the ability to dive deep for fish. It can dive deeper and stay under water longer than any other bird, and it can out-swim most fish. Loons have been known to reach depths of 200 feet. On the other hand, because of their solid bones, they are incapable of achieving flight from land and must patter along the water surface for some distance before becoming airborne.

A mating pair needs a considerable geographic area for reproductive success. During mating season, this area will be fiercely defended by one or both birds from any unwelcome intrusion by other loons. The clutch size is typically two eggs per season. While the research is inconclusive, it appears loons mate for life—often returning to the same nesting site year after year. Because of their superior skill as swimmers, they build their nests close to the water's edge. Loons will nest on hummocks, shorelines, or any spit of land adjacent to water. Islands are what they prefer most, especially along leeward shores where there's a deep-water entry.

As I say, except for that first night on Colby, the loon exists for me only in the imagination. And though the adage "you-don't-know-what-you've-got-till-it's-gone" doesn't technically apply here, since loons are still around, their disappearance from New York remains a real possibility. Otherwise, Annie and I wouldn't be here. And yet it's *because* loons still reside in New York, that the specter of extirpation carries with it no real sense of urgency. Not among people, anyway. (Ask a loon and you might get a different answer.) According to my calculations, we're still only in the "you-don't-know-what-you've-got" phase, having yet to cross over into "till-it's-gone." And until that time arrives, as far as I can tell, it's business as usual. Of course, it was business-as-usual that got us to this point in the first place.

In any case, it feels strange to know so much about loons without ever actually seeing one. It must be like what a paleontologist experiences when he spends a lifetime learning everything there is to know about a species that no longer exists, trying to imagine what its life was like. All those facts and mental images rattling around in his brain, you'd think they'd take on a life of their own after a while— spontaneously combust in some kind of chemical reaction whereby the ghost of species past would appear. At that point, of course, everything would change and what started as science would turn into a love affair, a case of romancing the dead. Seducing the genie from the bottle. And as is often the case in love affairs, there comes a point in time when there are no rules and anything goes. After a while, it's not even clear who the seducer is and who's the one being seduced. Sounds twisted, I know, but it can't be any worse than, say, driving an animal to extinction and then honoring it on the state flag.

It occurs to me that in the same way we reimagine the past or future to shed new light on the present, we can do the same with places. I'm thinking of a favorite place of mine just now, a certain redrock promontory in Utah overlooking the Colorado River, imagining what's happening there this very moment. I can almost *feel* the warm breeze rising out of the canyon, *smell* the juniper tree that grows along the ledge, *see* the serpentine course of the muddy river below as clouds sail through a blue sky.

My promontory was there last time I visited, it's there now, and barring any unforeseen cataclysm before sunup, it'll be there tomorrow. The same place at different times, all present in the same moment. Day, night, summer, winter, a hundred years ago, a hundred years from now ... take your pick. On a hot summer day, a driving blizzard howls across the promontory. In the dead of winter, a hummingbird drinks from the red flower of a prickly pear.

But I'm getting off point. And what's the point? We covered three lakes today and saw no loons. Almost two weeks now and still no sign of *Gavia immer*.

THE SAINT REGIS CANOE AREA is a sprawling area northwest of Saranac, with dozens of ponds and lakes fed by untold numbers of brooks and streams. Covering 19,000 acres, the Canoe Area is the largest (and only) wilderness canoe area in the Northeast. No motorboats or aircraft permitted. The Area lies within the Saint Regis River watershed, which drains into the St. Lawrence Seaway further north. The Saranac Lakes, on the other hand, drain into the Saranac River, which flows northeast out of town on its way to Lake Champlain. Both drainages boast an elaborate system of interconnecting waterways that include, at least in the Saranac watershed, a few strategically placed dams and locks.

Because of the wilderness character of Saint Regis, we decide to focus our efforts here in the hopes of finally seeing a loon. We start in the Paul Smiths area with a few small ponds that have easy access. But, again, we find nothing.

The day isn't a complete loss, though. At one point, we find ourselves in a swarm of Whirligig Beetles all gathered along the bank. They float on the surface like shiny black buttons, feeding on whatever they can find in the thin film of water at the top. As we draw near in the canoe, they become agitated and begin swimming in circles, creating quite a stir.

Later, we watch a Water Strider skate across the surface on its long thin legs. We're able to get close enough to see the tiny antennae at the head of its body.

The pangs of restlessness are with me tonight. I need to get off the grounds and move around some. Back in Albany, Frank issued me an extra set of keys to the Impala, so I ask Annie for the car.

Outside, crickets and cicadas are blowing to beat the band. I twirl the keys once around my finger and fire up the red coupe. It feels good to have the car to myself, cruising down the lane with the window open on a warm night. At the entrance, I turn right onto highway 86 and follow it into town.

Approaching the outskirts, I back the old girl down in front of a long row of houses, looking for the first side-street that can get me off the main drag.

Before leaving the house, I dipped into Door #1 for a little attitude adjustment, but I must have gone too far because in no time at all I'm stoned out of my gourd. It's all I can do to grip the wheel and maintain proper depth perception. The complicated road construction doesn't help matters. A long gauntlet of blinking yellow lights winds its way toward the middle of town, crossing back and forth between lanes. There are craters in the asphalt the size of manhole covers. The buildings along the road are dark and old, the brick dirty with soot, and I'm suddenly in some war-torn village in Belarus. The car rumbles over the pocked road, slow and exposed, like an easy target when it's anybody's guess where the next shell will hit.

But I'm not in Belarus, and, for all intents and purposes, I'm not in Saranac either. I'm back in my room at the old boarding house in Detroit, alone in the dark on a cold and windy night in late November, adjusting the contrast on the ten-inch screen of an old black-and-white television set, while outside, bare trees claw at a low overcast sky the color of rust. I change the channel on the TV, finding a late-night movie on channel 2, picking up the story … *as a midsize sedan turns onto a side-street in a gritty working-class town somewhere in the noir Northeast. The sedan moves slowly down the street. A squeak of brakes, as the vehicle pulls up to the curb and parks. The headlights snap off, the engine goes silent.*

Driver's door swings open. Out walks a man in blue jeans and a tee-shirt, his face hidden in the dark. He takes a few steps on the sidewalk before turning back to look at the car, skeptically, as if there's something not quite right with it. He starts down the sidewalk, slipping from shadow to shadow, avoiding the glare of streetlights.

No moon tonight, only a dim star or two peeking through shifting cloud cover. He makes his way along a row of shrubs and trees, stopping in the darkest spot he can find, the deepest shadow, everything obliterated but the grainy black-and-white snow from electrical impulses firing in his optic nerve.

He continues on, turning down an alley that leads to the center of town, walking to the very end where he stops just short of the lighted sidewalk along main street, ducking into a narrow shadow along the side of a brick wall …

I've always imagined myself as a character in a movie. Not sure what kind of movie, precisely, but probably a Western—something along the lines of *Shane* or *The Lone Ranger*—where the hero is a stranger, never feeling at home in the world. I know it's probably unhealthy to go through life this way, but at least it holds out the possibility of definition—some kind of role to play. Problem is, I can't totally buy into it. Not when I know I'm imagining my life as a movie that stars me. Not when I find myself constantly looking at myself looking at myself.

But now that we're on the topic, how *is* the hero faring these days with his badass credo of taking on all comers, fighting his way out of any scrape, gettin' while the gettin's good? Even he'd have to admit the credo wasn't exactly cutting it, here at the back end of the twentieth century. Failing miserably, in fact. Any shine of romance had worn off long ago, tarnished by eight gritty years of aimless wandering. And now, seeping in at the edges, a gnawing regret. And hard on its heels, the dull ache of despair. All of it lurking just below the surface, held at bay by a furious restlessness and some half-baked notion of pride that won't let him give in. Look at him now ... *cowering in the darkness outside a used-furniture store, watching for any movement, taking stock of what's happening around him: the raucous laughter from a second-story balcony across the street; a rusty pickup driving by with two malamutes in the bed, honking twice, the horn blasts reverberating between the rows of storefronts like thunder in a canyon. Slipping through the darkness, close along a brick wall, he steps onto the porch of a tavern, watching and waiting. A quick glance up and down the street, before he enters the bar ....*

The room is quiet, nearly empty. A man with white hair stands at one end of the bar with a whiskey glass. Someone is passed out at a small table in the corner. Your typical hole-in-the-wall.

"Draw," I say to the bartender, a scrawny guy with nervous eyes. He freezes in place behind the copper bar, pulls an imaginary pistol from his hip, then pours me a Cream Ale from the spigot.

The bar, dimpled with divots where the copper is nailed in place, stretches nearly the length of the room. Empty beer cases are stacked six feet high in a corner by the entrance, down where the old-timer stands with his whiskey. At the back of the room, a light shade hangs low over a pool table, the green felt stained with bottle rings. Not far from the table is a phone both with glass doors. But what catches my attention is the 12-point deer head mounted behind the bar and the collection of junk hanging from its antlers: beads, ribbons, feathers, garter belts, hats, chains, belt buckles, bear claws, a withered corsage, tambourine, baseball bobble-head, rusty pistol, masquerade mask, old boot ... all held together like some weird pagan altar.

"Guess I'll have a whiskey to go with that beer." I nod to the fifth bottle already on the bar. The old-timer rattles the ice cubes in his glass.

I look at the drunk passed out at the table. "Is that guy all right?"

"Snow? Oh, yeah. He's just napping."

The bartender looks skittish, wringing his hands with a bar towel.

"Kind of quiet tonight," I say.

"Everybody's down at the boat," he says. "They ought to be here any minute now."

He pours a beer and plants an elbow on the copper bar. "Snowhare!"

The guy at the table stirs, scoots to the edge of his chair where he gets comfortable and resumes his slumber.

The barkeep grabs a ballpeen hammer and whaps the lastcall bell. "That ought to get him up."

But the chair has other ideas. It buckles under Snowhare's weight and kicks out from under him. He grabs the table on the way down, only to have it fall on top of him.

The bartender slaps the copper bar with his open hand and roars with delight, triggering a fit of coughing. I have to laugh too, until he whirls around to face me. "What," he stares, "you don't like the way I laugh?" He grabs a mug and pulls the tap, bursts into more raucous laughter, touching off yet another hacking spasm.

"Come on up here," he says to his friend, "and get one on the house."

Snowhare picks himself up from the rubble. On his way to the bar he tries stepping over the fallen chair only to get tangled up again, this time bowing a metal leg that slingshots the chair hard against the upended table. Without looking back, he regains his balance and steps to the copper bar, takes the draught left by the cackling barkeep, and sits down on the stool next to me.

"Yessir," intones the bartender. "Got yourself a live one, there."

Snowhare drains half the bottle on his first drink, and it's just about then that my presence settles in like bad news. The bartender fidgets. The old-timer leans back and snorts something from a glass vial. Snowhare exhales and sets the bottle back on the bar. I look straight ahead, having played this scene a hundred times. The new kid in town.

"Name's Miles," I say.

As a general rule, it's not good to talk about yourself. Any information you divulge can be used against you somewhere down the line. There are times though when, for whatever reason, you can't help but blather on, tripping all over yourself to spill half your guts. It's a bit like loneliness. The only time a person feels lonely is when someone *makes* him lonely. You can be the last man on earth and be just fine with it, that is, until you remember the cute girl who sat behind you in fifth grade.

"I'm with the DEC," I continue. "Part of a loon survey that's being conducted this summer in the Adirondacks. I'm staying at the Colby compound with my partner."

"Loons?" says Snow, over a rising bubble in his stomach.

His blonde hair is scraggly and disheveled, his dirty t-shirt torn at the neck. "I saw two on Heart Pond just the other day. They's dippin' and bobbin', gearin' up to consummate their mutual affection. Listen to this."

He steps off his stool and cups his hands around his mouth in a finger-folding knot. He blows through a slit between his thumbs, sounding a hollow hoot. He tightens his fingers and the hoot grows sharper, more distinct. Now he opens a rack of fingers, and a howl rises and falls with the forlorn longing of a loon wail.

But it seems he needs a bigger venue—the dim and dank barroom just won't do. He charges out to the porch and blasts his loon call into the night. The eerie wail pierces the warm air, reverberating down the gauntlet of buildings along main street. The night answers back: a long, drawn-out *Snowhaaaare!* from somewhere up the street. Now he changes frequencies into something like a coyote howl, delivered with amplitude. He draws air and blows again, only this time the call is even more chilling. Somehow he's able to reproduce *two* distinct calls simultaneously in a hairraising cackle of yips and yowls.

Other voices now, from up the street. One in particular carries over the rest, deep and throaty. A smoky, alcohol rasp.

"Here they come," Snow says, returning to his bar stool.

I watch the ragtag of locals file in. Yukon, he of the raspy voice, hobbles over to the bar on a foot-cast and whacks the lastcall bell with the butt of his cane. Spot, a small tattoo on her cheek, helps herself to a shot of whiskey before springing up on the back bar to plant a kiss on the snout of the twelvepoint. Beaver, with a chipped tooth and hard gaze, sits down on the bar stool to my right.

"Line 'em up, Wire," barks Yukon, tolling the bell again.

"Spirits all the way around!"

"Why, thank you," Snowhare nods to his friend. "Don't mind if I do."

"Wait now," Yukon bellows. "I was only puttin' it out there as a suggestion. It ain't fair to take advantage ...."

"Wild Turkey," cries Spot. "I'll have a Wild Turkey! And one for the stranger there," she says, nodding in my direction.

I raise my mug in appreciation.

"Don't thank me," she says. "Thank him."

"But ..." Yukon starts, "I don't recall ever saying ...."

"Hot damn!" Beaver slaps his hand on the bar, turning to me. "Ain't that a pisser."

"But ...."

"What'd you say your name was?" Beaver asks.

"Miles," I say.

"He's with the DEC, counting loons," adds Wire, already lining up shot glasses.

Swaying on his bar stool, Beaver closes one eye and fixes the other on me. "And where'd you say you were from?"

"All over, I guess."

"All over or nowhere?" he says.

Now I return the gaze. "That's right," I say. "Miles from nowhere."

Meanwhile, the other conversation heats up.

"Come to think of it," muses Yukon, "it was Snow here said he wanted to buy the first round. That's how come he beat us to the bar."

Snowhare swivels on his stool, a dumbfounded look on his face. But I can't tell if it's serious or just a put-on.

"Counting loons, huh?" Beaver continues, heartened by my joke. "What for?"

Snow drains the last half of his draught before the jumpy bartender slides a foamy new one his way. The old man at the end of the bar takes another snort.

"Just count 'em," I say. "See if the population is going up or down or nowhere at all."

Beaver leans closer. "What are ya, trying to save the world?"

Snow turns abruptly in his seat. "Look at Spot," he says to Yukon. "She's got the fire in her eye. I say we give her a chance to make good on it."

I look long and hard at Beaver, as a thin smile stretches across his chipped tooth. He's hammered, true, but he's put his finger on something.

"Sure," I say. "Why not?"

"You'd both be wise to take it from old man Riley," Spot says.

Yukon pauses like he knows something's coming, but he just can't help himself. "Ain't he the one had his dog squashed by a tree that was struck by lightning?"

"That's right," she says. "I seen him afterward and he tells me, 'I just know the next one's on me.'"

"Jesus," Yukon sighs.

"Save the world," I say. And then I begin to laugh. First good laugh I've had in a long while.

Wire hops down from his seat on the back bar and grabs a bottle off the shelf. "That settles it," he says. "Spot's round."

Just as she points to her tab on the counter behind the bar, describing to Wire what he's already begun to do, I slip a ten on the copper. "Got it," I say.

Everybody's quiet as I get up from my barstool. I can feel them watching me, but I figure it's a good time to leave. Quit while I'm ahead. I tell them I have to make an early morning of it and duck out of the bar.

On my way back to the Impala, I turn up the wrong side-street. Must be I turned too soon or too late because after a block or two nothing looks familiar. And just like that I'm good and thoroughly lost in a town I know next to nothing about, with no money now and no way home. But it doesn't feel so bad, this wandering alone in the dark. There's different kinds of lost, and I could do a lot worse than turning up a wrong street. Feels kind of good, in fact. Nothing out here to answer to, nobody to judge. It feels good to be unaccounted for—lost on some empty back street with nothing to bother about but the fresh memory of a few yokels who were probably just putting me on anyway, what with the "save the world" malarkey. Where did *that* come from?

But none of it really matters, I'll be shut of this place soon enough. Like every other chance encounter that's happened my way, it too will fade into obscurity. Vanish in the dustbin of memory.

Eventually I get around to finding the Impala and drive back to Colby. Turning into the compound, I see something on the cobblestone pillars I hadn't noticed before. Embossed on each pillar is an oval of cement in the shape of some design. I stop the car and get out to take a closer look. On one of the pillars is a grinning theatre mask with an expression of glee so exaggerated that it looks sinister. The mask on the other pillar has a sad expression. If there's some other emotion attached to it, I can't say.

I cut the lights and drive the rest of the way in the dark.

TODAY WE RETURN to Saint Regis, following a two-track to a put-in on the upper lake. It's all very quick and easy—swinging the canoe down off the roof of the Impala, loading the gear, pushing off from shore.

We start along the shoreline before veering off in the direction of a nearby island. Coming around the lee side, Annie spots three loons in a small bay. We pull ashore, find a clearing beneath a large spruce, and lie down to watch with our binoculars.

Two of the loons are engaged in courtship behavior. Their gestures are synchronized, mirror images of one another. As they circle each other, they dip their bills three or four times, heads turned to the side. Then they dive together and surface side by side at the same moment, at which point they begin the whole ritual again. The only variation occurs when one bird stretches its wings across the water.

"It's preening," Annie explains, "straightening out its feathers."

Sometimes the birds sink low in the water so that only the head, neck, and top of the back are visible above the surface. "By pressing their wings together," she says, "they force pockets of air from their feather layers to make their body weight more dense, altering their buoyancy just enough so they begin to sink."

On the water the loons look sleek and powerful, brilliantly adapted to their habitat. Perfectly suited to their element.

Dip, rise, dip, rise, dip, rise … dive.

"Loons mate for life," I say, lowering my binoculars, trying to impress Annie with my newfound knowledge. "A pair will separate for the entire winter then meet up again when they return north. They'll come back to the same lake each spring and sometimes even the same nesting site. It's like they're married."

The pair surfaces and I raise my binoculars, trying to look the part of wildlife biologist.

Dip, rise, dip, rise, dip, rise … dive.

"Why is the third bird there?" I ask.

"Don't know," she replies. "Maybe it's an immature who's yet to find a mate, still thinking he's part of the flock. There doesn't seem to be any competition between the birds—no sign of aggression or threat."

"Maybe he's just lonely," I say. "No mate, no brood, nowhere to call home."

Annie remains still, watching through her binocs.

"Then again, maybe he just likes to watch," I add, immediately realizing this might be taken the wrong way. "You know, watch and learn. Like us."

But this only makes it worse. Change the subject.

"What about the pair?" I ask. "Shouldn't they be getting on with things? I mean, it's already June. Or do you think they've already done it?"

Annie doesn't answer right away, letting some time pass before replying.

"Done what?" she says. I can see a faint smile below the lenses of her binoculars.

"You know … mated."

"Spring migration can happen all the way into June," she says, "and they can mate at any time during the summer. But you're right, the sooner they can get on with things, the better chance the yearlings will have of surviving the fall migration."

Dip, rise, dip, rise, dip, rise … dive.

"What do you suppose they're doing down there?" I ask.

Annie lowers her binoculars and looks at me. "Checking each other out," she says. "Getting to know one another." Lying on her belly, elbows propped up, her silk hair falls over her shoulders. "Nature's way, don't you know."

Without fail, the birds reappear on the surface side by side.

And this is how we spend the afternoon—on an island in the middle of a wilderness lake, watching loons acting out a ritual of love and selection sixty million years in the making, driven by ancient urges wired deep in the blood and bones.

THE LEAK SEEMS TO BE GETTING WORSE. Not ten minutes on Black Pond today and there's an inch of water in the canoe. We get halfway around the lake before we're forced to pull up and bail. Just as we're putting back in, Annie notices a single loon swimming along the northwest shore. We finish checking the rest of the shoreline before doubling-back to investigate.

Thinking the bird might lead us to a nest, we watch from a distance with the binoculars. Annie spots what appears to be a chick swimming alongside the loon, but upon closer inspection, we realize it's a second adult partially submerged with only its head and the top of its back above water. We paddle closer and watch as the two birds dive, splash, and float in unison. When they sound, they stay underwater for up to two and three minutes. We try to anticipate where they'll surface, but rarely do we guess right. Never fails, though, they always emerge side by side at the same moment. Or so we hypothesize, since neither of us actually sees them the moment they reappear.

By the time we leave, the loons have moved into the middle of the lake. No calls from either one. Neither looks to be bothered by our presence, though one raises its beak at a slight angle, possibly indicating a degree of annoyance. There's only one small island to report on Black Pond. And no nest.

TODAY I RESOLVE TO FIX THE LEAK once and for all. On the advice of Flashlight, I bring it to a welder named Ray who keeps his shop in the garage of his house along the river. Says he can get to it tomorrow if I don't mind the wait. Together we lift the canoe off the car and carry it into the garage where we drop it on two sawhorses. Come by in the afternoon, he says, it should be ready then.

With some time to kill, I fill the car up with gas and swing by the market and hardware store for supplies, paying with state vouchers as I go. The clerk at the market says nothing when I slap a blue coupon on the counter and fill it out. In fact, he says nothing at all during the entire transaction. On the wall behind him is a Greyhound schedule. Looks like a bus leaves town every afternoon. Good to know, in case I want to blow this pop stand prematurely.

On my way back to Colby, I drop by the deli for a sandwich. Who should be working the counter but the girl Annie and I saw roller-skating with ski poles. Seated in sunlight next to a window, she looks up from a paperback when I walk through the door.

Tan and athletic, blue eyes to go with her blond hair, she smiles warmly and says hello. She wears a tight fitting, sleeveless white shirt, and I'm immediately thrown off guard, helpless as metal before a magnet. I order a sandwich from the chalkboard on the wall and dutifully answer her questions as she walks me through the order. White or wheat? Wheat. Cheese? Swiss. Pickles? Sure.

I watch as she makes the sandwich, and it occurs to me what I find so unnerving. The woman has poise. Even though she looks a few years younger than me, she carries herself with all the confidence and purpose of someone who knows exactly what they want in life. A wave of gloom passes over me, a vague regret that something has passed me by and I missed out because I made one choice and not another.

I go to the cooler and return with a six-pack. When I set it down on the counter, the *clang* of cans on formica sounds a little too loud. It's a sound that usually warms my heart, but not this time. No, not this time. I fumble around with the crumpled bills in my pocket before finally managing to pay her. She smiles when she hands me the change and returns to her paperback in the light of the window.

When I get back to the house, Annie takes the car on an errand. Alone at the compound with nothing much to do, I eat my sandwich and retire to the study for the better part of the afternoon.

Flashlight's done a nice job with the room, keeping it simple and cozy. I take a seat in one of the old-style reading chairs and plant my feet on the threadbare oriental rug. The picture window provides a nice view of the lake and hills beyond. This time of day, sunlight filters through the big oak tree out front and casts a dreamy light. Later, when the sun drops low in the western sky, the lake catches fire with sparkling light.

The built-in shelves are crammed with all sorts of books and magazines and binders. They could be better organized, I suppose, but you don't want to look a gift horse in the mouth. There is plenty of reading here, enough to keep me occupied for a long while: natural history books, novels and Shakespeare plays, stacks of *National Geographic* and *Boy's Life*, encyclopedias and field guides on animals and birds and fish, scientific papers on everything from the yawning habits of lemurs to courtship behavior in crocodiles.

As far back as I can remember, I've always liked to read. Holed up in the mountain cabin during winter storms, it was the only game in town. I started with comic books— *Superman, Batman, Spider-Man*—before moving on to kids novels: *Treasure Island, Tom Sawyer, The Red Pony.* And then later as a teen when life started to get complicated: *Catcher in the Rye, Siddhartha, On the Road.* Later still, on a bus or between jobs: *Notes from the Underground, Zen and the Art of Motorcycle Maintenance, Trout Fishing in America.* Pure escape, no doubt, but nothing wrong with that.

I pick up where I left off with the loon, reading about its communication system and four basic calls: wail, hoot, tremolo, yodel. The wail is used when one loon is trying to locate another. The hoot, vocalized in different pitches, is used in quiet conversation. The tremolo typically indicates alarm or distress in the presence of another loon or predator. Finally, the yodel is used to announce and defend territory. It may also function to indicate a bird's particular identity, as individual males have been known to display their own unique versions of this call.

Recent studies indicate that the yodels of males may also describe specific places. It's been shown that different loons display the same yodel in the same place. That is, a territory's yodel remains the same even when different males come to inhabit it. Not only that, the yodel is used nowhere else but in *that particular place.*

Because there may be dozens of variations on the four basic vocalizations, it's fair to say that the communication system of loons has yet to be fully understood.

I always thought of the world's creatures, only people knew language. At least that's what I was always told. By people, of course. And what could loons be saying to each other with all those different sounds? I am here in this place and this is what it looks like? Beware, here comes a raccoon? Get your tail feathers over here, it's your turn to sit on the nest?

Interestingly, loons remain mostly flightless during the winter, sporting a drab gray and brown plumage and living exclusively on the open ocean. Before flying north in the spring, they molt their winter coat and replace it with the familiar black-and-white checkered feathers of summer. These stiff flight feathers are strong enough to get the bird airborne and back to its northern breeding grounds.

A single loon has anywhere between 18,000 and 20,000 feathers. In addition to the black-and-white "contour" feathers, loons have soft "down" feathers that insulate the body. To protect these highly absorbent down feathers, the contour feathers fit tightly together so that drops of water can't squeeze between them. Loons also have an oil gland at the base of the tail that they regularly rub with their bills, releasing small amounts of oil that they then wipe across the outer feathers to make them even more water repellant. In addition to the checkered feathers, loons display a glossy black head, white-striped neck, and white underbody. The checkered plumage serves a survival purpose, providing camouflage for the bird on the sun-flecked surface of rivers and lakes. Even the diamond-shaped necklace is designed to mimic a V-wake on water.

Nothing wrong with camouflage. It's every bit as useful today as it was sixty million years ago. Still, it's crazy to think that nature could come up with such a wild design: checkerboard feathers, zebra-striped neck, spooky red eyes. It's like something from another world.

And what *was* happening sixty million years ago to produce such a bizarre creature? What kind of world was it?

I open up a book on the history of the earth and thumb through the pages until I get to the Paleocene, where I learn that something dramatic happened 65 million years ago to put an end to the dinosaurs. It may have been volcanoes or earthquakes or a meteor hit, but something occurred to cause the earth's climate to become cooler and drier, driving most dinosaur groups to extinction. Part of the problem for dinosaurs was their inability to get around. As opportunists, they were unwieldy. They couldn't scrounge and scavenge like smaller creatures. One such critter was a furry, shrew-like rodent that prowled the trees at night, feeding on insects. As an early mammal, this rodent would turn out to be the ancestor of tree shrews, flying lemurs, and primates. Humans included.

With dinosaurs out of the way, small animals and birds diversified into new species to fill the niches vacated by their dead predators. Some of these new species eventually became quite large. For instance, an array of flightless, meat-eating "terror birds" evolved, preying on smaller mammals and reptiles. One of these birds, the "terror crane," grew to be nine feet tall with a head the size of a donkey's. There were other predators to fear. The oceans were patrolled by *Basilosaurus*, an early ancestor of the whale that grew to be 80 feet in length with a mouth full of sharp teeth. A South American snake, the Giant Titanoboa, stretched 45 feet long and weighed over a ton. Bigger than a London bus, according to the book. (It doesn't say what kind of bus, so I'm guessing it's one of those double-decker jobs.)

Meanwhile, the continents were on the move. South America had detached from Antarctica and was on its way to uniting with North America. Australia was getting ready to break from Antarctica, while India was on course to smash into Eurasia. Sixty million years ago, there were no Adirondacks and the climate was warmer than it is now. A loon in these parts would have been neighbors to a two-horned rhino and a horse that stood sixteen inches high. Soon there would be mastodons and small-faced bears, saber-toothed tigers and American cheetahs. Meanwhile, out in the ocean, the megatooth shark was making a name for itself as the most fearsome carnivore ever. The megatooth grew to be over sixty feet long, larger than a whale shark. It had 276 teeth, each up to seven inches long, all packed into jaws that were seven feet wide and nine feet high.

So, for millions of years, the loon is minding its own business, when all of a sudden the ground beneath him starts to rise and keeps on rising until the Adirondacks are formed. This all happened about five million years ago, not a lot in earth years. Or loon years, for that matter.

Though the Adirondacks are relatively new mountains, the rock itself is quite old. To get the full story, you have to go back a billion years to when a shallow sea covered the better part of the eastern U.S. and much of Canada. The sediment on the sea floor piled up until it was fifteen miles thick. At the bottom of those fifteen miles, under intense heat and pressure, the hardened sediment mixed with other rocks and minerals to become metamorphic rock.

And then a lot of time went by. Hundreds of millions of years. And all the while there's this back and forth between uplift and erosion. Each would get the upper hand at some point or another. For instance, all those fifteen miles of sedimentary rock eventually eroded away. On the other hand, there was a period 400 million years ago when upstate New York was as high as the Himalayas are today. But even that would wash away. Long story short, about five million years ago, erosion stripped away the surface rock at the same time our billion-year-old bedrock was being pushed upward by forces deep within the earth. And when finally it broke through the surface, it kept on rising until it looked like one big turtle shell, a mile high and 160 miles wide. Throw in a few faults and glaciers and stream drainages, and there you have it: the present-day Adirondacks and its slew of waterholes.

Right about the time the Adirondack uplift was beginning, an ape in Africa got it in his mind to climb down from the trees and have a look in the grass. It would take four million years, but eventually he stood up on two legs and began to walk. It would take nearly another million years before the ape evolved into a man. In time, he'd find his way to all four corners of the globe.

The book on earth's history only takes me so far, so I get up and peruse Flashlight's shelves until I find what I'm looking for: a history of the Adirondacks. Returning to my chair, I turn to the chapter on early human inhabitants. According to the book, the first people to see the Adirondacks were the Iroquois who fled their homes along the St. Lawrence to get away from the Algonquins. The Iroquois eventually settled south of the Adirondacks in what is now central New York. It seems neither group had any real interest in occupying the mountains, both referring to the area as the *Dismal Wilderness*. As for the name "Adirondack," it translates loosely into *bark-eater*—a name given to the Algonquins by the Iroquois. Apparently, the Algonquins didn't amount to much in the way of hunting or farming, this according to the Iroquois. As for loons, they were pretty much left alone by Indians. Because they were fish-eaters, their meat wasn't valued.

The first European to see the Adirondacks was probably Samuel de Champlain, traveling up the St. Lawrence in 1607. Then came French trappers and Jesuit missionaries, followed by miners and loggers and farmers. Roads were built for stagecoaches, and by the early 1900s, the tourist trade was in full swing. Fancy lodges were built along the shorelines of lakes. Steamers brought hordes of vacationers seeking leisure and entertainment. Considered a nuisance by fishermen, loons were shot on sight, oftentimes by tourists from the rails of passing ships.

In response, loons developed a technique of exposing only their mouths above water when taking a breath. Quite the trick. And to think they learned this in short order: first, to figure out that people wanted to shoot them; and second, to devise a tactic to counter the threat.

Continents floating around the world, mountains rising and falling, oceans coming and going, the terror crane and megatooth and bloodthirsty tourists. The loon has survived it all.

By this time, I'm pretty worn out from all the reading. So, I return the books to the shelves and get ready to leave. Just as I'm on my way out, I catch sight of Flashlight's cardboard box with all the newspaper articles. Curiosity gets the better of me, so I grab a handful of clippings and flip through the headlines: "Revenge of the Virus"; "Killer Bees Are Here!"; "The Next Ice Age Won't Be So Nice"; "Cockroaches and Slugs to Inherit the Earth."

On the wall above the box is a large corkboard with a dozen newspaper photographs tacked neatly in place. The pictures show animals caught in strange situations and predicaments. One photo shows an alligator on a paved road beneath a sign that reads, "Slow Down! Alligator Crossing." Another tells of a horned owl that flies off her nest in a barn to distract the farmer every time he walks through the door. There's a picture of an elk in Sweden, drunk after eating too many rotten apples and biting a girl in the butt as she played in a sandbox. Not an uncommon occurrence, apparently. The caption reads: "A year earlier, a drunken bull elk was shot after it attacked an 8-year-old boy. Yet another intemperate elk laid siege to a schoolhouse."

Instincts gone awry, evolution run amok.

Next day, I drive to the welder's house in the afternoon where I meet Ray outside in the bright sunshine. He tells me it'll cost ten dollars. When I reach for my stack of blue vouchers, he shakes his head. "The state has owed me a hundred dollars for two years," he says, "and I've yet to see a dime."

So I pay him with my own money.

He asks what I'm doing for the State, and I tell him about the loon project. One thing leads to another and before long he's telling me about his army days and the corruption he saw in Vietnam. U.S. oil companies selling supplies to the enemy, that sort of thing. At one point he picks up four pebbles from the ground—a white one and three black ones. "This is what it was like," he says, "one American to three Vietnamese. One of the Vietnamese was on your side and the other two weren't. Only thing was, you couldn't tell who was friendly and who wasn't. Many of the people you passed on the street during the day, wore the black Vietcong suit at night. The idea was to trust no one."

Then he starts in about acid rain, how people in powerful positions make decisions based solely on profit. "There are at least two Americas," he says. "One for the ruling class, and another for everybody else."

I nod my head in agreement, partly because what he says makes sense and he's got the experience to back it up, but also because Ray the Welder looks to be one tough hombre. My suspicion is later confirmed at the Waterhole when I learn that, back in his wild days, Ray was apt to fight anyone at the drop of a hat.

That night I have a dream of being chased through the woods by a band of tomahawk wielding Algonquins, only to be eviscerated in a meadow by a saber-toothed tiger. It's a clean kill, my body severed neatly in half. I look on dispassionately, studying the cross-section of my torso—the globules of fat, the thatch-work of red muscle, the bundled fibers of raw nerves. There's no pain, only a textbook glimpse of the human anatomy.

No doubt, the dream was inspired by the graphic descriptions of prehistoric killers, courtesy of Flashlight's library. The price you pay, I suppose, for peering into the spooky ancient past of tooth and claw.

In the morning, Annie and I take the canoe out on Colby to check the weld job. It holds up just fine, the rivet seam sealed tight. Since Colby is on our list anyway, we paddle the entire perimeter of the lake. Good habitat, especially with all the hummocks at the far end of the lake, but no nest. Seems as though the loon that visits here at night lives on a nearby lake. McKenzie, maybe.

Toward evening, Annie informs me that she's off to town. I ask her if she wants the car and she says no, she'd rather walk. Which is good, because I have plans for the Impala. I watch as she starts down the footpath leading around the lake to the train trestle that'll take her into town. When she's out of sight, I pull the car around to the side of the house next to the garage, swing open the aluminum door, and get to work.

I find all the tools I need on the workbench: screwdrivers, pry bar, high-speed drill with attachments, heavy-duty extension cord. I grab the spray cans and masking tape out of the trunk of the car, and go to it. It doesn't take long to complete the makeover. I could have spent more time on it, for sure, but with the fading light I had to hurry the job. It gets the point across, anyway.

Later, after dark, I retire to the cupola with a rack of Genny Cream. Nestled nicely in a bed of ice, these chilly white cans offer all the nerve I need to tear into the journal and bring it up to date. Or at least come close. I've learned to cut a few corners by now. For instance, I don't bother mentioning all the lakes that we cover or all the places we go. If I did, I'd be here forever. Life happens too fast to write it all down.

Midway through the second beer, I feel the golden elixir coursing through my veins, making the world right again, and I get to thinking about what Ray said: Trust No One. Sound advice. As social currency, loyalty is all but dead in the late twentieth century. In fact, *disloyalty* is the order of the day, infecting all facets of life: business, government, marriage, gentlemen's agreements. With a divorce rate nearing fifty percent, a government that openly lies and then jokes about it, corporations that factor murder into their balance sheets, so-called friends who won't think twice about stabbing you in the back if they stand to benefit ... why, you'd be a fool to be faithful to *anything*. Be loyal and you get burned, simple as that. Used to be there was an understanding about how to get along. Help a person out if they're in a fix. Be honest, don't cheat. Stay true to your word .... Hell, nowadays, anything goes.

A guy gets wise after a while. A few rounds of being run through the wringer, and he gets to fashioning a few principles to help him through the pricker patch of treachery. You might even think of it as a code. Survival Tips in the Age of Free Agency:

RULE #1—Thou shall not promote, pedal, or otherwise hawk any product, belief, or ideology. To do so leads to bad things including, but not limited to, disappointment, disillusionment, over-exposure (see Rule #3), and that sinking feeling that comes when you realize you've just sold your soul.

RULE #2—Thou shall not join a group or maintain any group affiliation. This includes, but is not limited to, any organization, political party, religion, or cause célèbre. To do so is to surrender the ability to think and act for oneself, to abdicate personal responsibility, and to otherwise tie one's hands needlessly. This also, in letter and spirit, runs counter to the golden rule of *Keep Moving*.

RULE #3—Thou shall not stick out in public by wearing garish clothing or flashy frills in the way of studs, snaps, straps, clips, or other accoutrements added for show. Absolutely no brand names or other writing should appear on one's person. This includes, but is not limited to, any words intended as advertisement or promotion (see Rule #1). If you find yourself before a tailor—which you shouldn't—hold your ground and stay true to the manifesto: "I refuse to be a walking billboard, to use any part of my person as advertising space for any enterprise, but rather to present myself in accordance with drab anonymity."

Given the current state of affairs, it behooves the self-respecting free agent to shun the spotlight and seek out the shadows—all the better to move in and out of the spaces between. In this day and age when everything and everyone is for sale, it pays to blend in with your surroundings. The goal here is *camouflage*. If the need arises, and it will, you want the capability of slipping about unseen. Always maintain the option of going unnoticed, appearing in a thoroughly nondescript and average manner. Lie low, fly under the radar.

This strategy should not be confused with conformity. Not in the least. An undercover free agent should never demean himself to such an extent as to affect the appearance of his contemporaries, particularly when they look like they just stepped out of a magazine advertisement. You know the type: tight-fitting spandex in yellow and pink, with brand names plastered across the body. YUPPIES carrying themselves with all the discretion of a screeching cockatoo, flashing stiletto teeth, projecting the smug, let-me-show-you-what-I-just-bought arrogance that has come to infect this land like a plague.

Even loons know the art of camouflage and stealth.

SOME INTERESTING FACTS about the impala, handsome speed merchant of the African plains. Standing three-feet tall as an adult, this midsize mammal can run as fast as 55 mph, clearing bushes and other obstacles by soaring ten feet in the air and leaping distances of thirty feet in a single bound—a skill used to evade predators and also, it appears, to amuse itself. It seems *Aepyceros melampus* is not above tomfoolery.

Impalas gather in large herds—sometimes numbering in the hundreds—as a way of protecting themselves against lions, cheetahs, and leopards. When frightened or startled, the herd will leap about willy-nilly in order to confuse predators.

Males, or rams, grow long spiral horns up to three feet in length, that can be used to challenge other males in tests of strength. During rut, older rams establish a mating territory by herding groups of females (ewes), which they then guard against rivals. Weaker males are forced to live in what are called bachelor herds. Rams lure ewes by repeatedly sticking out their tongues. "Tongue flashing" can also be used to warn off other males.

WHEN ANNIE WALKS OUT this morning, she pauses at the bottom of the stairs to behold the new and improved state vehicle. *"What did you do to the car?"*

"Do you like it?" I ask.

"You painted it ... *gray.*"

"Not just any gray, that's flat primer gray. Do you like it?"

I was not insensitive to Annie's opinion. I wanted her to like the modifications: spray-painted chassis; black wheels and lug nuts where hubcaps used to be; hood ornament removed; the words "Chevrolet" and "Impala" ground down to a nub, defaced beyond recognition by the 5 1/2", 3-speed, reversible drill and accompanying sander attachment (#60 Coarse Grit).

I give her a minute to soak it in .... It may take a while, but I believe she'll come around.

To move things along, I unfold the "big board"—the 1:100 000-scale planimetric topo, 30 x 60 minute series— across the hood of the car and ask her where she wants to go. But I'm a little revved up on account of the paint job, so I just come out and suggest First Pond and Second Pond.

"We could cover Second first," I say, "unless you prefer First."

"Why Second," she asks, studying the map, "when it seems just as easy to start with First?"

"I just think there's a certain logic to covering Second first. That way we could do First second."

"Are you sure?"

"Not entirely," I admit.

By now, most of the smaller ponds we visit are covered with pine pollen. This is certainly the case with Second. On our way around the pond, we paddle past a lock that leads into Oseetah Lake, another reminder of the vast network of manmade barriers regulating the levels of these waterways.

By afternoon the water is perfectly still, reflecting a rampart of mountains beyond the opposite shore. I'm beginning to get a feel for the beauty and solitude of this Adirondack landscape—the rock and forests and lakes.

On the way home, Annie suggests we take a hike above town. First, though, I have her stop at a package store for some beer, it being that time of day.

From town, we follow a brick road uphill through one of Saranac's older neighborhoods, past big white houses with screened porches and towering evergreens on the lawns, continuing up to the base of Baker Mountain where Moody Pond sparkles blue in the afternoon sun. Annie parks along a dusty shoulder by the side of the lake. We each grab a can of beer and start up the trail for the top of the mountain.

The hiking is fairly easy but we pace ourselves anyway, settling into an easy rhythm, there being nothing else to do today. On the official end, anyway. I take the time to notice my footsteps on the soft forest floor, the luminescent canopy of leaves overhead, the throaty peals of a raven from somewhere deep in the woods. A jay scolds a cowbird before taking flight in a streak of blue.

On top of the mountain, the evergreens grow old and twisted, their boughs bent downwind. The walking is easy up high—flat granite, scattered patches of lichen and moss. We sit on an outcrop away from the trees where we can see the entire village below—the clock tower and row of brick buildings along main street, the road out to Lake Colby and our camp, the reflection of clouds on Moody Pond, the narrow straight connecting Lake Flower to Oseetah Lake. And beyond that, the formidable Ampersand Range and Lower Saranac Lake with its many tufted islands. Everywhere we look: a landscape of mountains and lakes bathed in the languid sunlight of a summer afternoon. A soft breeze sighs in the pine tree behind us. Water and rock, wind and sky. This is our place now, our time.

Two skewed eyeballs: one trained on me, the other directed out the window behind my bed. Each magnified by a windshield of thick eyeglass. It's Flashlight and he's beginning to hyperventilate.

"Did you read about the moose that got stranded in the deep end of an empty swimming pool? They had to get him out with a front-end loader."

He turns away and starts pacing in the room, hands behind his back. "The signs are everywhere—fish being born with two heads, weeds adapting to herbicides, rats eating rat poison for nourishment ... all happening with a vengeance to slap us into submission."

Then he stops and looks at me, standing perfectly still except for one eye that begins to slide sideways.

"Did you know that in England in the thirties, a number of birds learned how to open the tops of milk bottles left outside by milkmen, and almost at the exact same moment birds across Europe started doing the same thing? The coincidence occurred so quickly that it would have been impossible for one bird to travel all that distance in time to teach another how to do it. Not only that, the two populations were separated by the English Channel, and these were *not* migrating birds."

For the life of me, I can't think of anything to say.

"Mice are in the hot water heater again," he says finally, moving toward the door. "You might not want to take a shower this morning."

Today we cover Lake Flower and most of Oseetah, looking for an eagle's nest rumored to be in the area. We don't find any nests, belonging to either eagle or loon, but there's plenty of suitable habitat for both. Behind the wide expanse of marsh on the eastern shore of Oseetah, acre upon acre of untracked forest stretches clear to the horizon. To the south, the Ampersand, Seward, and Sawtooth Ranges rise blue and wide in the distance. It's not often that a person sees so much unpeopled space this side of the Mississippi, not without standing on some mountaintop. Kind of reassuring, this feeling of looking across all those miles without a sign of *Homo sapiens*.

There are a number of small private islands on Oseetah, accessible only by boat. Houses are built directly on top of rock, constructed according to the uneven topography. Decks and porches extend over outcrops. The shoreline is rimmed with boulders, providing convenient ledges for swimmers. By late afternoon, the day warms enough for us to jump in and cool off in the dark water.

On the back side of Oseetah, we find a slew of hummocks and islets in the large marsh. But no sign of loons. We see mergansers, mallards, and two broad-winged hawks rising on a thermal. Without a single flap of their wings, the pair circles higher and higher in the blue sky—a sight that hasn't changed from when the Iroquois plied these waters in dugout canoes ... or so it occurred to me then.

When we return to Colby, the acid rain techs phone to say they'd like to meet for a beer in town, so that night I take Annie to the Waterhole.

When we arrive, we find two seats at the bar and order drinks, waiting for our friends to show. As Wire pours our beers, Snow and Yukon make their way across the room to join us. They step to the bar and lean close, wanting to see what the new loon ranger is all about. It doesn't take long for Annie to win them over. She looks good in her snug jeans and batik shirt. Yukon clangs the last-call bell with his hickory cane, certifying that all is well at the Waterhole.

I leave them at the bar and step outside onto the porch, assuming my familiar position at the edge of things. Before leaving the house, I dipped into Door #3, so it's best if I keep close tabs on the state of my condition. I was never good at social etiquette, anyway. It always seems to get the better of me. The other day I stepped in front of Annie and opened the door for her, thinking it was the courteous thing to do. She paused and thanked me before telling me not to ever do it again. It used to be that opening doors for ladies was the proper thing to do—one of the hallmarks of civilized life.

When the acid rangers arrive, the four of us find a table in the corner. Roy and Ed are here for the summer to collect data for a study on acid rain and its impact on lakes in the northern Adirondack region. Like me, they are DEC grunts. Ed wears glasses—black plastic frames with white athletic tape wrapped around the bridge for reinforcement. Overkill, if you ask me, but who's to say? Other than the glasses, the two look pretty much the same. Blue jeans and pocket-tees, clean and pressed. White sneakers. The only other difference is that Roy has wavy brown hair that won't stay in place despite his best efforts to flatten it down with the palm of his hand. They're in the field a lot, spending half their nights in the backcountry. In fact, they've just returned from a week camped at a remote bog where they were airlifted in and out by helicopter.

Their job is to collect water samples from mountain lakes and check on any aquatic life they might encounter.

The samples are then taken to a lab and tested for chemical composition. The higher and more remote the lake, the better. This way, the state can begin to get a handle on the extent and impact of acid rain. To assist in the study, the DEC has leased two llamas from a farm in the Catskills. Ed in particular can't say enough about the llamas.

"We pack everything in panniers and strap it on their backs: field equipment, tent, sleeping bags, cooking gear, clothes, food and water. It's not easy slogging through thickets and swamps, swinging at no-see-ums, battling mosquitoes with sweat fogging your glasses and dripping into your eyes. The llamas are patient and low maintenance. They just bat their long eyelashes, munch some cud, and occasionally stop for a drink of water."

Ed pauses and takes a big gulp from his Iron City. Annie and Roy, meanwhile, are talking about the Albany office. I hear snatches of conversation about the bald eagle hacking project, funding for next year, etc. Roy sets his bottle on the table and goes back to flattening his hair. The yellow porch light comes on outside, shining in my eyes through the window. The room is louder now, as more people file in.

It seems bizarre that llamas should be in the Adirondacks, a world away from their ancestral home in the Andes. We humans yank them out of bunchgrass and coca and plop them down in sedge and spruce. And for what? So they can lend their hairy hide to an *acid rain study* of all things, toting state gear hither and yon, tramping mile after mile so that bug-eyed biologists can dip a glass vial in some mosquito-infested backwater for a tiny sample that's going to confirm what they already know. And all this data compiled and collated ... to what end?

"So some slick country-club politician can crumple it up and toss it in a wastebasket and tell his smarmy speechwriter to spin the story just so, then look straight into the lens of a television camera and reassure everybody there's 'no direct link' between the sulfur belched out of the Ohio Valley and the acid rain here in New York."

As a grunt, Ed has the advantage of speaking his mind without fear of reprisal.

I think about the newspaper stories thumb-tacked to the corkboard in Flashlight's study: An elk that charged its reflection in a plate glass window "only to find himself in the middle of a living room." A black bear "hooked on coffee creamer" that ransacked summer cabins, ripping off doors, overturning refrigerators, tearing cupboards from the walls. A horse that got trapped in a cellar, rescued by the boom of a tow truck ("the animal was declared safe and unharmed").

But all things considered, Ed would rather talk about the llamas. He leans forward and looks me in the eye. "You know, there's something incredible about these creatures. Spooky, even. They're very intelligent—you only have to show them once how to do something. They're curious and observant, and they have excellent memories. We have a female and a male, Millie and Fred, and sometimes they get frisky with each other. But they also like their time alone. They remind me of my parents. If Fred wants his space, he'll spit. They make a noise like a hum, and it's as if they're talking and you can almost understand what they're saying. I'm convinced they have a sense of humor, a knack for mischief. You can definitely tell when they're up to no good. Like I say, it can get spooky out there with nothing else around. Bottom line, though, they're outstanding in the field. They're troopers, very durable. They're not difficult like mules, they don't complain, and they can go all day."

"Truth be told," he says, looking over his shoulder. "They're better than my Pinto," he whispers, as if his car might be listening in. "More dependable and less maintenance."

By now, things are getting dicey. The top of the table is swirling. There's a buzzing sound in my head and a strange glow around the porch light. Door #3 is kicking in with a vengeance. I look at Roy hunched over with his big ears and eyes, his long fingers spread wide across the table. He looks like some kind of animal when ... *he turns into a tree shrew!*

He's still Roy the human, but his mannerisms belong to those of a large rodent. He's both man *and* rodent. I'm thunderstruck, unable to look away, both horrified and fascinated. It's as though a veil has been lifted and I've been afforded a glimpse of some awful, naked truth.

All I know is, I have to get out of there. I stand and push my way through the crowd—out to the porch and the farthest seat on the last bench where I sit with my back against a flowerbox, breathing heavily. I light up a smoke and take two big swigs of beer, trying to douse the fire in my belly.

It helps to be outside, the fresh air feels good. Across the street, shades of twilight play across the clock tower of the brick courthouse. Two teenage boys meet on the sidewalk, decide on something, and begin walking in the direction of the lake. A pickup drives by and blasts its horn—one of those custom, antique jobs. *Chu-hooga! Chu-hooga!*

Meanwhile, the barroom fills up fast. Groups of two and three crowd the copper bar, looking for a table to open up. Others mingle near the pool table, drinks in hand. It's Friday night and there's an electricity in the air, an atom random crackle. I can feel it building like a funnel cloud that starts out as a hornet's nest, then tightens into a rat tail.

Staying on the periphery, I make my way back inside. Annie shoots me a glance from the corner of the room, her eyes calm and steady. Hair curled behind one ear, she looks great tonight, and the thought crosses my mind to make a move. And I probably would under normal circumstances, but there's the job to consider and the whole business about starting fresh with a clean slate. And besides, she's a hard one to figure. You don't go fast with a woman like that. If it ever came to it, she'd have to make the first move, and even then it might be weird. There's something different about her, that's for sure. It's like she has one foot in this world and one foot in another. Sometimes she's talking and I'm staring into her eyes and I feel myself becoming hypnotized to the point that I start thinking about being hypnotized instead of listening to what she's saying. And then I have to turn away. Gaze into her green eyes long enough, and it's like peering into another dimension.

Someone told me once that our universe is only one of many, and we can't see the others because they exist in a different kind of space outside the four dimensions that we're familiar with. In fact, there may be a whole other universe operating in the very same place as ours, only we can't see it! Not only that, but there may be duplicates of everybody in these other universes. This very second, there might be another me writing in another journal about the me who is writing in *this* journal about *him!* Somewhere out there is a parallel Snowhare and a parallel Flashlight, and, of course, a parallel Annie—only she might be my sister or nanny or any number of things.

The strangest part about all this is that when I feel myself being pulled into the whirlpool of her eyes, there's something familiar about it. I don't know if it's her that I find familiar, or wherever it is I'm being pulled to. It's like the feeling you get when you see a complete stranger for the first time, and you could swear you know them from somewhere. Maybe Annie and I met in a previous lifetime. Maybe we're soulmates, and she's really me but in a different universe.

Maybe what I glimpse in her eyes is some hidden reality that only surrealist painters and shamans can see. Maybe she's my Siamese twin in a future life ….

Christ, listen to me.

I have but one job right now, and that is to not freak out. All I know for sure is that I'm not going back to the table, not as long as Roy is there. It's too risky. Right now, it's best if I avoid all eye contact. I am in no condition to mingle. A man can only take so much confab, anyway. It saps his energy, drains his battery. At some point it's unavoidable, I understand that, but it's best to keep conversation to a minimum. Choose when and how to engage. Estimate the amount of energy required against what there is to gain—like a predator who, when sizing up potential prey, must calculate the energy needed to kill the prey versus the energy gained from eating it.

I find a little space next to the phone booth, where I can drink my beer and monitor the room. Snow is passed out at a nearby table in a heap of hair and elbows, not far from a painting on the wall that I hadn't noticed before. The lighting is bad, so I step closer for a better look. The framed oil depicts a moose swimming in a deep river with water up to its neck. A massive rack of antlers towers above the calm surface, as a slice of wake trails behind. In the background, a wooded shoreline is barely visible in the mist, and I can't tell whether the shapes I see there are actual objects or not.

I look closer. It's clearly a moose by the shape of its rack, but there's something strange about the head. All the familiar outlines of jaw, nose, ears and brow are there, but inside the curving lines and colors, a whole other pattern emerges— trippy arabesques like something you might see in a Buddhist mandala. Divine and diabolical. All the more startling since, at first glance, I would have sworn it was only a moose head.

Snow stirs from his sleep, raising his head. A neat film of drool stretches from his lower lip to a tiny puddle on the table. One eye closed, he fixes the other on me. "Innocent of all charges!" he barks.

"No," I say. "It's only me, Miles."

"Huh?" He blinks and wipes away the drool, studying the slick he's left on the table.

"I was looking at this painting," I say. "It seems a little funny, you know, a *swimming moose?*"

"Let me tell you something about that moose." He leans back in his chair, takes a deep breath, and pauses in dramatic fashion. "But first let me get a beer."

When he returns, Snow begins his tale.

"I heard this story from a friend's half-brother who got it from his second cousin's ex-sister-in-law. It really isn't so complicated, but you're gonna have to take my word that it's true, true as I'm settin' here before your very eyes.

"This feller who lived up the mountain and two of his friends he knowed, they get the notion to paddle a canoe through the St. John's Wilderness and try their hand at lunker northerns. They figgered on paddlin' about a hundred miles of that river. Outpost to outpost, nothing but wilderness. Take their time, commune with creation, and come back all the wiser for it.

"So the first day is warm and clear, it being late August and already the trees changing color—the three of them in one of those fifteen-foot tri-seaters. They make good time that first day, cover twenty miles or so, wetting a line from time to time. It's truly beautiful in those parts, the tamarac bogs and evergreens. Beaver ponds, bear, bobcat ... nary a mosquito that time o' year, neither.

"When they make camp that first night, Ernie breaks out the whiskey. Now, Ernie's a good woodsman—can charm a ten-point off a salt lick. He's sportin' a scraggly beard, long hair, wiry frame, but rugged as they come. Whisper, my friend's brother, is the quiet type. Don't ever hardly say anything. He's the guy you want with you in the woods if you're huntin', but not if you have two lasses on the line and your tongue seizes up all asudden, you can't think of nothin' to say to save your life, and it's up to him to keep the ball rolling. Lefleur was the third—crazy Frenchman.

"So they get to drinking and carrying on, yippin' and yowlin' at the moon till they can't yelp no more and fall asleep. Fine. Next morning, they journey down the river another twenty miles, swimming and fishing along the way, until they set up camp for the night and pick up where they left off, drinkin' and cussin' to beat the band. God knows what all them critters back in the woods was thinkin'. Lefleur in particular likes to get the fire in his eye.

"On the third day they set off from camp when, wouldn't ya know, they commence to talking about how glorious the world is—how they're gonna mend their ways and start from scratch when they get back to civilization. Lefleur vows to fix that brokedown fence, like he's been aiming to do for a few years now. Ernie promises to swear off whiskey like his old lady's been after him to do ever since they swapped nuptials. The way I hear it, he mulled it over a piece before getting it straight in his head, that maybe just a little nip in the evening wouldn't do no harm, and maybe one at lunch would give him a helpful kick and, well, if he just studied it a while he could manage to drink his usual take but spread it out over the whole day so nobody'd notice, and it would be little rewards along the way, ya see, seein's how he'd be busy with all the good deeds he was now bound and determined to do to show he was an industrious sort, after all. See, back when he was four ...."

"But the story, Snow. What about the moose?"

"Oh yeah. Okay, so they hem and haw till about mid-afternoon, when they come across the damndest thing. They enter a wide section where the water's flat and spread out over the lowlands, and ahead of them they see what looks like two big *wings* in the middle of the river, powered by something big and brown there at the base. A nice steady wake is rippling behind, and they can't figger out what it is to save their souls, until they get right up on top of it and see that it's a dang *moose!* Well, they're flummoxed as all get out, until the Frenchman gets a bright idea. Like all them boys—and ain't it man's nature, anyhow—he gets to figgerin': why work when you got somebody else to do it for ya? So, while Whisper and Ernie are admiring the beast up close, it swimmin' along pretty as you please, Lefleur gets to tyin' a loop in the bow line. And just like that, he throws a lasso onto one of the spikes in the moose's rack!"

Snow pauses and takes a long pull off his beer. When Annie and I first arrived, there weren't but a dozen patrons in the whole bar. Now it's jammed with people, locals mostly, feeling their oats on a Friday night. A group near the bar erupts in uproarious laughter. A bottle smashes in the corner by the pool table. A couple in the throes of a scorching embrace crashes against our table, before Snow grabs the woman by the scruff and pulls them aside. All the while, he keeps his eye on me, focused on the story. With his outstretched arm, he fends off the swaying horde when it tilts too close, like some kind of backwoods messiah.

"Then what happened?" I yell over the noise.

"Well, now," he leans closer. "Lefleur's got the loop around the moose's rack, and he gets to hollerin' like he's discovered the greatest thing since the church key. The boys in the back get into the spirit, and before ya know it, there's an almighty ruckus going on in the canoe. They're all whoopin' it up, as the moose is towing them down the river! They're making fine progress too, the wake pickin' up real high, when a funny thing happens. In all their glee, the boys don't see it right off, but them big shoulders start to rise ever so slightly and that moose starts a comin' out of the water. Then they realize the beast has been angling for shore all along! Quick, Lefleur sets about retrievin' the line, but there's a torque on it like an iron bar, and before you know it, the water is cascadin' off the animal's back like one of them waterfalls in the gorge! The moose rises faster and the line climbs higher, until the bow starts coming out of the river, and Lefleur all the while heavin' and reefin' till that bow is plumb clear in the sky! He's hanging on as the moose lifts the canoe out of the river, their gear a tumblin' every which way, splashin' in the river and floatin' down with the current. By now the line is a good ten feet in the air. And steppin' out of the water, strollin' up on shore, that moose is the biggest godawful ...!"

But then a wave of bodies washes over Snow and pulls him to the floor. I watch him on his way down, both eyes open in bewilderment. And then I go under too, swept away by a tide of patrons, table and all. The last I see is Snow reaching for his spinning beer bottle, foam shooting out of it in all directions.

LAUNCHING FROM A BOAT RAMP on Little Clear Pond this morning, we paddle directly for the small island in the middle of the lake. On our way around the back side of the island, Annie spots a nest at the edge of the water. Two olive eggs, speckled blue, lay side-by-side on a patch of hardpan about the size of a dinner plate. The eggs are bigger than any bird eggs I've ever seen, each shaped like an elongated softball.

In the time it takes for us to register the nest, a submerged shadow slips beneath the canoe on its way to deeper water. It's the adult loon who has quietly abandoned the eggs without us noticing. As it swims away from the canoe, I see the white checkering of its plumage underwater and its feet extended from the rear, propelling the bird like a torpedo. The loon surfaces twenty yards offshore.

I back-paddle to bring the bow close to the nest, while Annie grabs the clipboard and begins to write. In less than a minute's time, we calculate the diameter of the nest, its distance to the water, the height of the nest above water, and the depth of the lake at one, two, five, and ten-foot intervals from shore. When we're finished, we paddle away from the island and watch as the adult makes its way back. At the sight of exposed eggs, a large raven alights on a nearby shrub, eliciting a sharp rebuke from the loon as it returns to the nest. At close range, its warning call—a resounding tremolo—chills the blood. Wings flapping, feet stomping, the loon gives the raven what for as the black bird scrambles through the brush in retreat. All this on a calm, misty morning.

"Did you see its ruby eye?" Annie smiles.

I'm just happy we finally bagged a nest. For now, anyway, the pressure is off. No more pangs of self-doubt as wildlife specialists. Now that we've actually seen what we're looking for, this should improve our chances of finding more nests. We *want* to find nests. Annie wants to see reproductive success. Me, I want to win. Not so much to win, but to *not lose*. Come in with higher numbers than the other crews.

After making a quick check of the rest of the pond, we head back to the boat-ramp. Coasting into the sandy shore, it occurs to me this loon business isn't all that bad. In fact, I'm beginning to like it. It could be that deep inside I feel the cobwebs of doubt unraveling, knots of despair untangling. The fog lifting on this rag-ass drifter's life.

That night I have a dream. Annie and I are lost, paddling in a thick fog. There's no difference between the fog and water, and it's as though we're floating in air, disengaged from earth. An island appears in front of us and we pull the canoe onto the bank. Then we lie beneath the pine trees in the dirt and have at it like a pair of wildcats for the better part of the morning, pulling and scratching at one another, dust rising in the amber sunlight. At one point, she grabs my hair by the scruff, looks at me and says, "Welcome to the last dance." Afterward, we lie drained and happy and half naked, watching and listening to the wind whisper in the pine branches above us.

All our wrestling has carved out a depression in the soft dirt. The few trees that grow on the island are spaced well enough to afford a view of the entire lake and its shoreline.

No cottages or docks or boat ramps, just an evergreen shore and the lonesome blue outline of distant mountains.

Annie drifts off to sleep, her body rising and falling on mine with each breath, her hair pressed against my cheek. I flirt with sleep myself but manage to stay awake, adjusting my shoulder slightly to make our bodies fit, watching the pine trees sway in the breeze overhead.

TODAY WE PUT-IN at Paradox Bay on Lake Placid, letting a stiff westerly wind carry us down the shore. The summit of Whiteface looms to the northeast at 4,865 feet, a white streak scarring its western slope. At the far end, a phalanx of mountains buttresses the lake: Moose, Alton, Eagle Eyrie. And to the east: Little Whiteface, Sunrise Notch, Moss Cliff. All aspiring, it seems, to the taller Whiteface. Halfway down the lake, a sheer cliff drops a hundred feet to the water. Staying close to shore with Whiteface in our sights, we pass beneath birch and pine trees growing horizontally out of the rock.

The wind howls, making Placid anything but. These are the toughest winds we've encountered so far. The canoe rolls and pitches in waves two-feet high. White clouds sail across the sky, pulling shadows across the green flanks of mountains. The wind pushes us down the rocky shore all the way to Whiteface Bay. We've heard that a single loon often appears here in August, but the rugged shoreline makes nesting unlikely.

Nestled among the mountains, Lake Placid is classic Adirondack. It's been said to remind some of the high alpine lakes of the Swiss Alps, though I've never been. A dyed-in-the-wool native son, I have no interest in the Old World. It's crowded, they let their wilderness go, and the brown bears are a shadow of their former selves.

I WALK OUTSIDE this morning to the *rat-tat-tat!* of a sapsucker rapping its beak on the metal roof of the house, a rapid-fire burst that soars across the lake like a jackhammer testament to futility. I locate the bird near the peak of the roof, its yellow belly shining in the sun.

An inauspicious start to the day, for sure.

In fact, today we make a mockery of the entire research project by surveying Mirror Lake. It's on the list, so we have to cover it. Hard beside the town of Lake *Plastic*, as Saranac locals like to call it, this modest waterhole has been overrun by human sprawl. The lake is heavily developed with clustered boxes, otherwise known as condo-bondage. This architectural atrocity seems to be the latest rage, though why one would want to live like a tenement rat is beyond me.

The only wildlife worth noting here is of the human variety, concentrated on the public beach. Most of the specimens we observe appear to be engaged in the early stages of mating behavior. The awkward gyrations of the male dance are especially evident.

I think it's fair to say there is absolutely no chance in hell of a loon nesting on this lake—at least not until one of Flashlight's viral plagues races through and wipes out all the humans, leaving nothing but a lonesome wind moaning through the rubble and scraps of refuse skittering like tumbleweed down deserted streets.

Not really sure why this lake is on our list, as we are wasting our time here, gawking at summer homes in a town that for all intents and purposes sold itself down the river long ago. For all its quaintness and glitz, this place is as phony as a wooden nickel. Not only that, it's an ugly reminder of why we're here in the first place. All this "development" (as if we're talking about some kind of improvement) is what pushes wildlife out of its habitat in the first place. It's bad enough we've only found one nest in four weeks, but to trot us out here like a circus act is to add insult to injury. We might as well be the moose stranded in the deep end of a swimming pool.

After a quick spin around Mirror, we decide to stop by the DEC Regional Office in Ray Brook, since we're in the neighborhood anyway. The facility, with its brown brick and evenly spaced windows, stands like a garrison on the outskirts of Lake Placid. Three flags for country, state, and agency snap in the breeze. Adjacent to the DEC building is a state police compound, and not far from that, the headquarters for conservation officers. A conservation officer, or CO, is a cross between park-ranger and cop. Think of it as nature fuzz, packing heat. All this law enforcement concentrated in one place makes me apprehensive, naturally, but at least it's good to know where the nerve center is.

Annie figures we ought to open a line of communication with the office here in case there's an opportunity to coordinate operations. If nothing else, it can't hurt to stop in and say hello. Besides, somebody in this building has our paychecks for the month of June. Frank sent them here with the idea that they'd eventually be delivered to Colby. By going directly to the source, we figure we can cut a little red tape and minimize the chances of any bureaucratic snafu that might delay the process. And while we're at it, we can top off the ungulate. Ray Brook has its own gas pump for state vehicles. Might as well fill up here, and not have to mess with vouchers.

We drive around to the back of the building, where we find the gas pump next to a helicopter parked on a patch of asphalt. Behind the helipad is a small corral on the lawn that holds two llamas. Fred and Millie, no doubt. Two leather halters hang from the iron bars of the corral. Nylon panniers are stacked alongside one another. There's a hay bale and a tub of food scraps—carrots, celery stalks, broccoli, grapefruit rinds, orange peels.

After filling up, we park the Impala and walk inside the building where we're blasted with ultraviolet light and the stagnant air of an office warren. I feel a pressure in my brain, like the low-grade pain you get when you walk into a large department store at a shopping mall—something felt more than heard.

Down the white cinderblock corridor we go, running a gauntlet of offices. At the first open door, we ask for Wildlife.

"You want *Non-Game*," a secretary intones. "This is Game. Non-Game is the next wing over," she points.

We turn around and retrace our steps, sneakers squeaking on the shiny tile, the UV bulbs buzzing overhead. We approach the glass door leading to the parking lot, the one we entered just moments before. Its tinted window filters the green woods and blue sky outside, making them appear darker than they actually are. Plus, it's cold inside. The climate control has been set too low. It's as if somebody decided to improve upon the sunny day and blue sky by first removing them, and then replacing them with bad substitutes.

We turn left down an adjacent hallway that leads in the general direction indicated by the secretary. Same white cinderblock walls, same shiny tiled floor. We pass the stainless-steel doors of an elevator. The corridor makes another left, turning back toward the bowels of the warren.

On the right side of the hallway, large glass windows are framed in black steel, and we can see into the cushy offices of administrators. We keep walking, looking for an entrance to the Non-Game wing, following the corridor nearly to its end before noticing what looks to be a lobby on the other side of the glass. A receptionist waves to us and I wave back. But there's no way to get there. I run my finger along the black steel sill and pick up a nice film of dust. At the end of the long corridor, we come to an exit door that leads outside. But the door comes with a warning: open it and an alarm goes off. Annie and I turn around and walk all the way back to the tinted door where we first entered the building. We step outside into the sunshine and rethink our approach.

This time we enter a different door on the side of the building. As it turns out, the Non-Game wing is a mirror image of the Game wing, with all the same cinderblock walls and UV lights and shiny floors. Even the hallways are laid out the same, only in reverse order. We make our way past another emergency door to the lobby where Annie introduces herself to the receptionist and explains that we're here to pick up our paychecks.

"Oh, yes," the receptionist replies, dark circles under her eyes. "We've been expecting you."

The receptionist escorts us down the hall to a room crowded with metal shelves and filing cabinets, all in the color of battleship gray. Manila folders and plastic binders are stacked in the shelves and along the floor. Through the black Venetian blinds covering the window, a glare of sunlight penetrates the room.

We're introduced to two men sitting at their desks. Stokes is our contact, the agency bureaucrat who has our money. He fumbles through a desk drawer and pulls out two checks. "You'll have to sign here," he says, extending a piece of paper.

"Exactly what are you two doing, anyway?"

"Common loon survey," Annie replies, signing the form. "We're based at Colby. There are two other crews around the state this summer—one at Blue Lake and the other at Racquette."

Meanwhile, the other worker pushes his chair back and stands, picks up his styrofoam cup and leans against one of the filing cabinets.

"Loons," Stokes says. "Why, there's plenty of 'em up here. See 'em all the time. Yeah, I'd say we've got our share."

Our man Stokes is overweight—a substantial paunch beneath his pale blue polyester shirt, pen clasped to the pocket. He sits slouched in his swivel chair, staring at the lines of sunlight glaring through the blind. When he turns to answer Annie, he looks at me instead.

"Our Albany office says you're helping track bald eagle pairs," Annie mentions.

"Yeah, we do a little of that," says Stokes.

"We've had a report of a nest in the area."

"A report?" he says, looking at me. "What report?"

"From some local people down in Sara—"

"Locals?" he smirks. "That's where you got your information?" Stokes glances at his co-worker who flashes a grin. "Somebody sees a hawk in the sky, and the next thing you know we have an eagle nest on our hands."

"She was only telling you what she heard," I say.

Stokes leans back in his chair, scans the array of metal shelves in the room and looks again at the blinds. "Well, maybe, but we get so many reports and none of them ever turns out to be true. This is how many nests there are in the entire state," he says, holding up three fingers. "One north of here, one in the Catskills, and one by Watertown. Take my advice and don't waste your time with locals."

"Do you ever investigate the reports?"

"Don't have to, it's a waste of time. Unless there are multiple sightings, we don't bother." He swirls the dregs of his coffee in his styrofoam cup. "Why do they have you doing a loon survey, anyway?"

"We're trying to establish reproductive success and population trends."

"What for?"

"So the State can classify them as either threatened or a 'species of special concern.' A lot of it has to do with the funding of recovery efforts."

"You're right about that," Stokes says, shaking his head. "It's all about the money." The smirk again. Subtle, but unmistakable. "Well, one good thing about loons, they bring more people up here. People like to hear them wail in the night. Gives them a feeling of the wilderness as they look out from their cedar decks."

"But that's a big reason why they're in trouble," Annie says. "Development."

"And that's why all asudden there's pressure to save them, so people can come up here to their summer homes and hear them! Who do you think is behind all the preservation stuff, anyway? Where do you think all the money is coming from? Locals?"

A peal of sharp laughter from the man at the filing cabinet.

"I don't think so," Stokes continues. "It's coming from the Sierra Club and a few other fluff outfits, and where do you think *they* get their money?"

"That's not the whole story," I say.

"Maybe not, but it's a big part of it. All I know is the last thing we need is another endangered species to manage. You can't imagine the headaches this causes."

I could care less about what he thinks or how many eagle nests there are between here and Timbuktu. But our man Stokes has copped an attitude that has worked its way under my skin to the point where I'm beginning to see red. Only thing is, this is not my element. I can't very well make a scene inside government headquarters. Not only that, but this is not my fight. I have no stake in the matter. Better just to remain calm, blend in. Fly under the radar.

But it's not that easy. Maybe it's the money issue or the way this bureaucrat wants to write us off, smirking for his flunky at the filing cabinet. Or maybe it's the fact he refuses to look Annie in the eye. It doesn't help, I suppose, that there's a kernel of truth in what he says. In any case, I feel a cold sweat coming on—an early warning sign. It's the same feeling I had in Albany when all that paperwork started piling up in front of me. And I guess it shows, because Annie takes me by the elbow and says it's time to go.

She leads me into the hallway and down the concrete corridor. At the end of the hall is an emergency exit door. I slam the metal bar and burst into the sunshine outside, hearing an alarm bell go off behind us. Walking quickly across the blacktop, a few steps ahead of Annie, I can guess what she's thinking. Making a beeline for the Impala, I *know* she's wondering about the change that's come over me ... *the flushed face and clenched fists, on the verge of some primal rage. When all we were doing was picking up our paychecks from the regional manager ...*

"There's still plenty of light," she says. "Might be a good idea to get back on the water."

We follow the highway west before turning onto a dirt road that leads down to Connery Pond, driving past a row of new lakefront homes, then parking where the lane ends just beyond the driveway of a large, pricey house—two stories, ten rooms easy. According to the map, this is the only way to get to the pond. The topo indicates no public access point, and the information we have from Albany mentions nothing about asking permission to cross private property. We can see the pond from the car, so I suggest we cut through the woods beyond the edge of the groomed lawn, keeping our distance from the house. I even chart a course through the tall grass and trees, using the enormous white satellite dish near the lake as a reference point. It's one of those huge 54-channel jobs, gleaming in the sun like a grail.

We start through the woods with the canoe, skirting the manicured lawn, guided by the dish. Annie carries the front while I take the back, my fingers curled under the aluminum cone behind the seat. We're making fine progress when a man bolts from the front door of the house and charges across the lawn, dressed in a button-down white shirt, khaki pants, and deck shoes. When he gets closer, I notice the alligator belt.

"What do you think you're doing?" he asks, as if we haven't a clue. "You're on private property."

As a matter of course, I let Annie handle all interactions with the public while I keep quiet in the background. Calmly, she delivers the company line: biologists working for the DEC, loon survey, checking on ponds in the area, etc.

But it's clear the diplomacy isn't going well.

"Why should I care? What does that have to do with me? I build a house on *my* property, and you people fight me every step of the way with your regulations."

His hair is closely cropped and slicked back with gel, flat against an oblong skull. A puffy nose with blackheads, and broken blood vessels on his cheeks.

"You're trespassing on my property. If you want to get to this pond, you go someplace else."

And we would have, had he left it at that.

"As far as I'm concerned, sweetheart, you and your monkey friend can go to hell."

And so I pop him. Not hard like a roundhouse, just a quick jab.

"Miles!"

Then the bleeding: a steady flow from the nose, down his chin, and onto the button-down shirt. The man tilts his head back as Annie runs to the car and returns with a towel. He pinches the bridge of his nose with his thumb and forefinger and wobbles toward the house, muttering some garbled threat I can't quite understand. But I pretty much know what it is.

Annie and I pick up the canoe and continue on our way, following an opening in the woods to the pond. We paddle the entire shoreline in less than a half hour. The banks are mostly covered with high grass, the trees set back from the water. We find plenty of frogs in a little stream leading down to the pond, but no loons.

On the way home, Annie turns off the highway onto a back road that takes us north, somewhere in the direction of Gabriels. After fifteen minutes of riding in silence, we come upon a stone cottage tucked in the woods with a small "Open" sign in the window.

We walk inside and find our way to a small taproom where two French doors open onto the woods. Honey sunlight pours through the doorway onto an oriental rug and knotty pine floor. The lacy stems of spider ferns, illumined in the golden light, cascade over planter boxes. A cast-iron woodstove stands in the corner on a small brick platform. As the only customers, we sit at a small oak table and order from a quiet woman, who returns with two beers before disappearing to the back of the cottage.

Left alone to our thoughts, Annie and I sit quietly in the late afternoon sunlight. I'm content to watch the tiny bubbles rise in the shining amber of my beer. A tough line of work, wildlife biology.

Annie looks at me coolly then turns away, her green eyes catching the sunlight. She looks at me again in a way that tells me she's working something out in her mind. I stare at the beer foam coating the inside of my glass, feeling the pilsner beginning to work, and it occurs to me to get to the bottom of whatever stands between us. There's a divide separating us, an awkward gap we've yet to ford—made worse, I'm afraid, by the punch at Connery. Ever since our first conversation on the drive up from Albany, I have felt some unfinished business between us. I like Annie, trust her even. It's just that we've been together for a month now, and something still doesn't feel right.

"Annie," I say, tilting my chair back, "what's the meaning of all this?"

She turns her head and I realize immediately that I've made a tactical blunder. This is not something to be tackled head on. Quick, change course.

"Exactly what are we doing here? I mean, I understand the science end of it—analyzing population trends and all that—but, in the long run, are we supposed to be *saving* this bird? Is that what we're doing?"

She doesn't flinch, not so much as a blink of an eye. And that's what's so unnerving. It's like she's operating on some other plane, tapped into some higher consciousness, a conduit to some energy force beyond this world.

"Don't get me wrong," I say, now clearly on the defensive. "I'm all for nature. I like animals better than I like most people. It's just that something doesn't add up about all this. First off, there's not a chance in hell that *anyone* can stem the tide of human domination. Let's face it, as a species we're going to reproduce ourselves silly and impose our will on as much of the world as we can, until nature says enough is enough and pulls the plug on our little party. Flashlight may be strange, but there's some truth in what he says—all that stuff about overpopulation, extinction, disease ... all those disasters looming on the horizon. If you listen to him, the planet is going to hell and there's nothing anyone can do about it. There's simply too much momentum."

No question, I can get on my soap box with the best of them. Only I tend to go too far, especially when it's clear I ought to zip it. But I've never been one to cut my losses. When I know I'm digging myself a hole, that's when I pour it on, adding fuel to the fire, until I get around to what I've been building up to do all along: put my foot in my mouth. Call it Hoof-in-Mouth disease.

The innkeeper returns and we order another round. Annie's not a drinker like me, but she'll tip a few if the occasion dictates. She's comfortable in her skin.

"What I mean is, nobody likes a blowhard who gets all high and mighty about saving the world, preaching do this and don't do that, when all along he's just angling to make things better for himself. I'm sure there are many well-meaning environmentalists out there, but don't you think there's something presumptuous about all this? Something self-righteous and hypocritical? You have to admit that a lot of the world's problems are the result of half-baked do-gooder schemes. I know he's an ass, but that office mole back in Ray Brook may not have been too far from the truth."

"'Office mole?'" she says, taking a sip from her beer.

"Yeah."

"So, what are you gonna do?" she asks. I can't tell if the question is rhetorical or not, but there's no stopping me now.

"I'll tell you what I'm gonna do—the same thing I always do: get on down the road, have a look around, and get my kicks in while I can. Nobody tells me what to do. I might not have a lot to show for it, but I'm free to go where I like, when I like. And I'm not afraid to call a spade a spade. It may not look like it, but I have my principles. I'm like a lightning rod, channeling all the energy of whatever is out there, good and bad. And I'm not afraid to go all the way, either. I've always said I'll try anything once."

I bring my chair down and lean closer, trying to level with her. "Annie, this 'saving the world' business is hard. I just don't think I'm cut out for it. It seems like it requires ... *manners.*"

I wait for a reply, especially to the offhand reference to Connery, but Annie says nothing. She just looks at me in that inscrutable way that makes me want to keep talking.

"Besides, it's a losing game," I say, "and it goes against my instincts to throw in on a pipedream."

She leans back from the table. "I guess I figured you wrong, Miles," she says. "I figured you for a romantic. You know, the kind of guy who goes down with the ship. Champion of wild things and lost causes."

This stops me in my tracks. I can't think of anything to say, prompting her to laugh out loud, a real honest-to-goodness laugh that lets me know there's no hard feelings and that maybe she's right about me. At least this much. And just like that, she's turned the moment around—removed any snag there might have been and put us in a whole new place with a fresh set of possibilities. The change is electric, I can feel it in the air. With all my yammering, I had backed myself into a corner, shrunk down my options, and in a single stroke of genius she opens a door I hadn't seen and shows me a way out of the cage. I feel a weight lifted from my shoulders, as if the world has just punched my ticket and welcomed me back.

Outside, the sunlight has turned a deeper shade of gold, filtering through the forest in glowing beams. A monarch butterfly flutters past. Birdsong is thick in the air—a wall of sound so dense it seems that if I just reached out far enough, I could touch it with my hand.

Annie leans forward, elbows on the table.

"When I was a girl," she begins, "there was a pond close to where we lived. I remember going there as often as I could, almost every day. There were dragonflies and bullfrogs and painted turtles. Red-winged blackbirds lived in the cattails, and I knew where the mallards nested in spring. I caught bluegills and sunfish and catfish with a net. I caught frogs, too, and they weren't afraid when I held them in my hand. I came to know the animals and birds, just as they came to know me.

"The pond was fed by a little crick where clams and crawfish lived. There were pebbles on the bottom that I imagined Indians used for decoration. I found arrowheads in the meadow next to it where cottontails and field mice lived, and sometimes I'd watch the hawks as they circled overhead before diving into the tall grass."

A change comes over her face, like the shadow from a passing cloud. There's a distance in her eyes.

"Next to the pond was a large weeping willow where I'd go to lie down and watch the clouds, looking for what I might see in them—animals and dragons and castles. They were all real to me. I'd go there at night to see the stars and fireflies. Sometimes I'd just lie there and dream, let my imagination take me away. This was my world. I was home there."

Now she stares outside, her hands cupped around the glass.

"Let me guess," I say. "Somebody trashed it."

"Shopping mall," she replies. "I came home from school one day and it was all destroyed."

"And it made you angry."

"I saw turtles and frogs buried alive, watched bluegills suffocate in oily mud. I remember throwing rocks at the bulldozer. That night I snuck out with a knife, the biggest one I could find in the house, and slashed the tire of a truck. I was twelve."

She looks into her glass, bubbles rising to the top.

"Annie, you mentioned once that you worked in some kind of rescue unit, but it didn't sound like any official organization."

"Oh, it was organized."

She squints her eyes, sizing me up. The same look she gave me in the car on the way up from Albany.

"I was an activist for a while," she says. "Direct actions. I was a bit of a mercenary, moving around a lot."

"What were you doing?"

"Whatever was going on at the time—springing traps, spiking trees, freeing dolphins from tuna nets. I was on one of the campaigns confronting whaling ships in the Pacific."

I pause to let this sink in. I'd seen the footage on television. Come to think of it, she reminds me of a pirate—with that roguish grin and mischievous gleam in her eye. Still, it's hard to imagine Annie ducking lethal projectiles on the high seas.

"That's pretty serious," I say.

"I suppose it is, but there was always something bigger at stake, a bigger question to consider. We all felt it."

She looks directly at me, her eyes calm and clear.

"Tell me," I ask, "how does a person reach a point where they'd risk everything to save wild animals?"

"Wild animals have as much right to be here as we do," she replies. "Maybe more. At least they've learned to live together in some kind of balance. We, on the other hand, are overrunning the planet. Eventually this will catch up with us, but in the meantime, it's the animals and birds and other living things that pay the price. And that's wrong. That's profoundly wrong. It's criminal."

"But to risk your life and break the law ...."

"You should know something about that."

"That's different."

Annie stares at me with dead calm eyes.

"Look," she says, "we all make our own decisions. For me, it's a matter of bringing my life in line with what I know to be true. I live with the injustice and destruction of the world, just as I live with all its beauty and mystery. I sit with them both."

Run, the old instinct tells me, *run fast* ...

"Does Frank know about any of this?"

"Not really," she says, "no one in DEC does."

"Except for me."

"Except for you."

"And why me? Why are you telling me this?"

Annie looks into the forest beyond the open doors. There's the distance again. "You don't think much of the loon survey, do you?"

"I don't have faith in humanity," I answer. "I think most people are out for themselves, and the system is rigged in favor of rich people. Push me far enough, and I'll say there's not much hope."

"I think you see more than you know," she says.

I look into her eyes for a clue.

"I have a debt to pay to society," I say. "That's what they tell me."

The sun slants low and floods the room in a warm golden glow. Birds sing away in the woods—warblers and vireos, a thrush from some secret recess. At the moment, I'd be hard pressed to find anything out of place in the world. If my number were to come up just now, well, it could be a whole lot worse.

"I'll promise you one thing," I tell her. "From now on, I'll do my best to be a good partner. You have my word on it."

A MONTH INTO THE STUDY NOW, and we've settled into a routine that goes something like this. Sometime in the half light of dawn, Annie patters down the hallway, grabs the knitted pillow with the state seal on it from the chair next to the telephone, and whirls it at me as I sleep. This is sometimes followed by a soft giggle that dissipates in sweet gradations as she walks down the stairs to the main floor. Truth is, I'm usually awake by the time she throws the pillow. But it's part of our routine, and I let her have the satisfaction of thinking she's awake before me.

I leave my clothes on a bedside chair for easy access, so that I'm dressed and down the stairs before she finishes her orange juice and toast. An opportunistic omnivore, I'll eat anything I can scrounge in the house or scavenge later in the way of bar food. Regarding the former, I have no compunction about foraging any and all foodstuffs left in the refrigerator by visiting state officials who periodically convene here for meetings. I think this rankles Flashlight a bit, as he likes to run a tight ship. But, hey, propriety goes to hell when hunger enters the equation. I've always done most of my eating on the run, anyway. If it were up to me, there'd be a little door attached to the stomach where a person could insert food, much like shoveling coal into a furnace. Just be done with it, quick and easy.

As we get ready for the day, Annie plays the vinyl record of Eastern bird songs on the phonograph, so that we may hone our auditory skills and contribute to the Audubon survey.

When I first heard the record, the songs all blended together and I couldn't tell the difference between a Titmouse and a Bobolink. Lately, though, I've begun to concentrate less on the drone of the narrator's voice and more on the nuances of warbles, chits, and squawks.

If we have the ingredients, we'll make sandwiches. Otherwise, we pick something up at the deli in town where the young woman works the counter. We've seen her a few times now, skating along Highway 3 in her new-fangled, high-tech gear. Although I can't say for sure, it's probably safe to assume she's an elite athlete, training for the Olympics in one of the Nordic events. She certainly has the physique for that level of competition, not to mention the dedication.

While the warped and scratchy 78 spins on the old RCA, we eat breakfast in the den and plan out our day. Oftentimes these strategy sessions take place the night before in the cupola, but even so, we're sure to take a few minutes in the morning to go over everything. We start with the 30 x 60 topo for the big picture, then turn to the more detailed 7.5 maps for launch sites. Most of the lakes have public access. If not, we go to the state-issued directory to find the names of landowners whose permission we must obtain before crossing their property. This is usually a formality. It's always satisfying to impress homeowners with the moral imperative of our mission. Most of the time, anyway.

A final check to make sure we have everything: lunch, water, maps, clipboard, forms, binoculars, bug juice, bird book. (Unbeknownst to Annie, I also carry a "travel bag" of assorted goodies from the three doors of redemption.) Canoe lashed to the top of the Impala, paddles and life jackets piled into the back seat, and off we go.

We have a system in the field as well. Upon arriving at the put-in site, we untie the canoe and swing it down from the roof of the car. (I've shown Annie how to do this by herself in case there's a time when I'm not there to help.) Once the canoe is down, we carry it to the water where we load the gear, get ourselves ready, and push off. Annie sits in the bow while I man the stern. She takes care of the technical side of the survey, while my primary responsibility rests with the safe operation of the canoe. I've rigged up a comfortable backrest with the spare paddle, wedged between seat and stern, and a life jacket for padding. All in all, I'd say we execute our duties with the style and panache of an elite military unit. A lean mean reconnaissance machine.

We can cover up to three or four lakes on any given day, depending on access and acreage. For the sake of efficiency, we'll target a number of adjacent ponds if they're small—fifty acres or less. The maps are crucial. We carry at least one 7.5 topo with us at all times, along with a clipboard and field forms to enter all the pertinent data: lake name, loon sightings, loon behavior, nest location, number of eggs or chicks, distance between nest and edge of water, water depth at different intervals, etc. If we encounter other wildlife or bird species, we enter this information as well.

To get to Osgood Pond, our destination this morning, we park at a bridge and paddle a half mile upriver from Jones Pond. Well worth the effort. Osgood is a classic alpine lake with many bays, its shoreline crowned with peninsulas sloping down to the water. The peninsulas line up in sequence, each with a slightly different hue—from the deep greens of nearby forests, to the smoky blue of distant ridges. There's one island on the lake with two houses on it. We say hello to a man in front of one of the houses who says he's seen loons on the lake in the past. A familiar refrain, by now. *Do loons hide when they know we're coming? How do they know we're looking for them?* It may be that loons spotted on Osgood actually inhabit the nearby St. Regis lakes.

In the afternoon we paddle Barnum Pond, a small body of water filled with lily pads at one end. Some of the lilies have white flowers. Not unlike the sacred lotus of the Far East, Annie says. With its roots in the mud, the lotus rises through murky water to flower in the air above. For Buddhists, this symbolizes a spiritual awakening from earthly attachments and desires. Out of the muck of existence come beauty and purity of mind.

Though Barnum lacks the isolation associated with loon habitat, we spot a large raptor in the distance that we're unable to identify. The northern Adirondacks are home to a number of raptor species: Bald Eagle, Osprey, Turkey Vulture, and American Kestrel. Among the hawks are Red-Tailed, Broad-Winged, Red-Shouldered, Cooper's, Northern, and Marsh. The Cooper's Hawk feeds on songbirds it plucks out of the air. Like the loon, the eagle and osprey share a taste for fish. The Turkey Vulture is easily identified by its featherless head, all the better for removing the innards of a carcass.

Speaking of food, I drive to the market that evening to do some shopping before the holiday. The clerk greets me at the entrance with his customary indifference. I look away to avoid his deadpan, glancing at the bus schedule on the wall behind him.

Things are going pretty well as I make my way through lunchmeat and dairy—pickled bologna, Velveeta, chocolate milk—but when I get to the produce section, everything changes. A few of the bins are empty, with only scraps of corn husks and dried onion skins. A half-dozen shoppers linger nervously, squeezing tomatoes, sniffing melons. No one moves and I can't get through to the lettuce. Somebody wheels a cart behind me, boxing me in. I begin to panic. A woman in high heels looks at me and snarls. All in my imagination, of course, but it doesn't make it any less real. I'm having a vision. A man in overalls grows fangs and attacks a frail old lady by the cauliflower, biting her in the back of the neck as blood smears across his face. She collapses to the floor with the dazed look of fallen prey.

I abandon my cart and hightail it out of there, exchanging glances with the clerk on my way out the door.

TOMORROW IS THE FOURTH OF JULY. Annie has taken the Impala down to Albany for a few days, leaving me alone with the bicycle and leftovers in the refrigerator. But I'm not feeling especially domestic. And I'm not keen on the bicycle, either. So when the sun goes down, I hike the path around Colby and cross the trestle, following the road into town to the Waterhole.

A good crowd tonight in anticipation of the Fourth. All the regulars are present and accounted for. Snow has an idea about tomorrow and wants to know how many are interested in his plan. Says he knows of a nice location for viewing the fireworks, but it will take some work to get there.

"See, we take the houseboat down Lake Flower into Oseetah and all the way to the south bay. At that point, we tie up and proceed on foot to the top of a mountain that looks west over the High Peaks. From there, we ought to be able to see the fireworks from both Saranac and Placid. We'll bring us a grill and cook out."

He's got the shine in his eyes, so I tell him to count me in.

"There's the grill and food and beer to carry. I figure there might be six of us, so that's at least three cases. Not impossible, I suppose, but it sure would be nice if we had some way of transporting all that weight without having to hump it ourselves."

I tell him I might have an idea about that.

Independence Day breaks clear and bright, sun blazing in a bluebird sky. Anticipating a long day and night, I ride the bicycle to town where I meet Snow waiting in his van outside the bar.

"Boat's all ready to go," he says, as I slide into the passenger seat with a bag of carrots and celery stalks. My cutoffs snag on a metal spring protruding from the vinyl seat. "Yukon's keeping an eye on things. Everybody else should be there by the time we arrive. Only thing left to do is procure the balance of the cargo."

On our way out of town, I notice red-and-white bunting on a few of the store fronts. Old Glory hangs from flagpoles secured to the wooden frames of porches. Patriotic whirligigs sprout like weeds in the grass.

Snow has removed the bench seats from the back, transforming his van into a spacious metal shell. He's custom fit indoor-outdoor carpeting on the floor, wall to wall. Two old blankets are folded in the corner.

"What do you use that for?" I ask, pointing to the police scanner on the dash.

"I like to keep tabs on things," he says. "You never know what might come across it."

"How does it work?"

"You just find the right frequency and listen in," he says, looking at me. "It's all about tuning into the right frequency."

He taps his fingers on the steering wheel. "You sure this is going to work?"

"Piece of cake," I tell him. "What could go wrong?"

When we arrive at Ray Brook, the parking lot is empty. Everyone is gone for the holiday, just as I suspected. Snow drives around the side of the building, past the helipad and gas pump, slowing down as we approach the corral holding the llamas. If they are anything like horses, they'll spook at the first sign of jitters. Relax, I tell myself. Stay calm. Go slow.

Snow opens the sliding door nice and gentle, then waits by the van. "Have at it," he says with a grin, "I'm just the door man."

I free the latch of the iron gate and walk inside the makeshift corral. "Have any preference?"

"How about the perty one," he says, nodding to the black-and-white paint.

"That would be Millie," I say, "if I'm not mistaken."

I extend a few carrots in the palm of my hand. The llama steps forward and snatches them with its upper lip. "Looks like we have a winner," I say. Millie already wears a halter, so all I have to do is clip on a lead line. Her face is black with white markings, dark around the eyes. She has a gray coat and white belly, black feet and spotted white legs.

I walk out of the pen with the llama in tow. "Spread those blankets out," I say. "Give the old girl a soft landing."

As we approach the van, Millie hesitates. "Gorgeous thing," Snow says, petting her flank. A beautiful girl, indeed. Luminous brown eyes, long lashes, Mona Lisa smile.

"What's wrong?" I coo. "Never rode in a van before?" I tap my hand on the indoor-outdoor. "Here ya go, baby doll."

Millie steps into the van and sits down, tucking her legs beneath her. Once she's comfortable on the floor, I walk to the storage shed behind the corral and grab a stake line, saddle and pad.

Millie rides like a queen all the way back to town. No fuss. When we get to the launch, I guide her out of the van and across the lot to the dock where Spot, Yukon, Wire and Beaver are waiting. We pull the houseboat flush with the dock, open the gate, and coax her aboard. She sits down on the green, plastic grass of the houseboat just as she did on the indoor-outdoor, front legs tucked underneath. We pile all the gear on the boat—beer, food, grill, and boombox. Snow fires up the outboard. I free the line, step aboard, and off we go.

Nobody knows how to act at first. We all stare at Millie as she stares back. "It's like she's reading my thoughts," Yukon says.

Snow keeps the throttle low, as we putter our way down Lake Flower. Beers are cracked, conversation begins to flow. Millie stays calm, resting. At one point, when our noise begins to build, she raises her head and snorts.

After an hour in the houseboat, we tie up to a tree in the south bay of Oseetah alongside a flat bank where we disembark. The others haul the gear ashore while I walk Millie off the boat and set about dressing her. Just like a horse, I say to myself, thinking back to the summer I worked at a ranch in Colorado. First the saddle pad: a wool cushion, leather on top, with internal stiffeners to distribute the weight. Then a soft pack with cinch straps and D-rings (two on each side) to clip on the panniers. Now the nylon straps to tie the panniers in place.

The grill folds up small enough to fit in one of the panniers. We break down the cardboard boxes and load the cans of beer individually. Hamburger and hot dogs and requisite fixings. All told, no more than sixty pounds for Millie.

I take the lead line and guide her along the trail, as Snow and Beaver carry the big cooler loaded with ice and beer.

Yukon hobbles along in his foot-cast with the aid of his cane. Millie's an angel, sure-footed and quiet, her movements fluid and graceful.

It takes about an hour to get to the top of the mountain, where a panorama of peaks and lakes and rolling hills unfolds in all directions. We find a grassy flat, wide enough to accommodate our foolishness, and spread out a few blankets. I stake Millie off to the side, where she can have her space and plenty of green grass in addition to the carrots and celery I've brought.

Reggae plays on the paint-spattered boombox, Yukon sparks up the grill, Snow packs his meerschaum pipe, and the festivities commence. I clear a space on a blanket and divvy up six piles of fungal scraps gleaned from Door #3. Spot watches with reverence. "Sticks and stones may break my bones ...."

Out of the blue, Yukon raises his can of beer to the rampart of high peaks in the west. "Here's to big country!"

Snow cups his hands around his mouth and unleashes a soaring loon wail.

"Big country and *wild things*!" Spot adds.

"Don't Tread on Me!" Beaver follows.

Now it's a free for all.

"Freedom from tyranny!"

"*E Pluribus Unum!*"

"Down with the man!"

"Up with people!"

"Today is the first day of the rest of your life!"

A steady breeze agitates the ground cover on our bald mountaintop. Looking closer, I see three layers of grass, each with its own little dance going on. At six inches high, thin stalks bounce in the wind like the steady back-and-forth stroke on a musical washboard. A middle layer of grass spins in circular fashion—the graceful pirouette of a lady's gown at a Victorian ball. And close to the ground, a stubby short grass twitches in sudden bursts. Three different kinds of grass, three different layers, three different rhythms. Each working in concert with the others.

A red cardinal alights on the branch of a twisted pine. Its feathers ruffle in the breeze—primaries and secondaries mussed like fine hair, reassembling in perfect alignment.

I wander over to Millie and sit for a while in the grass, pounding a beer to quell the buzz in my belly because now #3 is coming at me in waves. Looking at Millie helps to settle me down. I find my nerve in the calm mien of a llama. Curled eyelashes, sanguine eyes, grinning lips. Elegant ungulate. Dislocated ruminant of the high lonesome. So far from home, Millie, do you ever grow heartsick? Does any ancestral memory register in your blood and bones?

Native to the highlands of Peru, llamas were domesticated by Andean peoples 6,000 years ago. Go back further in time and the story gets even more interesting. Llamas are descendants of ancient camelids that lived on the North American plains 40 million years ago. These camelids migrated into South America when the volcanic isthmus of Panama rose up from the sea floor 3 million years ago to bridge the formerly separated continents, all part of what's come to be known as the Great American Interchange.

And now here you are, Millie, back in North America. Cloven-footed wonder. Pack animal *extraordinaire*. Tell me, *does it feel like home?*

Gazing at the chain of mountains to the west, I wonder about my own roundabout journey that's landed me here on this breezy mountaintop. What volcanic isthmus pointed the way for me? And what are the chances of ever getting back to *my* ancestral home, wherever that may be? Any thought

I might have had of a triumphant return, horns blaring in a hometown parade to honor the local hero, seems remote now—the possibility more unlikely with each passing day. Like trying to line up all the events of your life, studying them in reverse order to find the chain of cause-and-effect that's produced the here and now. It just doesn't work—the events pile up faster than the ability to make sense of them.

When darkness falls, we watch the fireworks from both Saranac and Lake Placid, just as Snow said we would. Placid relies heavily on the plume variety and its cascading showers of color, whereas Saranac goes more for the loud *BOOMs!* preceded by a white flash.

One particular firework of red and green reminds Yukon of Christmas. "A tribute to the yule!" he proclaims. That's followed by a black and orange affair that prompts Spot to say, "Halloween!" Soon, everyone's in the spirit. Green and white for St. Paddy's Day. A purple-yellow sparkly for Boxing Day. Yellow and green tracers for Secretary's Day.

When the grand finale ends in a cloud of smoke, we pack it in and start down the trail. Through it all, Millie behaves wonderfully. Poised, elegant, stylish. The belle of the ball. She rests her head on the boat ride across Oseetah. We have her safely back in the corral by midnight, no worse for the wear.

THE HOLIDAY OVER NOW, we're back on the job in the morning. Annie returned to Colby sometime last night and looks fresh as a daisy. I'm moving a little slow, sluggish from all the festivities.

We drive down to John's Cabins on the peninsula separating Kiwassa and Oseetah, just a few miles south of town, where we're greeted by an odd fellow whose family runs the small business. The operation consists of a half-dozen cabins set neatly back in the forest. When we tell him who we are and what we're doing, he invites us up to the screened porch. Says there's something he wants us to see.

A lanky sort with a quick smile, he leads us onto the porch where we sit in wicker rocking chairs. The porch is old with dark and worn floorboards. Potted geraniums hang from the eaves. He offers us lemonade and then disappears into the clapboard cottage. The whole compound here—cabins and cottage and well house—looks as though it was designed to complement the big spruce trees and pines. Not the other way around. None of the structures seems intrusive. The cottage has an old rustic smell, and the cold lemonade puts me in a good frame of mind. I could have rocked in my wicker chair the rest of the day, listening to our friend go on about how the world was unraveling before our very eyes.

"When I was a child back in the forties, I remember the forest had a bright, blue-green tint that was most vivid right after electrical storms. Well, that bright tint is gone,

Acidic moisture has dissolved the protective waxy layers on leaves and conifer needles, leaving them saturated with water during periods of rain and unnaturally dry in periods of hot weather. I also remember when the black spruce was a common species in these woods. Now it's difficult to find. When I told a forester at DEC about this, he told me the species doesn't grow here."

At this point, our friend leads us into the back yard where he shows us a living specimen of black spruce.

"And it's not just the trees," he says, strolling on the lawn. "The wildlife has declined with the diminished beech stands. Butterflies are in decline, too, though I think that has more to do with increased spraying."

Inside the porch again, he shows us a Ph-gauge he bought for two dollars in a pet store, pointing to the 4.5 reading he's recorded at the onset of electrical storms. "I've even conducted experiments with plants. I water a few plants with neutral-Ph rain, and then I water plants of the same species with acidic rain. Judge for yourself."

The "neutral" plants clearly look healthier.

"Look over at the forest there," John says, gesturing to the deep woods across the yard. "How does it look to you?"

No question, the forest looks brown. I gaze at the mountainside opposite. Same thing. The trees appear more brown than green. This is July, the time of year when the forest ought to be at its healthiest.

Rocking away, lemonade in hand, I picture a steady flow of carbon dioxide, nitric oxide, and sulfur dioxide pouring out of giant smokestacks from coal-burning power plants down in the Ohio River valley. At the same time, I hear the drone of politicians assuring the public that no direct link has ever been proven, that more studies are needed, and that without a direct cause-and-effect, well, what have you got?

It gets me to rocking the chair pretty hard, I guess, because next thing I know, Annie and our friend are looking at me funny. So I tone it down a bit, as our host continues.

"Hawkeye Whitney, grandson to Eli, is a friend of mine. He lives out near Gabriels where he likes to tinker with old American engines. Once when I was visiting, I noticed he collected rainwater in a barrel. I told him the water was probably too acidic to drink. Next time I visited, I brought my gauge to prove the point."

I ask him about other oddballs that live in the area.

"As a kid, I remember watching Albert Einstein fish for bullhead in a rowboat on Kiwassa Lake. He'd go out by himself dressed in a long coat. I remember once seeing him on the lake, fishing in the rain."

If there was ever a question about John's credibility, this puts it to rest. As far as I'm concerned, Albert Einstein fishing for bullhead in a rowboat seals the deal. Listening to our friend expound on butterflies and beech stands, pH gauges and protective waxy layers, it's hard to escape the conclusion that everything's going to pot.

THREE LOONS ON COLBY this morning. They dip and preen, with an occasional foot waggle thrown in. Supremely at ease with one other. Can't tell if it's a pair visiting the Colby bird, or whether they're all immatures simply wiling away the day without the care and worry of raising chicks. Who knows, maybe we'll get a nest on our lake after all. I think I speak for Annie when I say I hope our lone Colby loon finds a mate, settles down, and gets on with his biological imperative.

Gentle breeze from the west today. Brilliant blue sky. We put in at the bridge separating Kushaque from Buck Pond, checking the shoreline and islands of Kushaque while enjoying the view of Little Haystack cliffs. Across the lake, a motorboat changes course and heads in our direction.

"Looks like CO's," Annie says.

When they get close, I notice the boat: sixteen-foot Boston Whaler, 40-horse outboard, steering counsel, teak trim. Two spinning rods lean against the console. I also take note of the .38s in their holsters.

"Ahoy," says the officer standing in the bow. "How are things today?" he grins.

Once again, I defer to Annie when it comes to making conversation. Not that she's the chatty type, but we both know it's in everyone's interest if I keep my trap shut. She tells them who we are.

"Oh yeah," the friendly one says. "The loon rangers. We've heard about you. Haven't we, Stryke?" His partner behind the wheel has closely cropped hair, pudgy cheeks, squinty eyes, a red hue.

"All good, I'm sure," Annie smiles.

"Of course."

It seems we're in tight with the CO's and there's nothing for me to worry about. We're all brothers-in-arms in the service of the State.

"You guys look like you have it pretty good," she says. "Cruising around in a nice boat."

"All in the line of duty," he jokes.

"Judging from your gear," I say with a nod, "it looks like you make arrests on occasion."

"Yep," he says. "We pretty much have the same authority as police officers when it comes to law enforcement."

"And how does one get to be a conservation officer?" Annie asks. Annie doesn't usually go out of her way to extend a conversation, which makes me think she's up to something.

"First, you have to have a stellar personality," he smiles, "and then you have to successfully complete a seventeen-week training course."

"I see," Annie says, chewing her bottom lip. "Say, we couldn't talk you into helping us with one of the bigger lakes, could we? Say, Upper Saranac? There's a lot of shore to paddle and the lake is fairly well developed, so there's probably not going to be a nest. If there is a nest on the lake, we'll know where to look for it."

"Sure," the friendly one says. "Be glad to. We're always looking for things to do." He pulls a pad and pen from his shirt pocket and begins to write. "I'll give you our number." The CO tears a page from the pad and reaches across the gunwale to hand it to Annie. "Name's Bradley," he says, "and this here's Stryker. Just give us a call when you want to go out."

Annie thanks him and gives the Whaler a push. As we're drifting apart, it occurs to me that but for a turn or two in the road, that could easily be me in uniform packing a .38. Stryker, the hard ass, lacks a sense of humor. Bradley, on the other hand, seems decent enough, and it's good to know he's the brains behind the operation.

From Kushaque, we portage to Buck Pond where bog laurel grows lush along the bank. We paddle past the public beach to the far end where we find lots of snags and deadfall, seeing plenty of good nesting habitat in the way of hummocks and islets, but no loons. We check the shoreline all the way to the peninsula and Buck Pond hill, before tying the canoe off and starting on foot through the trees in search of an eagle's nest rumored to be in the area.

The woods are thick with underbrush and fallen trees, the ground covered with moss. The forest consists of spruce and pine near the pond, giving way to a large birch stand deeper in the woods. We split up, walking in different directions, which is good because I'm dying for a smoke. It's not that I'm trying to be a sneak about it, it's just that the habit seems unbecoming of a wildlife professional. It's all about perception. People expect their scientists to be clean-cut and free of vices.

I start uphill with the hope of finding a better vantage point to scan the trees. Slathered in bug juice, binocs and map in hand, I pause on a knoll to get my bearings. Mosquitoes swarm relentlessly until it's clear that this is not the place to take a stand. Better to keep moving and live to fight another day. I walk all the way to the back of the bog and glass it thoroughly. A great blue heron glides across the tops of dead trees, but I find nothing that resembles an eagle's nest. I think of our man Stokes back in Ray Brook. Smug bastard.

On the way to the canoe, I stumble upon the wooden stakes and blue tags of what looks to be a road planned for the woods around Buck Pond. I consult the map, concluding that this is not the Gabriels-Onchiota trail, and proceed to pull up the stakes and tear down the tags, burying the whole mess in the ground with the aid of my trusty Buck knife.

Back in the canoe, Annie and I paddle out to the middle of the pond and glass the woods again. A cloud blocks the sun in the west, as shafts of golden light pour onto distant mountains.

HEART POND IS A BEAUTIFUL LAKE located in a small basin in the mountains of Saint Regis, accessible only by a long two-track off the paved road. We drive all the way to the end, parking next to a DEC truck and a brown sign informing us that we are now on the property of a state fish hatchery where camping and fishing are strictly prohibited.

Carrying the canoe to the water, we hear a tremolo coming from somewhere on the lake. With her binoculars, Annie spots a loon drifting between two small islands. We paddle straight for the near island, watching as the loon retreats. We find nothing on the first island and so we start for the second. We're close now, thirty feet away, when the loon unleashes a bloodcurdling laugh—so loud that it makes the hair stand up on my forearms. Then it disappears underwater. Rounding the back side of the far island, we watch as a second loon plops into the lake. Drifting closer, we discover a nest at the edge of the water with two speckled eggs.

The second loon surfaces thirty yards away. We take our measurements and get out of there fast, paddling far enough away from the island to allow the loon to return to the nest. We hear another tremolo from the first loon, this time from the other side of the lake.

"That's two," Annie says with a smile. "Two nests."

We complete a quick tour of the rest of the lake, knowing full well we're not going to find another nest. Heart is simply too small to support two mating pairs. As we're paddling along the far shore, I notice a small makeshift dam—more like an improvised fish barrier and spillway—constructed at the outlet where a brook drops down into the woods. The construction is rather primitive, just some concrete, an iron frame, and two-by-twelves stacked on top of one another to hold back the water. It occurs to me all someone would have to do is to slide one of the planks free to lower the lake level by a foot or so. This is not the first of these contraptions we've seen in the Adirondack backcountry.

Across the lake is the hatchery facility, partially hidden in the trees. A small clapboard house sits directly above it on a hill. I'm guessing the pickup truck in the parking lot belongs to the caretaker.

Later, at the Waterhole, I run into Beaver who suggests that we change venues and try another bar. He says I should see a different side of town than what the Hole has to offer. The Rusty Nail is where he wants to take me, located down by the river. Spot, overhearing our conversation, says she's game. So, the three of us finish our beers and step outside.

"How're you liking Saranac?" Beaver asks as we walk.

I tell him I like it just fine, but I've noticed there's a high percentage of screwballs living here. I mention Flashlight and the market clerk as prime examples.

"That's because he's taken a vow of silence," Spot says, referring to the clerk. She then proceeds to explain that a number of religions honor this practice—Trappists and Hindus and Buddhists, to name a few—but, to the best of her knowledge, the clerk's vow is "nonmonastic" in nature. "He's just doing it to become more aware," she surmises. "After all, silence is the mystery of being."

"I once had a beer brewed by Trappist monks," I say. "It was delicious."

Spot carries herself with a certain verve. Her strawberry blond hair catches the sunlight, and her smile is infectious. When I ask where she learned so much about religion, Beaver informs me that Spot graduated at the top of her class. "She won a full ride to college," he says through the gap in his chipped tooth.

When we arrive at the bar, Beaver leads us to the back and an outside deck overlooking the river. Over a pitcher of Canadian lager, he explains to me that when the river gets high enough, they like to come here and jump off the railing into the river. "You ought to see Snow," he says. "He's perfected a wicked back flip."

NICE DAY TODAY, sunny and warm. After a late start, we drive north out of town to Moose Pond. Because it's the only lake we'll cover today, we take our time in the canoe, enjoying the calm afternoon, drifting slowly along the shore.

I stare at the reflections on the glassy surface of water: the green lattice of shrubs, the overhanging branches, the dark woods and blue sky—all reflected back in a soft, impressionistic watercolor. Gliding through this liquid mirror is like flying through air—a dream-space filled with myriad shapes of light. The sky is an ocean, and the reflected branches are trees of coral. I am freediving in the Caribbean, flying over forests and deep canyons. Realms of light and color, each with its own mysteries. I see in two dimensions what the eye is trained to see in three ....

And that's about the time I run the canoe up on a log.

From the bow, Annie gives me one of those *what-the-hell-are-you-doing* looks. But she knows that sometimes I need to look at things crossways. She understands deviance and subversion. I dare say she's got a little of that in her, too.

We watch an army of salamanders scurry across the sandy shallows along the bank. After repeated efforts to capture one (in the interests of science, of course), I abandon the project and we continue on our way. There is one island on Moose, but its shore is too rocky to provide any suitable habitat for nesting.

As we start back for the launch, a loon flies in and lands on the water, grooming itself in the middle of the lake. This is the largest individual we've seen. It dives once before returning to the surface and stretching its wings, exposing its white belly. Then it starts running across the water, thrashing and flapping its wings, until it gains enough speed to launch into the air. The loon circles over the lake three times, delivering four quick tremolos before flying off to the south.

LISTENING TO THE BIRD SONGS on the phonograph is paying off. From the raucous *squawk* of a blue jay to the *cheep* of a hummingbird, we hone our skills of song identification. The more we become attuned to the various nuances and intonations, the more we understand in the way of communication. It's like learning a new language—stepping through a door into a whole other world.

Most birds use a range of sounds, from courtship songs to calls of alarm to locating a mate. Many of these calls have become second nature to us. For instance, the song of a male Red-Winged Blackbird (*o-ka-leee* or *conk-la-reee*, followed by a buzzy trill) is synonymous with cattail wetlands. The song of a meadowlark is also easy to recognize: *see yer* or *spring-o-the-year*. The signature tune of the male bobwhite (*bob-white!*) is a territorial and breeding call. Bobwhites use a different call when separated from a flock or covey. This separation call probably denotes mild alarm, coupled with a desire to make contact with other birds. And there are other common calls: the *ahonk ahonk* of Canada Geese, the *quack-quack-quack* of mallards, the *weet-weet-weet* of sandpipers, the whistled *perchickory* or *perteeteetee* of goldfinches as they swing upward in their undulating flight pattern.

And then there are the songs that are more difficult to identify: the *witchity-witchity-witchity* of the yellowthroat, the *drink-your-tea* of the Rufus-Sided Towhee, the *sweet-sweet-sweet-I'm so very sweet!* of the Yellow Warbler, the *fire-fire where-where here-here see-it see-it* of the Indigo Bunting.

Lately, I've been working on the subtle difference between the hermit thrush and wood thrush. Both songs are flute-like and melodic. The song of the male wood thrush begins with several soft notes that lead into variable melodic phrases, ending with a high, buzzy trill. Something like: *tutut-eee-o-lay-o-eee*, or, *tutut-eee-ay-eeee*. It's the introductory notes and concluding trill that I listen for in the field. Each male has several different song patterns that aren't sung in a fixed sequence, and rarely are successive songs repeated.

The song of the male hermit thrush, on the other hand, can be recognized by a drawn-out whistle preceding each flute-like ramble of notes that vary in pitch. Listen for the whistle at the beginning, that's the key. I also think the hermit thrush has more of a flute tone than the wood thrush. When alarmed, a hermit thrush responds with an emphatic *churt*. Another of its distinctive calls is a drawn-out, nasally *wayy*. Though the purpose of this call is unknown, it is heard at dusk from solitary birds. A lonesome lament, perhaps.

Annie and I note all the songs that we can identify in the field—from swallows, finches, flycatchers, woodpeckers, wrens, and more. The most common call of the scarlet tanager is the two-parted *chick-bree*. The male song is presented as a series of hoarse, burry whistles, slurred together and delivered quickly. It sounds like a robin with a cold. And then there's my friend, the Yellow-Bellied Sapsucker, whose drumming display serves both territorial and breeding purposes. The display starts out fast, then slows down in uneven fashion. Sapsuckers often beat on metal signs (or metal rooftops, as the case may be). During social interactions, including aggressive encounters and courtship, aroused sapsuckers make harsh grinding sounds to the tune of *shreeek-shreeek-shreeek-shreeek*.

There are still a number of songs that stump us, including most of the cheerful melodies in the extended warbler family.

But we're working on those, confident that with due diligence we can someday crack the code. Deciphering the language of birds is good science—something that people can be doing in their spare time.

Sometimes at dawn on a small pond, we paddle into a chorus of birdsong—different voices all intertwined, each with its own range of calls, and for each call, untold nuances and shades of meaning. Because we can't see into the woods, we rely less on our eyes and more on our ears. There's a lot of communication going on, both among birds of the same species as well as those of different species. No doubt, Annie and I become the topic of conversation from time to time as we pass through the various avian hamlets. We do our best to be good neighbors, keeping still and quiet. This is not random, senseless noise we're hearing. These birds are *talking* to one another, engaged in serious conversation, relaying vital information about location, threats, desires. Who knows, maybe they tell jokes ... *Why did the wildlife biologist cross the road?*

And it's not only birds. We bear witness to a world that, in all its particularity and dynamics, rivals any acid trip I've had. A big wild universe to be explored out there. Just yesterday, I watched a sandpiper walk the length of a fallen log angling into the water, only to realize the bird stepped over the camouflaged shell of a behemoth snapping turtle. And then to see the reptile plop into the drink and swim under the canoe in the dark depths, its ironclad claws and prehistoric tail suspended in flight. Or seeing two broad-winged hawks ride a thermal on a warm day, spiraling higher without a single wing beat. Or at dusk, gliding in a reflection of pale sky laced with lilac clouds, the watery tableau unfurling behind in a slow, rolling wake. Or drifting close to shore beside a luminescent filigree of bleached branches and upturned root tangles, mirrored so exquisitely across the black water that it's hard to tell where the object leaves off and its reflection begins ... and the only sounds to be heard are from drops of water rolling off the paddle onto a placid surface, and two swainson thrushes trading melodies from opposite shores, running their organ-pipe flurries off the scale into the ethereal space between sound and silence. There's a *presence* here. Everything in its place, down to the last detail. Always turning, always *moving*.

THAT FIRST DAY IN ALBANY we were assigned a list of 125 lakes, each with its own data regarding size, location, point of access, and other information provided by the two wildlife techs who conducted the same survey three years earlier. Trouble is, the two techs had a falling-out with Frank before the survey was completed, prompting them to sabotage their data by omitting or scrambling key information. Come to think of it, maybe this is why Frank is so adamant about collecting our journal at the end of the summer. In any case, in addition to the armful of policies and procedures and directives issued to us back in Albany, we were handed a box of papers with the expressed warning not to believe everything we read. Which is fine by me. All the better, in fact. This way, the data Annie and I collect becomes that much more important. Our findings carry weight, the entire survey hinges on the raw data we gather in the field. As the days go by, I can see why our predecessors might have wanted to distance themselves from Albany. I can't speak for Annie, but the more time I spend in the field, the further away I feel from the State bureaucracy. We go at our work blindly, losing ourselves in the task at hand, utterly committed to gathering as much information as we can.

At night, we convene in the cupola and pore over the topos. Huddled over the desk in the light of the candle, we meander through the intricate ins-and-outs of lakes and streams indicated on the colored map. Pens and highlighters in hand, we chart our days according to the mountains and waterways of the northern Adirondacks. Every symbol on the topo resonates with significance, drips with purpose. Every elevation line, slough demarcation, railroad grade, primitive road, access point, portage route ... all become a piece in the puzzle of our common destiny, Annie and I. Flesh to bone.

We've had good weather for a few weeks now, dry and warm. Our plan today is to cover the two Pine Ponds, then follow a river upstream to Rock Pond. Although we're not certain the stream provides suitable access, it looks to be the quickest way into this remote lake.

After an hour's drive, we arrive at the put-in under a hazy sky. The air is humid. As we unload the gear in the parking lot, I notice two fishermen standing by their boat like a couple of four-star generals in full regalia, their fishing hats and vests decorated with colorful spoons and plugs. When we carry the canoe to the launch, I ask them about the fishing.

"Not bad," says one.

But something's not right. Their boat is beached beside the launch. Neither man moves. They just stare across the water. Annie returns to the car for the clipboard, while I load the paddles and cushions.

"Going out or coming in?" I ask.

"Getting off," the man says, still looking across the lake. "Heard thunder."

But the sun is shining, and except for the haze that's moved in and a bank of clouds to the west, the sky is clear.

Annie and I take our seats in the canoe and push off. When we're out a ways, I look back at the generals still staring across the water.

We cover East Pine in short order (no loons) before making the half-mile portage to West Pine. It's hard work, with a steep hill to climb and an army of mosquitoes to battle. The trick with mosquitoes is to keep moving. Stand in one place for very long and they'll find you, their high-pitched whine growing louder. We stop only once—at the top of the hill—where we load everything into the canoe. Annie takes her seat in front and I push from the back, bobsled style. The canoe slides nicely over the packed pine needles on the trail. As it gains momentum down the hill, I hop in and we ride it out to the bottom.

We paddle halfway around West Pine before starting up the inlet to Rock Pond. It's a fast and narrow stream, and the going is slow. Trees lean in on both sides and we have to duck under branches. I pole with my paddle as Annie pulls us upstream by the branches.

Eventually, the stream grows wide enough that we can sit upright in the canoe. There's an old wooden causeway we have to portage, but above that is open marsh. A blue heron takes flight in the direction of our destination, the sough of its wings in the heavy air.

We portage around three beaver dams, ankle-high in mud, carrying the canoe past tangles of branches and limbs. All the while, the prospects of reaching Rock Pond grow slimmer. The waterway has been reduced to a maze of rivulets, hummocks, and brush. We snake up a tiny stream no wider than a paddle length. My shirt is soaked with sweat, but to stop now would incur the wrath of biting insects.

"Wait," Annie says, wiping a lock of damp hair from her face. "This isn't working."

The heat kicks up a notch. I hear the whine of black flies and mosquitoes.

Not far is a small knoll supporting two dead pine trees. I climb my way between them, using their limbs as steps, balancing my weight from one tree to the other. Brittle twigs *snap* like lady-finger firecrackers. I climb high enough to see over the entire bog—the beaver ponds and hummocks and rills.

Atop the two dead pines, a gentle breeze cools my forehead. I close my eyes until I can picture the crooked topo lines in the candlelight of the cupola. I had talked Annie into taking this route, convinced her that there'd be enough water to get to Rock Pond. Now we have to turn around, retrace our steps, and come at it from a different direction. Still, with that sweet breeze cooling my brow, I feel good that we at least tried. Dammit anyhow. Even though we failed, it was *our* idea to come this way. Nobody telling us different.

By the time we escape the swamp, paddle back to the car and start down a utility road, the sky has darkened to charcoal gray.

"Looks like we can get there by way of Floodwood," Annie says, studying the map. "But there's still a lot of bog and river to navigate. It's practically wilderness in there, miles from anything."

At the end of the two-track, I park alongside the adjacent railroad tracks and cut the engine. A light rain begins to fall. Mosquitoes bounce off the windshield, looking for a way into the car.

Annie stares at the flat surface of Floodwood Pond, rubbing the edge of the map between her finger and thumb. "It's going to take a while to get up there," she says, "and there's no telling what this weather's going to do."

According to my calculations, to cover Rock Pond now will save us an extra trip out this way. This is the farthest we've had to drive for any lake on our list. We've already spent two hours trying to get to the pond, and now we're within striking distance. Besides, Rock Pond is small. Once we get there, it shouldn't take long to paddle the perimeter.

And we'll be going downstream on our way out.

"You didn't tell anyone where we'd be today, did you?"

"No," she replies. "Why?"

"No reason."

I like it this way, on our own and far from everything.

The drizzle stops, the sky brightens. Enough, anyway, to convince us to go. We put-in and paddle to the inlet leading up to Rollins. The stream narrows as we grind against the fast current, inching along, looking for eddies as the whitewater slaps the aluminum hull. A glassy tongue whips around a sharp bend, and it's all we can do to pull ourselves upstream by the willow branches reaching across the water. The river flattens out above the bend, and we continue on.

But the sky darkens again, and thunder rumbles in the distance like a stampede of oil drums. When the rain comes, we make for shore. Under a lacy awning of fir, I open my raincoat and pull it over us like a blanket. There's nothing to do but wait it out, close together under the coat.

The rain stops and we get back on the water. But I can tell those old thunderheads aren't done yet. Somewhere in that dark brooding sky, they're rearing back on their heels, gearing up for the big load.

We portage a train trestle and start across another bog, paddling through a misty fog, etching a V across the smoky glass of water. A merganser appears out of the mist and skitters ahead, feigning injury. It moves in spurts, letting us get close before swimming off again with a limp wing.

Marking the entrance to Rock Pond is a massive boulder the size of a boxcar. Scarred and sculpted, it looms above the outlet like a giant gargoyle, steam rising off its back. When we pull alongside it, it feels like we're passing through the gates of hell.

The steep banks of the pond are tangled with fallen trees piled up like matchsticks. Around the logs we go, looking for any sign of a nest along the shore. I keep my technique steady: two hard back paddles port-side, then hard by starboard until the submerged log is deep enough to cross, then two back thrusts starboard, hard by port again, until the canoe is parallel with the log and pointed straight for the bank. Annie knows exactly when to drag and pull in front. The canoe pivots and turns according to the features of the convoluted shoreline.

A light rain begins to fall, teasing the surface of the water. The sound is hypnotic—like needles falling on glass. By now the lake has turned a sickly hue, the shade of yellow you see in the sky before a tornado hits.

We make the long turn at the far end of the pond and start back toward the outlet, looking for a nest in the shrubs between slabs of granite—a nest we know we're not going to find. And that's when the lightning starts, followed by crackling thunder.

"Annie ..." I say, but that's all I can muster. Danger has scared the words out of me. We're sitting ducks on the water.

"Just the other side of this ledge," she says.

We paddle hard for a place where we can land and take shelter in the woods. But there's no landing to be found. Whole trees, roots and all, lay jack-strawed along the bank. We have no choice. The rain is falling hard, the lightning has moved on top of us.

Annie loops the bowline around a fallen tree and ties a quick knot. I watch as she starts up the slippery trunk on all fours, using branches and knots for handholds. Halfway up, though, the branches end. It's bare trunk the rest of the way. The bark has long since peeled off, leaving the wood smooth and break-ass slick in the rain. Annie shimmies up the log. At the very top she stands and pulls herself up by the branches of two pines growing at the edge of the woods. She gains solid ground and turns around to look.

Now it's my turn. I scramble to the front of the canoe, grabbing the clipboard and map and binoculars, wrapping them up in my raincoat as lightning explodes around us. I climb the lower half of the log, pausing where the handholds end. But I'm still a good twenty feet from Annie, too far to toss the coat.

"You're going to have to stand!" she yells over the pouring rain.

I get one foot beneath me and start to rise, my eyes fixed on the tree trunk. Finding a balance on the log, I take a step, then another, reaching with the bundle ... *when my foot slips out from under me and I fall, banging my head on the log in a shower of white stars ... crashing through branches and limbs, hitting the ground with a* THUD. *Lying there, a sharp pain in my ribs, looking up in the rain, the sky blurry in black-and-white watercolor ...* "Get up!" ... *rising from the mud and broken deadwood, kneeling ...* she pulls me to my feet, taking me by the arm, helping me up the bank into the damp forest under a dripping canopy, leading me to a small clearing where we lie down on matted leaves.

She pulls her raincoat over us. "Be still," she says.

We lie close together under the coat. Muted bursts of lightning flash through the blue nylon. Thunder booms and trails off. I lift the zippered edge of the coat to see rain drilling the lake, white daggers of lightning piercing the air between us and the far shore. We're caught in the lap of an electric storm, dead to rights.

Annie reaches out from under the coat to catch raindrops in the palm of her hand. I'm close enough to see the pupils in her eyes open and contract with each drop that falls. I pull on the stem of a dead maple leaf and watch the seconds tick off on my cheap digital watch: 21, 22, 23 … the glass face of the watch is fogged, smeared with bug juice … 27, 28 …

KABLAM!

A white-hot jolt through the legs, a rush of adrenaline and tingling of nerves …

"What?" Annie says.

Thunder echoing through the mountains, rolling down the valleys.

"What happened?"

The patter of rain on her coat.

"Lightning …."

"Did you *feel* it?"

"My nerves …."

"Shhh, listen," she says, almost in a whisper. The rain is letting up. Peals of thunder rumble in the distance. Water drips off the trees onto the raincoat. "I think it's moving off."

We wait until the sun breaks free of the clouds before making our way back to the canoe. Gingerly, I slide down the slippery tree trunk, pain knocking at my ribs with each breath … *a skeletal x-ray image, white against black, ribcage curved like the wooden strips of an antique canoe hull lacquered shiny and stout.*

We drain the water, load everything back into the canoe, and push off. Rock Pond is calm again. A blue mist rises in the woods as we glide across the glassy surface. Shafts of sunlight pour through the forest, illuminating drops of rain still clinging to pine needles. A redwing blackbird flies from a cattail, pivoting mid-flight before a swarm of insects. The merganser hen reappears, this time with a string of chicks in tow.

"Look," Annie says. "Over there."

A steady stream of smoke billows from the bank, too thick to be fog. We change course to get a closer look. It's smoke, all right, coming from a small fire at the base of a white pine that's been struck by lightning. Chunks of fresh wood float in the water around us. The tree is split down the middle, upper half gone, its lower limbs splintered. Smoke from the fire rises in the forest, twisting through glowing bars of sunlight.

I WAKE THIS MORNING to a sharp pain in my ribcage, like a pair of steel jaws clamped tight to sinew and bone. Bruised ribs, hopefully nothing more. Either way, I'm rendered useless for the day. Annie says we could use the rest, anyway.

Yesterday's storm has scrubbed the sky clean, leaving a picture-perfect day. Blue sky, warm with a breeze. After breakfast I saunter outside and ease myself into a chez lounge, slow and careful. On top of bruising my ribs on the fall, I cracked my head open, resulting in a slight concussion. Nothing a little vitamin D can't cure. Still, every pulse of blood pounds in my skull like the *boom* of a bass drum. I hurt, all right, and it's not made any easier when Annie comes to check on my wounds. It's been a while, you see, and I've got half a mind to open negotiations on her abbreviated tank-top and cutoff corduroys.

"Hold still," she says, leaning close to examine the cut on my head, all that luscious silk hair falling down her shoulders. She dabs a wet washcloth on the cut.

"You're good at this," I say. "Administering care."

She loosens the caked blood around the wound, pulling it free from my hair. She's close enough that I catch a whiff of her skin, see the rise and fall of her breast when she breathes. Her arms are smooth and tan. She wears a locket on a chain that rests on the white fabric of her t-shirt. When she leans close it swings freely, and I tell her how pretty it looks.

"It's from my grandmother," she says. "A family heirloom."

"It must be special."

147

"It is," she replies, "but only because it was hers."

"Oh?"

"She grew up during the Depression. The locket was the only thing she owned of any value." Annie pauses and touches the chain. "There's nothing quite like old wisdom."

She goes back to working on my wound, and I get the feeling that's all she wants to say about it.

"You ever wanted a family of your own?" I ask.

"A family? You mean kids?"

"Yeah, kids."

"Sure," she replies, "when the time is right. But a few things have to happen first."

I can feel her fingertips massaging the scalp around the wound as she applies the vitamin D.

"You mean like meeting a guy?"

"That would be useful."

"And how will you know when you find the right one?"

"Probably the same way you'll know when you find the right girl."

"I never said I wanted a family."

"I see," she says, returning to the job at hand. *Dab dab, smooooth it out.*

"You ever been in love?" I ask.

"My, aren't we nosy. And why would you ask a question like that?"

"Just curious," I say. "Well, have you?"

"Once, maybe."

"What happened?"

"I guess you could say we went our separate ways. People move around a lot these days, you know."

"Didn't you want to stay with him?"

"Sure."

"Well?"

"Well what?"

"What happened?"

She pulls back to look at me, the tube of vitamin D in her hand. "Think of it as random energy. In any case, we went our different directions."

She returns to dabbing the ointment.

"Seems like it's hard to keep that kind of thing together, anymore," she says, speaking to herself as much as to me. "And what about you?"

"Once, definitely," I answer. "But I was a little naive about it."

"Oh?"

"It never really happens the way it's supposed to. You meet somebody, fall in love, then expect that to take care of everything. But love can't keep up. We want to believe there's this perfect match out there, this soul mate, and it's just a matter of finding that person. But it's not true, it's just another fairy tale. People don't stay together anymore. Infidelity has gone mainstream. Love has become negotiable, something to be leveraged."

"You don't say."

"But it makes sense, if you think about it. The problem is that we confuse love for something that it's not."

"And what might that be?"

"Biochemistry. Love can all be explained by chemicals. I was reading how hormones released in the brains of voles during sex are what make the pair faithful to each other. When these hormones are injected into females, they immediately fall in love with male voles, even those they've never seen before."

"And where did you learn about … *vole love?*"

"In the library," I say, motioning to the house. "Flashlight has a whole section up there on current science."

She leans closer to resume her doctoring.

"And it's not just voles," I continue. "Scientists think it might be the same for humans. We have chemicals in the brain that act like a love potion. It makes sense, if you think about it in evolutionary terms—get people hooked on drugs so they procreate. It's nature's way of maximizing the efficiency of mating. You know how it is when you fall head-over-heels for someone, it's like you're out of your mind. They've done MRIs on horny people, for crying out loud. Current studies suggest there may be two different kinds of love chemicals: one for the initial infatuation stage, and another that produces the feeling of peace and comfort that comes from being with someone a long time. We'll call that the nuzzling chemical."

"The nuzzling chemical."

"Yeah, it's the drug that's released while cuddling with your longtime partner. They've done other studies as well. Smell is important. A woman is attracted to the smell of a man whose genotype is dramatically different from hers. This is good because it increases the chances that her offspring will be healthy. Don't want inbreeding, now do we? Attraction is also about symmetry—face, ears, elbows, wrists, hands …. A rugged looking man is attractive because strong muscles indicate a good supply of testosterone, which means a healthy immune system. From a woman's perspective, this translates into healthy children. On the other hand, men are attracted to a woman's curves in the waist and hip region. The right symmetry means higher fertility."

As I'm saying this, I realize I'm staring directly at the round swell of Annie's breasts.

"And then there's the State."

"The State?"

"Yes, the State has an interest in seeing that its subjects pump out babies. It's good for business—more workers, more soldiers, more consumers. Bigger markets. More power over other populations competing for the same resources."

At this point, I'm feeling pretty good about my analysis.

"Sounds like you have it down to a science," she says, patting my scalp, putting the finishing touches on the wound. "You're all done," she giggles. "Get some rest and call me in the morning."

"But don't you think it's true?"

Annie rests her hand on my shoulder, and for a split-second I see that faraway look again.

"I don't know," she says. "It sounds like you've been run through the wringer once or twice. You want to pick love apart piece by piece, put it under a microscope and analyze it away. Okay, so maybe you've learned to see through the illusions and false promises. So what? What do you have to show for it? Give it a rest, man," she says, turning away. "Nothing lasts."

And with her soft giggle trailing behind, she returns to the house to collect her water bottle and waist pack. When she reappears outside, she bounds down the steps and starts for the footpath that leads around the lake, sunlight gleaming in her hair.

"Didn't mean to open old wounds," she says over her shoulder. "But we must think of the poor voles," she smiles.

And off she goes, disappearing into the mottled light of the forest under a canopy of translucent leaves (*look how green!*) past a white blur of water lilies at the edge of the bog, following the path along the lake as it winds around granite boulders and decaying stumps, a warm breeze carrying the fecundity of water and earth.

A mare's tail twists in the blue sky, as she combs the shoreline for any sign of a loon (*even the marsh reveals nothing, not a telltale twig or feather anywhere*) to add to the data that contributes to the evidence that officially seals its fate—one more abandoned lake, one more piece of habitat gone in the slow, methodical demise of natural systems *(and yet, why shouldn't there be loons here? With so many hummocks and islets for nesting, a whole family could be living here without anyone knowing it)* because every night when the haunting wail soars across the lake, piercing the darkness, she hears it too. Call of the loon, voice of the wild. Timeless lament of primeval earth.

For the ancient ones (they too haunt this land) the loon was a bird of magical powers. Divine messenger. Omen of death. When water covered the world and the Creator decreed that there should be land, he told the animals to dive into the watery depths and return with mud. But the waters were too deep and the animals failed. Even the loon—best diver of all—emerged disappointed, believing that it too had failed. But as the loon turned to go, waving good-bye, all noticed the glimmer of mud on its foot.

For the Cree, the wail of a loon represents the voice of a fallen warrior denied entry into the next world. The haunting cry of the dead, caught between worlds. Destined to wander without a home.

And what difference now and a million years ago, now and a million years hence?

I've spent the last few nights alone in the house. My routine has become ritual: pack the cooler, turn out the lights, climb the stairs to the cupola, drink beer and think.

Annie has taken the car again, leaving me in this spooky funhouse by myself. This has been her pattern lately—disappearing at night, not returning until the wee hours. No idea where she goes. Normally I wouldn't mind, but there's too much history in this house, too many empty rooms. When the last light goes out at the kids camp, it's as though I'm the only one left on the whole compound.

Topo maps are folded and stacked on the desk. Heaps of data forms are scattered nearby, slightly luminescent in the dark. The window is pried open with a stick, as it has been since we first arrived. I've kept it this way, even though rain sometimes blows in to wither the maps and smudge the data.

Tilting the wooden chair back against the wall, I gulp down half a can of Cream Ale and ponder life's in-betweens. In the darkness I can't tell if I'm buzzed or not, so I light a candle on the desk, take out the journal, and begin to write.

It takes a while but eventually the crickets begrudge me a place in their chorus. Before long, I'm just one of the gang. When I thump down my can of beer on the desk, the *clang* complements the cadence in their rhythmic drone and I feel like I'm part of the orchestra. But then an owl glides in, alighting in a nearby tree, and everything goes silent. Gradually, the keening and croaking start up again (this time in a different key) as the entire ensemble (frogs and crickets and katydids) moves over a chair to make room for the newcomer. A fish slaps the surface of the lake like a cymbal crash from the percussion section. This is my tribe, they don't judge me.

Two things to consider tonight.

One, I'm anxious to get back in the field. The bump on my head is feeling better, and the pain in my ribs is subsiding. For the most part, I can move around all right. But when I bend over or reach for something, the muscles in my back tighten like taut cables crimping down on the ribcage. Annie and I have agreed that we should give it one more day of rest.

Two, Annie was only half right about what she said the other day while tending to my head. She was right about some things, I'll give her that. But I think I have a perfectly good handle on the past, her perorations notwithstanding. True, I've been reluctant to swallow the standard fare of a steady job, house in the burbs, dutiful wife, 2.3 kids ... all the essential building blocks of the American dream. I've taken 'em off the table, rejected them outright. Why? Because—and here my theory departs from Annie's—they've been shoved down my throat from day one. There's no debating whether we should even want these things. To question any of them is heresy. You might as well let the flag touch the ground or carry on with a communist. Safety in numbers, you see. Everyone wants to be part of a crowd, no one wants to be left out in the cold. Me, I'm not a joiner. The idea of conforming to *anything* raises the hackles on the back of my neck. As a matter of principle, I'm not going to do something someone tells me to do, even if it might do me some good.

But this is where it gets tricky. Lately, I've been feeling that maybe I *do* want some of these things. Maybe I *do* want to get on the straight-and-narrow. After all, isn't that part of the plan? Clean the slate and start fresh? On the other hand, maybe what I like is just the idea of it—having it out there as an option, just in case I want to settle down and play it safe. My ace in the hole.

But who am I kidding? There was never anything about a steady job or house or kids that really appealed to me anyway. For me, the American dream was never a viable option, even though there was a time there when it seemed I was ready to embrace it, going as far as to work at a brokerage firm on Wall Street, albeit as a gopher, only to become disillusioned with the whole idea of funny money. Greed is good, they told me. But I could only stomach so much of that.

(A gibbous moon throws a ghostly light over the lake, illuminating a thin veil of fog rising off the surface. Water like

glass, the lake recedes into the darkness and a faint silhouette of mountains in the distance. Somewhere along the far shore, a loon wails ...)

The chair squeaks when I move, but the crickets don't seem to mind—the symphony continues without a hitch. It feels good to be part of the gang, even if it is just a loose arrangement of insects and amphibians gathered beside the lake. A place for everything, everything in its place.

(The lonesome wail carries over the water, ringing in the night air ...)

In my element now—drinking beer in the dark, slowing the world down, contemplating the big picture and what got the ball rolling in the first place, knowing full well I could begin at any number of places. Roll the roulette, see where it lands. Spin the globe and put my finger down ... *there.*

I could go back to those warm summer nights at the Crow's Nest, watching the light shows from massive thunderheads towering over the Plains fifty miles away—cumulonimbus eight miles high, unleashing all that electrical fury, sparking a desire deep in my bones to get out into the world. Or, I could return once again to the hardscrabble cabin and Billy chained up all day, howling at the sun until he was hoarse and half dead.

But it was Jessie who made me pick up and leave the Keys to go north, setting me on course for what turned out to be a wild goose chase. She stole my heart, god bless her, leaving me helpless as a puppy. Blond and daring, lively and footloose, she was game for just about anything—cocaine nights and Bloody Mary mornings, shacking up with an older guy who swung a hammer by day. But then it was back to college for Daddy's darling and an image to uphold, a future to think about. The letters that went unanswered, the rendezvous that never took place, the final conversation from the pay phone across the street from her dormitory.

Go down with the ship, just like Annie said. Maybe she was right. The more I try to make sense of my past, the more I find myself running in circles. There is no starting point and there is no end. There's only the moving from town to town, the drifting from job to job. The endless wandering with nothing to show for it.

(*A second wail, closer now, rising out of the incandescent fog obscuring the boundaries separating air from water, water from land. The wail—ancient, tragic, magnificent—like the voice of darkness itself …*)

Champion of lost causes, that's me alright. Just like the loon out there, caught between worlds with no place to call home. Star-crossed and under the gun, who can't fight what he doesn't see. Who doesn't stand a snowball's chance in hell. Been here, what, sixty million years, only to return one spring to find a split-level going up where he and his distant kin have come for eons to raise their young. Maybe he'll stick it out for a week or two until the whine of a table-saw, day in and day out, gets to be too much. And then one day, he'll just fly the coop. *Never to return.*

And if it's not a split-level, it'll be acid rain or ozone depletion or any one of those doomsday scenarios Flashlight has cooked up. Take your pick. Loons and cats and two-toed woodpeckers all going under fast, no matter what anybody has it in their mind to do about it. Because all the signs point to it.

(*… but doesn't it sing to your soul, this haunting cry rising and falling in the night like a current running through your nerves, this conduit to the dark heart of the world?*)

I open up another beer and tilt my chair back. The yellow moon hangs low in the western sky on its way to setting behind the ridge. And what other axe to grind tonight? What other bone to pick? What other shadow to fight in the dark? Tough guy with the big talk. Fight your way out of any scrape. Take on all comers. Look anybody dead in the eye and tell them *exactly* what you think. Tough guy with the big bad talk ...

A blood-curdling scream shatters the stillness of the night, ghastly laughter reverberating in the cupola, startling me so much that the chair slides out and I fall to the floor, spilling my beer ... as the echoing tremolo dissolves back into the night.

And then all is quiet. The crickets and katydids have gone silent, waiting for the loon that's hidden in the fog somewhere along the near bank. The lonesome loon of Colby. Lord of the northern woods, spirit of mountain waters. Snuck up on me unawares. Swam right up to the house to unleash his lunatic yowl and scare me half to hell.

But I don't get the sense he's alarmed or that he's defending his territory or anything like that. As strange as it sounds, it seems as though the loon wants to communicate something, like there's some message he wants me to hear. He's aware of my presence, that much is clear. He's down there now on the water, slipping unseen among the lacy silhouettes of shrubs along the shore. A shadow in the mist. Betrayed only by a riffle of water when he pivots and dives, stealing away into the night.

I've been reading the novel *1984* to help pass the time while I recuperate. I found the book in the library, and I figured I'd read it because it *is* 1984, after all, and maybe I could learn something. But if the writer was trying to predict what 1984 would be like, he got a lot of things wrong. For instance, there aren't televisions everywhere spying on people. There's no Ministry of Love or Ministry of Plenty. There's no Newspeak or Thought Police telling everyone how to think. And as far as I know, there's no one removing words from the language.

One part I find interesting, though, is this business of *doublethink*—when a person believes in two different things that contradict each other and yet he doesn't see any inconsistency. It seems to me he should at least suspect something's off, but I guess not. So I try to imagine a few examples of what this might be like. Let's say you go along with what the group wants even though deep down you know it's not what you want, but, because it's the group that wants it, you go along with it figuring that if the group wants it, you must too. Or, you have to destroy something in order to save it. Or, you spend day after day doing something you know is wrong, but, because you've been told that it's always been done that way, you willingly keep doing it because, well, it's always been done that way.

Bottom line is, you *know* that what you're doing doesn't square with the facts. And whatever shape or form that may take, it boils down to the same thing: living a lie.

A STORY COMES TO MIND just now, though I'm not sure if it has to do with anything ...

While I was in the Keys, I worked for an outfit that specialized in repairing wooden hulls on sailboats. We were set up at a small marina a mile or two off Highway 1, deep in the mangroves, working on the hull of an old schooner that was dry-docked there. All of us on the crew were a bit destitute, so, as part of the deal, we were given access to the living quarters below deck. Basic bunks, nothing fancy. Anyway, we rigged up a ladder so we could climb up at night and sleep on board—this after a long day of sanding and patching with fiberglass and resin, running up and down the ladder whenever we needed something from the cabin.

One night, me and this other guy catch a ride to a tiki bar out on the highway where we proceed to get good and thoroughly looped. My buddy was a farm kid from Indiana with dirty blond hair and a crooked nose. Anyway, when the night had run its course and it's time to catch a ride back to the schooner, I walk outside and notice a rustling going on in the sea grape. And there, amid the grape and palm trees, blind with rum and purpose, my friend the Hoosier is trying his damndest to scale a thirty-foot palm he thinks is the ladder to the schooner—like it's time to bunk down, and if he could just get a foothold on one of the rungs, he could get some shut-eye and be ready first thing in the morning.

Now, how do you figure something like that?

Maybe it's not so strange after all—him shimmying up that tree trunk only to fall back down again. Right idea, wrong place. Maybe that's the way things really are, only they don't come to light so much. Maybe that's what dreams are all about—the truth bubbled to the surface out of some black and murky water, and even then, it's so bizarre that none of us can make heads or tails of it.

TODAY I RETURN TO THE CUPOLA with the more practical objective of putting papers in order and making plans for the coming days. I collect all the Audubon forms and bind them with a paper clip and then arrange our field forms into two stacks—those that have been completed and those that remain blank. The piles look about the same, so I consult the master list of all the lakes Annie and I were assigned back in May. We're definitely making headway, having surveyed 60 lakes out of 125.

We've been going about our mission with some efficiency, covering lakes in close proximity to one another in order to cut down on time spent in the car. (Nothing against the Impala, worthy ungulate.) But there's always a lake or two that slips through the cracks—the rogue waterway that requires a special trip. Lately, Annie has entrusted me with the task of planning our days and sometimes I don't get it right. And then there are times when I mess things up on purpose in the interest of subterfuge. Call it "fly in the ointment" syndrome. Already I've "overlooked" a pond or two, prompting us to retrace our steps to survey a lake we could have easily covered on an earlier occasion. I think she may be on to me, but there's something bigger at stake. I could sit here and extol the virtues of chaos and perturbation and why too much order is dangerous to the fate of all living things. If you listen to Flashlight, our species is hard at work driving the planet to hell in orderly fashion. But this is not what motivates me.

It's like this. I have an insidious worm in my brain that prevents me from being reasonable all the time. There's just something there that makes me want to upend the apple cart. I want to believe it's all just harmless fun, but I'm not sure that's the case. Sometimes I think how nice it would be to cut open my skull and root around until I corner the little bugger and extract its long pincers and teeth from the soft gray matter upon which it feasts. But that's a stretch, I know. All I can really do, the only feasible option, is to treat the symptoms. And that's where the three doors of redemption come in. That's where I find my peace, even if it's only temporary. Why? Because the worm survives. And as long as I remain at its mercy, I'll do whatever I can to ease the pain and keep myself amused. This includes acts of subversion. Danger helps, too. Think of it as a public service—a way to release pressure that might otherwise fester and build until it erupts into some major calamity. So what if I mess with the plans when the mood strikes? All things considered, it could be worse.

Having organized all the papers and decided on a plan for the next couple days, I sit down and begin writing in the journal when who should appear at the doorway but Flashlight. He stares at me with a blank expression, saying nothing, so I invite him in.

"I was just getting caught up with the journal," I say, "describing what happened at Rock Pond."

"I heard," he says. "Annie told me you got zapped by ground current."

"Yeah. Plus, I cracked my head and bruised my ribs on a fall." I finish the sentence I'm working on and put down the pen. "I'm having a hard time describing what happened, trying to put into words what it was like."

His expression doesn't change. "It's not surprising that you felt a charge," he says. "Our bodies are better conductors of electrical current than most of the ground is. We generate electricity in our bodies, you know. That's what keeps the heart ticking. Even after we die, electricity is still moving through the body."

He glances at the journal, as if he's expecting me to jot down what he's saying.

"Yeah, well, it didn't feel too pleasant and it's hard to put into words," I reply. "Besides, I'm feeling like maybe I dodged a bullet. You know what they say, lightning never strikes twice in the same place. That's why it's good to keep moving."

Flashlight stares at me, his eyeball holding steady. There's an awkward pause and something tells me I screwed up the whole "lightning strikes twice" theory.

"There are certain alignments of energy in earth's magnetic field called ley lines. Birds and fish use them for navigation on their migration routes. These lines are believed to produce low-frequency vibrations that affect our minds and bodies. The energy is especially pronounced where two or more ley lines intersect, producing energy vortexes that some believe may be portals to multidimensional realms. Ancient civilizations built sacred structures along ley lines in places like Stonehenge, Easter Island, and the Egyptian pyramids. Thunderstorms are also known to generate paranormal activity. It might be that any changes in human perception that occur during storms can be traced to the increase in electrical energy. Or, as some believe, it could be that spirits become especially active during such times."

Once again, I'm rendered speechless in the presence of Flashlight.

FEELING BETTER TODAY, good enough to get back in the field. Under threatening skies, we park at the southern end of Upper St. Regis Lake. The wind is down, the water flat. Unloading the gear, we watch as a loon dives in advance of a speeding motorboat near Birch Island.

On the water, we come upon a snapping turtle near the put-in with some sort of parasite—beige in color—stuck to its shell. The turtle has its head hidden beneath a log along the shore. I pull on its scaly tail but the turtle doesn't move. I go after the parasite with my paddle, trying to dislodge it from the shell, but it won't budge either. The parasite remains firmly attached.

As we approach Birch Island and two nearby islets, the loon reappears. By now, the ceiling of clouds has dropped ominously low and it occurs to me to take shelter. Coming around the leeward side of the first islet, thinking maybe I've grown gun-shy of lightning, I see the black-and-white back of a loon, not a paddle's length away, sitting perfectly still on a nest at the water's edge. The loon bolts from the nest and runs across the water in front of us, flapping its wings. Then it kicks its feet and rises up, rearing its head back in what is clearly a threatening posture. Finally, resigned to our presence, it swims out fifty feet where it splashes and shakes its beak while we take our measurements. There are two eggs on the nest.

After breaking for lunch on a small isle along the western arm of the lake, we circle the rest of the islands before entering Spring Bay. Earlier, on our way out to Birch Island, we flushed a great blue heron in the strait between Ward Island and the mainland. This prompted an immediate rebuke from a nearby loon in the form of a tremolo. Now, as we enter Spring Bay, we see the loon swimming along the western shore. We start our search in the southeast end of the bay, looking closely in the hummocks, when a different loon comes running across the water in front of us with its wings flapping, just as the previous bird did near Birch Island. In all its hell-bent fury, the gangly bird trips on a protruding tree branch, momentarily disrupting its momentum. It eventually settles on the water about twenty-five feet away, unleashing a cavalcade of tremolos as we go about our business.

It's one thing to observe these large birds at a distance—even from far away, their power and grace are impressive, especially if accompanied by a tremolo or wail—but to have one so close with all that insane laughter ringing in your ear, well, that's a whole other matter. It sends chills down your spine. It's just not natural to be this close, even if your intentions are good and you have important scientific tasks to perform.

This loon is especially exercised. It rises up and flaps its wings, dives periodically before surfacing *right next to the canoe.*

Something is up.

We stop what we're doing, letting the canoe drift. And that's when we see the chick, a little fuzzy ball of black and brown, swimming straight for us at an impressive clip. It comes right up to the side of the aluminum canoe, bumping along the hull.

Annie and I stare in amazement. Even the adult bird has stopped its antics to watch. The chick bobs along the surface next to the canoe, all the while getting closer to the stern where I sit. I don't dare move. It's so small that I could scoop it up and hold it in the palm of my hand—a tiny ball of feather, with beak and feet and eyes.

Now a second chick falls from the nest. It's a big drop to the water, a foot or more, easily the highest we've seen. This one doesn't fare as well, emerging wet and water-logged from the plunge. Unlike its sibling, this chick begins to chirp, setting the adult into a tizzy of whitewater dancing and hair-raising tremolos. Meanwhile, the other adult keeps its distance on the other side of the bay, never once making any sort of call. Annie and I slip away without taking our measurements.

WE START THE DAY AT FOLLENSBY CLEAR, a big lake with a number of bays and islands. Probably a great blue heron nests here. Perhaps a loon, too, though we don't find a sign of one. The lake is plenty big enough to accommodate two nesting pairs, so it might be a good idea to come back here another day and check again. My suspicion is that if a nest were to be found on this lake, it would be located on one of the bigger islands.

From Follensby, we follow Fish Creek up to Little Square Pond. No portage necessary, but the upstream paddle is long and arduous. We spy a king bird nest with two speckled white eggs, situated in a scrub pine that juts over the water. We also see two dark birds flying off in the distance. Because of their quick take-off, they can't be loons. Still, we're unable to make a positive identification.

Paddling along the northwest shore of Little Square, we spy a loon fifty yards away. Riding low in the water, it dives and reappears at a slightly greater distance. The bird repeats this behavior three or four times, until we lose sight of it somewhere along the opposite shore. We comb the lake carefully, checking some areas two and three times, but find no evidence of a nest. The only islands here are near the inlet leading to Floodwood. By afternoon, low gray clouds cover the sky, turning the day overcast and cold. On our way out, after the sun has set, we hear a single wail coming from the south shore of Follensby.

Later at the Waterhole, I run into the Acid Rain techs, Roy and Ed. They ask about the loons, and I tell them we're starting to see more now that we're spending time in the St. Regis area.

When I ask how they're doing, Roy shakes his head. "We're finding the impacts to be pretty extensive. Some of the lakes are dead, especially the smaller ones where there's no limestone," he says. "Sometimes we come upon a fisherman who's fishing a lake that's completely devoid of life, and I don't know whether to laugh or cry. I mean, what am I supposed to say?"

Like everyone else around here, they rattle off the names of lakes where they've seen loons: Oseetah, Little Polliwog, etc. We talk for a good half hour, before they drink up and wish me luck with the survey. Not a word is mentioned about the llamas. I stay longer than I should. The last that I remember is driving between the theater masks with one eye closed.

BEWARE SUMMER, for it opens the heart to hope and other dangerous propositions. With the sky so blue, the earth so green, the days so long and warm, you can't help but crack open the door of trust and let some light in. Wildflowers burst forth in showy displays, birds sing their hearts out. Full steam ahead, summer seems to say, come what may.

We spend the morning in the field before knocking off early. Annie rides the ten-speed into town in the afternoon to get more bear grease for her boots. Doesn't want to be caught short again, she says, after the "fiasco at Rock Pond." Our plan is to meet later at the Waterhole.

The sun is still high when I close the front door and walk outside. White clouds saunter across the blue ether like fleecy daydreams. The lake laps against the shore in hypnotic licks, gems of liquid light flashing across the water. Damn near idyllic. Makes you wonder why it can't always be like this.

Showered and preened, gingerly optimistic about my prospects, I sally forth into the afternoon. Turning the corner, perhaps. Ready to step out of the shadows and grab life by the horns, twist it around to my way of thinking. Two months of paddling and my arms are strong, my back feels like a million bucks. I move like the catamounts of old, swift and powerful. The survey is going well. We're more than halfway done, with a number of breeding pairs to report. As wildlife specialists, Annie and I have hit our stride. Found our groove.

I pump the accelerator once and fire the engine, guiding the ungulate down the driveway, alert to what's happening around me: a black squirrel running through the grass, a nuthatch walking down the trunk of a cedar tree, a raven dipping its wing overhead. Driving between the comic and tragic faces, I turn right out of the compound on my way to town—picking up speed, snaking through the curves of highway, approaching the construction and long row of blinking yellow lights. A lumberyard sprawls beside the road, just past the railroad tracks. An old cobblestone house sits back on a hill between two weeping willows shading the groomed lawn ... feeling good in my adopted hometown, like I have a place and a purpose here. Wildlife biologist. Loon ranger.

Cruising through the village past garages and apothecaries, slowing now for a traffic light where two older men in blue shirts tilt their chairs back against the wall of the firehouse, stopping behind a rusty pickup truck idling at the light, a wisp of smoke rising in the air ... looking at the row of buildings lining the street, I mean *really looking* as if seeing them for the first time: the gray weathered wood, the old brick and mortar, the lichen on a crumbling stone wall buttressing a vine-choked hill, weeds sprouting from cracks in the sidewalk. All of it gracefully aged like tarnished silver (*the smoke denser now, too thick to be exhaust from the pickup that pulls away when the light turns green*) this is not the filthy grime of old eastern cities, no, this is the look of antiquity and elegance (*smoke rising from under the hood, billowing in thick folds ...*)

My God, the Impala is on fire!

I drive onto the sidewalk, cut the engine and charge out of the car, pulling the latch to raise the hood when a burst of flames surges *three feet high in the air!* I can't see where the fire is coming from, but it's somewhere near the carburetor and gas line. I could run until the fire blows everything sky-high, or I could tear into the engine right now and try to put the fire out. A few onlookers have gathered on the sidewalk. A siren wails from the firehouse, blasting through the quiet streets.

I prop the hood and clear the smoke from a pile of dead grass on top of the manifold and carburetor. Flames tear through the grass as yellow smoke smolders below. I peel off my shirt and shove it into the engine, hot ash scattering. Fiery embers ricochet off the steering box, dropping to the sidewalk. I stuff the shirt deeper into the flames, attacking each clump of burning grass until I smother all that I can reach and the smoke abates … whipping my shirt through gaps in the engine to flush out any ashes trapped below.

"Watch out," someone says. "Don't get burned."

I turn around to find one of the firemen standing behind me.

"It's hot," he says. "The engine, I mean."

There must be a dozen people watching from the sidewalk. I'm sweating and breathing hard.

"Looks okay," the fireman says, inspecting the engine and ash and charred grass. "Looks like you got it."

I swipe the engine clean, make a final check, and close the hood. The fireman turns and starts toward the station.

"Wait," I say, pointing to the clumps of dry grass underfoot. "What *is* all this?"

"Don't know," he muses. "It seems you had a bunch of grass piled on the engine block. Clippings from a lawnmower, from the looks of it. Once the engine heated up, it all caught fire." He glances down at the "state vehicle" embossed on the front license plate, before looking back at me.

But I'm in no mood to stick around. I shake out my shirt, get back in the car and drive toward the river, turning onto a side-street until I find a parking space that's hidden on three sides by shrubs. I back it in until the tail-lights nestle in the branches, then lock all the doors and start down a path leading to a bridge where the river flows quietly between grassy banks. I walk across the bridge to the other side, keeping to the backstreets in an easterly direction toward the center of town, turning onto main street before ducking into the alcove of a shoe store with big glass windows on either side—recalling the odd way the fireman looked at me after noticing the Impala was a state vehicle.

And who the devil has it out for me, anyway? I mean, who would go to such lengths to carry out such a devious plot?

All signs point to a premeditated act. Dried grass—so brittle you could snap it between your fingers—packed tight and piled on the manifold so that it would catch fire after a mile or two of driving. Ready-made tinder. Time-delay combustion. *Ingenious.* But to place the grass so close to the carburetor? That shows malice. Intent to harm. Assume otherwise at my own peril.

So, who could it be? One of the yokels at the Hole? Doubtful. No one there seems the type, especially since I haven't done anything to anyone. Flashlight? Hardly. The guy is so freaked out by his doomsday fantasies that he wouldn't have the inclination, let alone the guile, to hatch and execute such a plan. He wouldn't know the makings of a prank if it bit him in the ass.

(... *stepping out of the alcove now, walking to the end of the block before turning up a side street, heading for the alley that runs alongside the Waterhole ...*)

Think now, must think. Who's going to have the motive, the means, the opportunity? Motive is unknown, at least for now. Means are not an issue either—dried grass clippings can be found anywhere. That leaves opportunity. The sabotage had to have been committed on the Colby grounds, that much is clear. The perpetrator, then, is likely connected to the compound.

(... *turning into the alley, slowing down, not yet ready to enter the fray of small talk inside the bar ... passing garbage cans and wooden pallets, milk crates and cardboard boxes ... pausing beside a brick wall to survey the sidewalk ahead, eyeing each passerby for anything suspicious: a snicker, a sideways glance, anything out of the ordinary. A couple walks past, arm in arm. A rattletrap pickup drives by. Now strolling onto the sidewalk outside the bar, looking both ways before walking across the porch to the steps that lead down into the barroom ...*)

Annie and Snow are seated at the far end of the bar next to what looks like a lumberjack sporting a black beard, dirty blue jeans, and red t-shirt. I nod to Annie and she waves me over.

"Miles ..." she starts, and then stops. "*What happened to you?*"

"What do you mean?"

"Your shirt," remarks Snowhare, turning toward me. "You're lookin' somewhat ... *feral.*"

"It's just dirt," I reply.

Annie drags her nails across the charred spots. "These are *burn* marks."

"It's nothing," I say, noticing that the lumberjack has taken an interest in the conversation.

"This is Black Bart," Annie says, "from ... where'd you say?"

"North of the Algonquin Range."

"Yeah, north of the Algonquin Range. Bart doesn't care much for government agencies."

"They restrict my freedom," he says flatly, placing a meaty hand on the bar that makes me think of the grip on a crosscut saw. We size each other up like dogs. There's dirt under his fingernails and tobacco stains between his teeth. A devil-may-care glint in his black eyes.

I grab the beer Wire has waiting for me and walk outside to the porch. Across the street, the white clock tower catches the late afternoon light. The sky has turned overcast, the air humid. A family waits for their order at a table outside the deli. Teenagers loiter in front of the market. Older folks, tourists from the looks of it, mingle in front of shop windows before falling in with the slow stream of pedestrians moving along the sidewalk. Next to me, a night watchman nurses his draft, foam clinging to his handlebar moustache … waiting for darkness to fall and the start of his shift.

I look inside. Two guys in white overalls, dusty with drywall, drain whole beers before Wire can return with their change. Another man sits next to them, flecks of silver hair beneath his baseball cap, his work boots caked with mud. At the other end of the bar, Annie and the lumberjack are deep in conversation.

A couple in their thirties sits down next to me on the porch, dressed in tennis gear. They sip mixed drinks and smoke clove cigarettes. YUPPIES, if I've ever seen any.

"Jesus," Yukon says, joining me by the geraniums, "what happened to *you?*" Even when he means to talk softly, his throaty alto booms.

"The Impala caught fire. There was a bunch of dried grass piled under the hood, and once the engine got hot it all went up in flames."

Yukon looks across the street. "How'd the grass get there?"

"Don't know," I say, taking a swig. "Any ideas?"

"Bowersox!" he yells.

A skinny kid in black high-tops runs across the street and hands Yukon a joint, before rejoining his friends on the other side.

Yukon smiles blissfully. "Crazy man."

By this time, the tennis couple is laughing and talking loud. "I tried to avoid it," the man bellows, "you saw me. But it ran right in front of the car. I can still see it flying through the air!"

The woman, with poofed hair and a pink headband, doubles over in laughter, spilling some of her gin and tonic.

"Uh, no," Yukon says, "no ideas. But it reminds me of the time we stuck a dead carp under the hood of a CO truck. Same deal. It was a hot day and after a few minutes of riding around town, it got to stinkin' pretty good."

"Damn thing got blood on my bumper," the yuppy continues. "I hope it didn't leave a dent. I mean, aren't they supposed to keep those things in the barn? That's what it was, right? A barn cat?"

A rusted Electra coupe passes slowly by. The driver asks how the view is, and Yukon salutes him with his beer bottle.

"I was on McKenzie the other day and saw two loons," he says to me. "I'm pretty sure one of 'em was that solo buck on Colby. The McKenzie loon flies over occasionally to check on him, and sometimes they fly back together. Just so long as the Colby bird don't get too close to the nest on McKenzie, they seem to get along all right. When they're flying overhead, I can hear them talking down to the bird on the nest."

A low rumble of thunder sounds in the distance.

"I wasn't gonna give that old fart the time of day. He's a farmer, for chrissakes. It's not my fault that he can't keep his animals in the barn."

The woman laughs and chokes on her smoke, starting a fit of coughing.

"Speaking of the devil," Yukon smiles.

I look across the street to see an officer walking down the steps of the courthouse. "That's Stryker," I say. "What's he doing at the courthouse?"

Yukon shrugs. "He doesn't care for all our shenanigans over here."

Stryker returns our stare. When he opens the door of his truck, his boyish face looks contorted.

"But did you see the way he ran after us? No, listen, this is the best part. He was holding a *pitchfork*. It was like a horror movie!"

The woman wheezes, trying to catch her breath. She spills more gin on her tennis shirt, as they cackle like geese.

A gust of wind blows down the street, picking up dust and ruffling the table umbrellas in front of the deli. Traces of distant lightning flash in the darkening sky. The Olympian walks outside and cranks the umbrellas shut, her long blond hair tied in a ponytail.

"You and Annie getting along all right?" Yukon asks.

"Yeah." I look at him. "Why?"

"Just wondering."

"Why do you ask?" I say.

"Just checking, no big deal."

Inside, the lights have come on and the barroom is crowded. It's mostly a younger crowd—locals in their twenties, dressed in jeans and t-shirts. Day laborers, housepainters, nurses, waitresses ... working class folk who've come down to catch up and see what's on for the night. They all seem to know one another, sitting around tables or leaning against the bar, mingling effortlessly. The women wear their hair long, down over their shoulders. The dapper white-haired gentleman stands at the end of the bar, rustling the ice in his glass of scotch, reaching back for a snort from his glass vial. A light rain begins to fall.

Annie is alone now with the lumberjack who is doing his best to convince her of something, his hands dangerously close to her hips. He leans in, chest hair protruding from the neckline of his shirt. Annie sits back in her barstool, one hand clenched to her breast. Is she in trouble? Does she need rescuing? I remember the way she glared at me when I tried to open the door for her.

I make my way to the back of the room, where a group of teenagers dressed in black leather has gathered around the pool table. I find a place against the brick wall where I can look across the room. It feels good to have my back against the bricks, with everything in front of me. The lamp above the table casts a pyramid of light over the green felt and colored balls. The leather-clad punks mill about the table, restless and fidgety. Only they're not pool sharks, not good with a cue at all. But that's hardly the point. They're here to hang with the tribe. One sports a Mohawk, the crest of his hair dyed white. He wears thin black gloves with the fingers cut out, and three silver rings in his left ear that reflect the light when he bends over to line up a shot.

They've purposefully set themselves apart from the mainstream, brandishing their studs and leather like badges of honor—tokens of the alienation that binds them together. The walking wounded, finding refuge amongst themselves. No one talks big, no one makes a scene. They move around me like I'm not even there. It's as though they've had their youth taken away too early, and they've banded together in a last ditch effort to make a stand. Or maybe they just see through all the self-serving hypocrisy of the adult world—a world, like it or not, they're soon to inherit. They look serious, except in those brief moments when they drop their guard and laugh, the weight of their lives suddenly lifted, the pain forgotten if only for an instant.

Jesus, listen to me. The grass fire has me rattled, alright, more than I might have supposed. Here I am, playing outsider to the outsiders. Time to reset, get another drink … *keep moving.*

The copper bar is crowded, two deep all the way around. The only place I can get reasonably close to Wire is a little gap between the lumberjack and Annie who's now facing the other way, talking to Yukon. Black Bart has his back to the bar, and I can tell by his goofy grin that he's had a few.

All I really want is to have a beer and relax, maybe track down Spot and make small talk, get close enough to catch a whiff of the musk she dabs on her neck beneath her strawberry blond hair and dangling silver earrings. But something tells me it's not going to happen. The prickly complications of social dynamics intervene. I feel like some out-of-place knight who needs to defend the honor of his damsel-in-distress, but even that's not clear. It could be his chivalric advances are not even wanted.

I sneak into the gap without Annie noticing, but the lumberjack sees me coming. He doesn't move when I put my empty bottle on the copper. Bart's odor is bad—a potent mix of alcohol, tobacco, and stale sweat. His shirt is stained under the arm pits. And when he says what he does, it's like being handed a script and told to read the lines. Read the lines and act out the part.

"Comfortable?"

"Yeah," I say, turning to face him. "Comfortable."

"Let me just get out of your way then."

But he doesn't move. When he grins, his bloodshot eyes say: *come right ahead, 'cause I got nothin' to lose.*

"I'm talking to the little lady there," he says. "Do you mind?"

Annie is still facing the other way.

"Looks like she's busy," I reply.

"Oh, a tough guy," the lumberjack sneers. He's close enough that I can smell his rancid breath. "DEC tough guy."

(*And then, as if in a dream, the lumberjack reaches back and cold cocks our hero, sending him crashing into the bar to the sound of shattering glass and the clank and rattle of an empty beer bottle rolling across copper. He falls to the floor, next to the shiny brass foot rail, peering up at the circle of faces looking down at him, all of it in slow motion—a late-night movie he watches with detached interest, indifferent to the outcome. Rising to his feet, one hand clenched to the edge of the bar, he's grabbed from behind and pulled backward. Somewhere on the periphery he hears a woman's voice calling his name—distorted like the muffled cry of his young sister, reverberating in the galvanized culvert, begging for him to come out and meet her on the outside, her words drowned in the amplified sibilance of his rubber boots sloshing through sand and gravel, until, in the pallid light near the end of the tunnel, he comes upon a pool of clear water and a cutthroat darting from side to side. Dipping his hands, careful to slide his fingers gently under the iridescent belly, he raises the trout out of the water, its gills gasping, and all the while his sister calling from the end of the culvert, pleading ...*)

"Outside!" Wire leaps across the bar to stand between us. He must have been watching, seen it coming even before I did. "Take it outside!"

We're not three steps away from each other, but the press of bodies makes it difficult to move. Bart pauses and stares over the crowd, like he's weighing his options, swayed finally by the urgency of the moment. *'Cause there's nothin' to lose.* The black glint returning to his eyes, the goofy grin back in

179

place, goading, he says loud enough for me to hear, "We'll just go outside is all."

Yukon releases his hold on me. "You don't have to do this, you know."

But he might as well be some stranger I pass on the street. Yukon and everyone else. All part of the sea of faces you see, whizzing by the station on a speeding train. When Bart rolls his shoulders and shambles toward the door, his eyes promising black disaster, I follow him out.

We walk to the alley next to the bar and face each other in the rain. Bart takes off his red shirt and begins to circle me.

"Tough guy," he smiles. "DEC tough guy."

And then we box, clean and civil, trading jabs like textbook fighters. Blood trickles from the corner of his mouth, shining in the light when he passes by the streetlamp. I'm bleeding too from a cut under my lip, leaving me with the taste of metal mixed with rain.

We go back and forth like this, no roundhouses, just clean jabs. Bob and weave, slipping punches. There's no lunging or grabbing or tackling, and it occurs to me we're caught in some kind of bizarre dance. What one does the other repeats, until it no longer feels like a run-of-the-mill barroom fistfight with some grungy lumberjack. In this strange, mystical two-step, there doesn't seem to be much difference between us.

I have to stop, if for no other reason than the whole thing is too weird. I think Bart feels it, too. "Had enough?" he says, looking up at the rain. He seems content, reverent even. "I know I have."

He walks toward me. With the streetlight behind him, all I see is his silhouette. If he's got a mind to, he could lay me out. He could floor me right then and there, and I wouldn't even bat an eye because by now I'm real close to not giving a damn.

He puts a hand on my shoulder. "Hey," he says, catching his breath. "It's nothing personal. I just like to fight." My vision swims in the rain and light. Black Bart is a blurry shadow, leaving tracers of streetlight when he moves.

"Forget it," I find myself saying.

The porch is crowded with people who have come outside to watch. All I know is I have to get out of there. When I start down the dark alley, I hear Annie's voice behind me.

She catches up to me and grabs my arm, holding on as we walk. That's when I realize I'm shaking pretty bad.

"Stop," she says, "let me look at you."

Her hand clenches harder and it calms me a little, like recovering a lost memory of something.

"Look at you," she says, reaching in her pocket. "My partner all beat up."

She takes out a bandana and dabs the blood above my lip. Then with her fingertips, she pats the knot rising over my eye.

"Come on," she says, leading me down the alley, the rain falling harder now. Thunder follows close on the heels of lightning.

Annie drives the Impala back to Colby and helps me to bed. She brings a bucket of ice to my room and makes a cold pack with her bandana, placing it above my eye so the cubes fit the curve of bone along my brow and cheek. "Hold this," she says. Then she leaves and returns with the first aid kit and a small music box, which she places on my nightstand. As she opens the kit, she begins to sing to the jingle of the chiming bells:

The moon shines tonight on Pretty Red Wing
The breeze is sighing, the night bird's crying

She dunks a cotton swab into a bottle of disinfectant and applies it to the gash that's opened on my other cheekbone. Wincing, I look into her eyes.

"This is getting to be a habit," she smiles, "nursing you."

Close now, she dabs the cotton on the cut over my lip, patting the peels of skin into place.

For afar, beneath his star, her brave is sleeping,
While Red Wing weeps her heart away

She sweeps my hair out of the way, back across my head, and pauses to look at her work. The music winds down. I close my eyes, listening to the rain falling on the metal roof, feeling the weight of her on my chest and her hair when it drops across my shoulder. The soft brush of her lips on mine.

(SHE APPEARS IN THE DISTANCE, *a vision in the night with her blond hair and white cotton dress, walking toward him. A gentle trade wind rustles the palm trees, ocean waves lap upon the beach. She walks barefoot in the sand, as strobes of lightning flash in the darkness behind her. She steps closer, eyes beseeching. Come, she says, in the sigh of wind and sea.*

A warm breeze pushes the hair across her face. She curls it behind one ear, her gaze calm and steady. Blue eyes transfixed.

"Miles."

The wind grows stronger, swirling around them. She moves closer, her body against his, the sound of her breath as she whispers his name. Don't leave, she says. Her long blond hair blowing in the wind, radiant in the black night. In the wind and lightning flashing over the dark sea ...)

"Miles."

Annie walks across the room and sits on the edge of my bed.

"Our man Stokes just called. He says a farmer phoned him this morning about a loon on the side of the road near Gabriels. Says he didn't know who else to call."

I rise to a splitting headache and the lingering resonance of my dream, waiting for the moment to catch up. Congeal. "What's a loon doing on the side of the road?"

"I guess we'll know when we get there," she says.

183

The farmer is holding vigil when we arrive, standing beside his mailbox at the end of a long dirt road that winds through spruce trees up to a farmhouse and barn. Thirty feet away, a loon rests on the sandy shoulder of the highway.

"Hallo there," he says. "You the loon folks?"

"That's us," Annie replies.

"Well, here's the critter."

It's an adult (single male, if I had to guess) sitting perfectly still on the shoulder.

"I think he's getting used to me by now," the farmer chuckles. "Been with him since daybreak. We had that rain last night, so I was checking on the garden and doing my morning rounds when I see him fly over. He starts to circle above, and then he glides in low over the road here. He drops down even lower till he sticks out his feet like he means to skid on water. Well, he's got his feet out and wings spread wide to slow hisself down, when he hits the golldang blacktop full bore! The landing goes well enough for a few feet, a nice smooth skid, until it proves too much and he somersaults onto the shoulder."

As he tells the story, the farmer removes his railroad engineer's hat and waves it in a circle like a haymaker, rocking back and forth on his heels, emphasizing the highs and lows of the incident. Arms waving, he pauses once to look at the loon, scratching his head in wonderment. He's a beefy man, stout as a barrel. Broad chest and round shoulders. Bald on top, the bushy gray hair along the sides of his head protrudes above his ears. At eight o'clock in the morning, he's working up a sweat, blue eyes burning.

"So, he goes into this tumble with feathers flying every which way, but he lands right-side up, just as you see him now. And that's basically it. Like I say, I've been watching him all morning, keeping my distance. He just sets there, not movin'. I don't know if he's broke or not. Can't tell. He just sets there quiet as a church mouse. Skinned a little bark off'n his beak, it looks like, but the critter don't do nothin' but *stare*. It's the darndest thing. I been here two hours, wavin' cars down so as not to startle him too much, and in all that time there weren't five minutes that he didn't have at least one eye on me. Tell ya the truth, those red eyes are kinda spooky. If I didn't know it was just a case of him taking a wrong turn, I'd think he was sent here to check on me."

The three of us stare at the loon, looking for signs of higher intelligence.

More than anything, the bird seems curious. Not terribly frightened, anyway. Just curious and maybe a little embarrassed at being put out this way. His back feathers are ruffled, though the wings look to be folded properly. Road grit mars his white belly. A black-and-white feather blows across the road.

"Darndest thing I ever seen," the farmer says. "But I figure it's got every right to be here. Just as much as us, anyhow."

I wonder what we must look like from a distance—three grown adults along the side of the road, bending over, staring at a bird like it's some kind of alien from outer space.

"Okay, what's the plan?" I ask.

"Pick it up and put it in the back seat," Annie replies, starting for the car. "We'll drive it over to Heart Lake."

"Are you serious?"

She stops to look at me. "You have a better idea?"

Lest I forget my place, it's up to me as grunt to secure the cargo. I approach the subject cautiously, speaking in reassuring tones. "Good loon." Up close like this, I'm reminded of how big and strong a loon is, how at any moment it could wheel and pluck my eye out.

I reach out to pet it, my hand shaking from the night before. I'm just about to touch its checkerboard back, when the loon turns and cocks its head. I back away, realizing that a leap of faith is required here. Once I commit myself, there will be no turning back.

The loon seems more at ease the second time around. It flinches when I first touch it, but otherwise remains still. Perhaps it realizes the predicament it's in, the fact that without my help it's up the creek. Its neck is beautifully emblazoned with white stripes. The power of this bird, its shimmering black and white beauty, the bizarre markings and ruby eyes ... only sixty million years of evolution could concoct something so fantastic.

Annie brings a towel from the car and together we wrap it around its body. When I pick it up, the loon shows no alarm. Maybe it's the farmer rubbing off on me, but I have the eerie feeling it knows exactly what's happening.

The bird watches as Annie opens the back door of the Impala. Wings tucked under my hands, I hold it steady while she clears a space on the seat among the cushions and paddles and papers. Through the threadbare towel, I can feel its heartbeat—or maybe it's my own that I feel. I set the loon down on the seat between the two seat-belt fasteners.

The farmer shakes his head, turning to go. "If that don't beat all ...."

Annie thanks him and tells him we'll call with any news. As the farmer walks off, she asks if we should buckle up the loon.

"Buckle him up? You mean with a seat belt?"

"Yeah, fasten him in."

The loon stares blankly.

"*It's the law*," Annie says, mimicking the public service announcement on television.

As she reaches for the belt, the loon opens its wings like a morning flower, sweeping the towel aside.

"Maybe not," she says.

I start the car while Annie slides into the passenger seat, keeping an eye on our friend. We drive like this all the way to Heart, Annie watching as the loon stares straight ahead. When we arrive, I stop the car beside the water and go to the back seat, noticing the DEC truck parked in the lot. I place my hands over the wings and pick up the bird. Once it's out of the car, it begins to squirm and Annie quickly puts her hands around mine. We wade out till the water is up to our knees and lower it in the lake. The loon paddles out a ways, makes two staccato *cheeps* and disappears beneath the surface. The last I see is the crimson scuff on its foot as it sounds. A little road rash shouldn't hurt too much. We watch and wait until the loon appears thirty yards offshore, stretching its wings.

When we turn back toward the car, we find an agency man standing on the gravel lot next to the ungulate. He's DEC alright, dressed in government green. The drab olive contrasts sharply with his orange, bristly hair. I notice the Fisheries patch on his shirt.

"Let me guess," he says, as we approach. "The loon people."

"That's right," Annie says. "Non-game. I'm Annie and this is Miles."

"Oh, I know who you are," he laughs. "You've made quite a reputation for yourselves," he says, looking at me.

"All good I hope," Annie smiles.

He glances over my shoulder and motions toward the loon riding low in the water. Only its head and neck and the top of its back show above the surface. The white necklace shines like war paint.

"Where'd you find *him?*"

"Out by Gabriels," Annie says. "He was on the side of the road."

The man chuckles and scratches the orange stubble on his chin.

"What's so funny?" I say.

"Loons," he says loudly. "Loons is funny. They'll do that, you know. They'll be flying overhead and look down on a road, especially if it's wet with rain, and think it's a river. They come flying in low, drop their feet, and skid across the asphalt just like they would a flat black river."

"Really?"

"Really," he snickers. "Only they don't land so smooth. I imagine they take quite a tumble," he laughs. "Maybe that's why they call 'em loons."

There's something about our Fisheries man that rubs me the wrong way. He's a little too cocksure for my taste. He has a way of subtly reminding you that he's in the know and you're not. A bureaucrat and proud of it. Turn him inside out and you'll find the same thing, like one of those reversible winter jackets. No telling how he landed this job farming fish, but he's got a grip on it like a vice.

"This is where we raise fish for stocking," he says. "We bring the fingerlings here in a truck and release them by the thousands. Then we collect 'em after they've grown, take 'em away in the same truck and stock the area. It's all tightly controlled. We have a barrier dam on the far shore to keep it isolated. And that's how it gets done. Gotta keep the fishermen happy."

I look across the lake for our loon, but he's disappeared. Chances are this isn't his lake, anyway. Heart is too small to accommodate more than one pair, and we've already seen a nest on the far island.

"Loons don't bother the operation?"

"Naw. Oh, they'll eat some fish, but there's enough in here to feed a million loons. If they ever gave us any real trouble, then we'd have to do something. But it's fine the way it is."

"How long has that nest been out there?"

He sticks his chin out and scratches the stubble on his neck. "Been there a while. As long as I can remember, anyway. We don't pay them any mind."

The Fisheries man studies us one last time. "Well, gotta go," he says, and starts across the gravel lot toward a trail that leads into the woods. "Oh," he says, turning back to look at us. "A tip for you, free of charge," he winks. "There's loons all over the place up here."

When we get back to Colby, Annie makes another ice pack for the lump over my eye. We climb the stairs to the cupola where we sit and look out across the lake. The wind teases the leaves of the big oak tree, casting a lazy dance of flickering sunlight into the cupola. Annie sits at the desk near the pile of maps, staring out the open window. Things are different now, that's for sure. So much for my grand plan of lying low and keeping out of trouble. So much for the straight and narrow.

A gust of wind sails across the surface of the lake, racing over the water like goose bumps on skin. The grass along the shore is beginning to fade, no longer the vivid green of June. The dog days of summer are upon us. For the first time since I've been here, it hits home that our days at Colby are numbered.

We're ahead of schedule, with another dozen or so lakes to cover. Once we're finished with the list, we'll return to those sites where we saw nesting activity, make our final entries, pack it in, and head back to Albany.

That afternoon, Flashlight comes by to give us our monthly checks, and I tell him about the loon that tried to land on Highway 86.

"Not surprising," he says. "It's just like the prophecies say. Everything is turned upside down and mixed up—animals popping up in places where they don't belong."

Maybe so, but I try to see it from the loon's perspective. From the air, the wet asphalt is going to look like a river winding through forests and fields. Sixty million years without blacktop, and you can't expect a loon to identify a highway overnight. Its wiring can't possibly account for pavement, at least not yet. Give it some time. My guess is it'll figure things out soon enough.

When I ask him if he's heard of any suspicious behavior on the part of the campers, Flashlight shakes his head no.

DRIVING BETWEEN THE THEATER MASKS this morning, we spy a loon flying overhead on a course from Colby to Mackenzie, and I imagine what the Impala must look like from the air: a silver canoe floating toward the confluence with Highway 3. At eight in the morning it's already hot, ninety-degrees or better. I suspect the turtles will have a good day, letting it all hang out in the sun.

When we arrive at Upper Saint Regis Lake, we put-in at the southernmost point and follow the shoreline west, until we come to a trail marking the portage to Bear Pond. On the bank, Annie grabs the cushions and paddles, while I lift the canoe by the center thwart and flip it upside down over my head, balancing the gunwales on my shoulders. With my head inside the canoe, I can only see ten feet in front of me, so Annie takes the lead and starts down the trail. The tall ferns bend and release when she brushes against them with her thighs. It feels good to be in the shadows of the forest. The needle-packed trail is soft underfoot, the air sweet with the aroma of pitch.

After a half mile or so, the sunlit water of Bear Pond appears in the distance through the trees. A glacial pond, Bear is the color of turquoise, reminding me of the azure waters off the Keys.

Annie drops the cushions and paddles on the beach and retraces her steps to a small flower in the woods. I swing the canoe down and set it next to the gear, rolling my shoulders to get the blood flowing, before joining her beside the flower:

a pink lady's slipper growing among tall pines. The plant has two leaves at the bottom and a big magenta flower.

"Look," I say. The walk through the woods has put me in a goofy mood. "A solitary slipper in a den of cork-booted giants."

The flower looks especially delicate next to the big pines, and yet there's something about its fragile beauty that gives the trees pause, like they know they need to be on their best behavior.

Annie kneels before the flower, tucking her feet beneath her.

With each passing day, our time in the woods draws down like sand in an hourglass, and I realize I should savor moments like this—make sure they're stored properly in memory for those times when I might need a little hope. But, honestly, I'm not sure it's in my nature. It goes against that part of the credo that says the only thing you can ever be sure of in this world is what's directly in front of you, and even that's a bit suspect. Chances come and go. Luck might be on your side, or it might not. And even if it is, it won't last long. So better just to stay on the bounce and keep moving. Sure, there will be good things that come your way, but they won't last. Why? *Because the whole damn world sees to it.* Pretty flowers exist to get crushed and driven into the ground by the boot heels of progress.

But maybe that's all changing. Maybe the credo needs adjusting.

I look at the alabaster beach beside the turquoise water, the cool recess of forest, the way the sunlight angles through the trees like stained-glass windows in a cathedral.

"It's crazy," I say with a sweep of my hand. "I mean, look at all this. It can't just be an accident. There has to be a *reason* for all this."

It's hard for me to know if I believe what I'm saying, but it feels like I do. I *want* to believe in something good. I *want* to sound sincere. Then again, maybe I just want to impress Annie.

In any case, something comes over me and I begin to jabber away like there's no tomorrow. I pontificate on all the bad in the world and why it has to be this way. The pain, suffering, injustice, you name it. It has to be this way simply because *it is*, I say. It's as though humans can't help themselves. They keep doing what they're doing no matter the consequences, even if they know it's not what they should be doing. Meanwhile, as Flashlight likes to say, we're all going to hell in a hand-basket. We're going to hell and dragging half of god's creation with us. It's true. It's *all* true. You come into this life, take stock of what you find, and then decide for yourself. Ya gotta have an idea in this world—an idea and a little sand to back it up.

The whole time I'm talking, Annie doesn't look up once. She keeps her eyes fixed on the flower like she's in some kind of trance, staring into a future of collapse and ruin haunted by the specter of extinction, and it occurs to me why I'm carrying on this way. For the first time, *I'm* the one looking on the bright side. *I'm* the one championing all that's good in the world. And I have to say it's thrown me through a loop, like I've been backed into a corner and left to my own devices, and so I keep yammering as if the longer I talk, the more my uneasiness will go away. I blather on about how people are animals too, subject to the same kind of mating dances and songs and carrying capacities as any other species, only maybe it's time we get down off our high horse and ante up. Greed will be our downfall, I say. Arrogance and willful ignorance will seal the deal. And before you know it, I find myself in a place I could not possibly have predicted, but in order to keep the ball rolling and drive home the point, I have to come up with an example of how everything is going to hell and the only thing I can think of is the drunk reindeer in Sweden who bit the schoolgirl in the ass.

Annie looks up, a hint of the gypsy in her eyes. "Maybe we should get to work," she says.

As we're loading the gear into the canoe, I notice a long line of damselflies parked along the shore, like a battalion of helicopters standing guard. These electric blue whirlybirds are nearly 300 million years old as a species, going back to the days of Pangaea. The phalanx parts nicely when we slide the canoe down the beach into the water. Once we're afloat, a squadron breaks ranks and escorts us around the perimeter of Bear. Seems they're partial to the drops of water dripping from the paddles between strokes.

The pond is so clear that we can see the play of sunlight on the sandy bottom, thirty feet down. If the sprawling Saranac Lakes evoke the peninsula-strafed wilderness of voyageur lore, then Bear Pond is the Caribbean oasis of the Adirondack backcountry—a secluded lagoon of bright light, white sand, and turquoise water.

From Bear, we make the short portage to Little Long Pond. Little Long has five islands, any one of which could provide suitable habitat. All are low islands with plenty of hummocks and dirt patches upon which a loon could stamp out a home. Not to be, however. No loons on Little Long, either.

I read in one of the articles that in places like Minnesota and Canada, populations are pushed to their density limits. Loons everywhere. The sky speckled with them, flying high, hooting pleasantries to their compatriots below as they pass overhead. Maybe not as numerous as passenger pigeons, whose enormous flocks were said to blot out the midday sun.

But still. The habitat at Little Long looks ideal, so where are the loons? I remember what the Acid Rangers said about dead lakes, and I wonder if that's the case here.

From Little Long we portage to Green Pond and from there to St. Regis Pond. I set the canoe in the water as Annie loads the gear. Just as I'm stepping in, she points to the tree behind me. I turn around to see a bright red bird, hopping along a pine branch, not thirty feet away.

"Scarlet tanager," she whispers.

Its vivid color is offset by the darker tones of the forest behind it. No camouflage for this bird, not in these parts. His plumage is too bright, too brash. The tanager hops along the branch, long enough for us to detect the black wings and tail, before flying away in a streak of red.

Don't think I'm not picking up the signs. With the beautiful blue of Bear Pond and now this scarlet tanager, things are looking up. Maybe it does come down to the power of positive thinking. You know, put your faith in doing good and the world responds in kind. And why not? Why *shouldn't* good things come my way?

We check a small island with a dead birch tree standing in the middle of it. I poke the shrubs along the water with the fat end of my paddle. No loons, no nest. Not on this or any other island. What we do find are campers—plenty of neon polyester tents beside thin streams of campfire smoke. On the two islands that have no humans, we see rusted tin cans and the coals of recent fires.

On our way back to the portage, we sight a pair of loons on the pond. We change our course to get closer, until we're only fifteen yards away. Annie quietly slides her paddle inside the canoe, and I follow suit. The water is calm, the sun slanting low in the west. For the next half hour, we drift on the glassy surface, observing the pair as they watch us. The loons, ruby eyes aglow, rear back and stretch their wings. Then they bend and roll their heads, as beads of water roll off their backs. They take turns diving through the liquid gems of sunlight reflected on the surface, the checkerboard plumage blending nicely with the blinking light, casting a hypnotic spell, so long as I keep my gaze steady and don't look away. The play of light on the black-and-white checkering reminds me of something an old Indian told me once in Gallup. He said that when a person dies, his spirit travels to the underworld where everything is the mirror image of this world. If it's night here, then it's day there. If it's winter here, it's summer there. Everything is turned inside out like an x-ray image. What's black is white, what's dark is light.

It's been a long day. By the time we reach Green Pond, the sun has set. We slice through the placid water, making good time. The canoe pulls a rippled V through an impressionistic reflection of forest and sky. Up ahead, we see another wake moving across the water. Through the glasses I make out a shadow at the front of it, just beneath the surface. A head emerges, and then a big flat tail to slap the water. CRACK!

The North American Beaver (*Castor Canadensis*). Largest rodent on the continent, weighing up to 100 pounds. Ruthlessly trapped for their pelts in the 17th and 18th centuries, until they were nearly extirpated. Distant cousin to the Giant Beaver (*Castoroides canadensis*) that flourished in the Ice Age before dying out 10,000 years ago. These 400-pound beauties were the size of black bears and sported serrated teeth six-inches long.

The forest darkens in the gathering dusk. A yellow moon rises in the east, perfectly reflected on the lake. Our canoe sails through the skywater, smooth as a hawk on the glide. Up ahead, hard by the St. Regis portage, a braid of fire smoke rises from the beach. As we approach the camp, close enough to hear the crackling embers, a man starts for the outlet with the gait of a bear, canteen in hand.

"Greetings," he says with a hint of French in his accent. "I'm fixing up some tea just now, care for a cup?" The man squats to fill his canteen. "I haven't spoken to another soul in three days."

It's nearly dark and we're still a good piece from the car, with two more portages to make. But the fat moon promises to light the way, casting a ghostly hue among the shadows of the forest.

"Sure," Annie says.

We pull the canoe up on the beach and follow the man to the fire.

"I don't mean to hold you up any, but you don't strike me as campers. You don't look like you're out here just for fun."

"We're wildlife biologists," Annie explains, "conducting a loon survey."

"Ah," the man sighs, adding water to the pot on the fire. "And what has your *biology* shown you?"

Annie and I look at each other. His question puts me on guard, but there's something about him that seems guileless. I don't sense any sarcasm in his tone. He's including us in any irony there might be behind his question, and he seems genuinely interested in what we have to tell him.

"Nothing conclusive yet," Annie replies. "We really won't know anything until all the data is in, but, overall, we're not seeing the numbers we hoped for. It seems the loon has lost ground since the last survey was done five years ago. We know they've abandoned some lakes."

The western sky fades to rust and lilac. It's a small fire he's built, but it burns well.

"I'm sorry to hear that," he says, "but I guess it's not surprising. Seems to be the way things are going."

The lid on the pot pops up, ejecting a spurt of steam into the air. He pours a little more water from his canteen.

"And you," Annie asks, "what brings you out here?"

"Oh, I spend most of my time in the woods. I guess I'm what you'd call a hermit, at least that's what folks call me. There's a tradition of that in these parts, you know. You've heard of Noah Randeau, I'm sure. The truth is, I like spending time alone in these mountains. I winter in a cabin not far from here."

Short and stout, he moves quickly about his camp—tidying his bedroll and bag, pulling tea bags from a sack, adding wood to the fire, poking the coals. When he lifts the pot to pour the water, I reach for the travel bag in my pocket.

"Here," I say, pinching a couple stalks and caps between my fingers, "we can add this to the tea."

He looks at the shriveled caps, then back at me. "Okay," he says, setting the pot back on the coals. "Looks like we have a choice, leaded or unleaded."

Annie gives me a quick glance. "Leaded's fine," she says.

The man picks up the lid with a pad in his hand, as I pluck another cap from the canister and drop everything into the simmering water. He returns the lid and nestles the pot on the bed of coals. "We'll just let that settle a bit."

Annie looks at the three-quarter moon, and I know she's wondering if we can get back all right. But it's a warm night and there's plenty of light. We've had a good day and it seems only natural to keep it going.

"You ever get lonely out here?" I ask.

"Sometimes," the hermit replies. "But lonely is like a cut that starts to infect. You have to nip it at the bud, lest it festers. The more you brood on it, the worse it gets. Let it go long enough, and it might drive you stark mad."

For a hermit, he sure has a way with words. Not shy either.

"I have to admit, there are times when I miss good conversation and companionship. Then again, I'm always running into folks in the backcountry like yourselves. Anymore, it's getting to be a bigger challenge to *avoid* people out here. But I love to talk. Sounds like a contradiction, doesn't it? A hermit with a knack for confab. Anyway, my name is *Henri*."

"Miles," I say. "And this is Annie."

"Pleasure to meet you both." He opens the lid and looks inside the pot.

"Loneliness though ...." He squints like he's thought long and hard on the subject. "There's no reason why you can't make a truce with it, you know. Reach an understanding. If you don't ask too much, that is. It's like everything else out here, the forest and lakes and animals, even the shadows at night. But you have to be careful with them, they don't always play fair. Spirits, I mean."

He laughs and checks on the brew, stirring the sludge of mushrooms with a fork, studying the amber color of the water. Satisfied with the state of his concoction, he pours the steaming tea through a metal strainer into a coffee pot, then adds a bit more water to the clot of soggy fungi left over in the first pot. His movements are graceful for such a powerful man. He looks as strong as a bear and every bit as nimble. When he isn't fiddling with the pots and fire, he stands with his hands in his pockets, shadows from the firelight streaking his face. He strikes me as some kind of backwoods warlock, stirring up a cauldron of wicked stew. But in a good way.

He lets the new batch simmer a few minutes before pouring it into the coffee pot and swirling it around. Then he sets the pot in the coals at the edge of the fire, reaches into his sack and pulls out a pair of tin cups. "It's all I got," he says.

"That's alright," Annie says, "we'll share."

He pours the tea into the battered cups and sets them aside to cool. By now, a few stars have appeared in the purple sky, as the last blush of day reflects off the lake. The moon hangs above a black, serrated edge of conifers etched against the sky. At the far end of the lake, a silhouette of mountains rises above the trees.

The hermit hands us one of the cups, mumbles something into the fire, and drinks his down. The tea has a strange organic flavor, not bad considering what's in it.

"Out here, there's always something to keep me company—a bird or animal, a change in the weather, a shooting star …. There's always something going on. Everything is *alive*, you know. If you listen and watch, you can pick up on it. It speaks to you, but you have to be tuned in to what it says. You have to know something of the language."

I'm content to let the hermit ramble, looking off now and then at the moon and the stars as they appear in the sky. But mostly I stare into the fire. I notice Annie looking at the fire, too. The coals change color with the fluidity of vapor, from orange to silver to black, like there's something *breathing* inside the burning wood. A thin wisp of blue flame appears and vanishes within a split second. Back and forth like this, the flame flickers in the dark until it slowly assumes the shape of a thin blue ghost—partly of this world, partly of another.

Henri stands and places another limb on the bed of coals. Shadows from the firelight creep across his face, creating a sinister effect. He must realize this because he sits down again, and he's no longer the evil hermit but simply Henri. I can't help but laugh.

"It's true …" he says. "Everything's true."

Many times in the canoe, we've passed a tree along the bank that has fallen over with its root structure completely intact. The elaborate network of intertwining roots, weathered white by the elements, stands vertically beside the water like a wall of tangled bones, reflected perfectly on the calm dark surface of the lake. Roots and reflections become one and the same—an intricate latticework of interlocking limbs, branching into endless configurations, like tiny fingers of fungus spreading web-like through a forest floor; a living organism with no center, alive and aware, expanding outward in all directions, gathering and relaying information in pulsating waves and frequencies that are themselves plugged into an underlying energy field that makes it possible for everything in the universe to interact and communicate with everything else, throughout all time.

I've seen a salmon carcass washed up on a beach, writhing and squirming from a swarm of maggots eating away its insides.

The flames in the fire flicker like a neon light on the fritz. In the glowing coals, there's a silhouette of dancers in a lit room behind a pulled shade. Tattered ash clings to the burning wood, flapping wildly, like trees caught in the hurricane wind of an atomic blast, or the tentacles of sea anemones on a shallow reef with the water swaying this way and that, this way and that.

Now the glowing embers are blocks of sandstone in a redrock canyon, with secret defiles and keyholes, and I'm flying through a labyrinthine slot canyon of orange luminescence, past a creepy gargoyle with blinking black eyes, turning down a narrow corridor that suddenly opens onto an Old World village, with tall stone-and-plaster buildings towering over cobblestone streets. But all is not right in paradise. A young man peers down from a third-story window, heartsick, a casualty of youthful love. Smitten with the girl next door, his desires go unrequited. He wants to flee, light out for the territory, just he and his mount ... ride along a canyon rim and never feel the sting of love again.

"The world ..." Henri says, reverb in his voice, "forever on the verge of revealing itself, as it makes itself anew. But never quite. There's always something there that eludes us."

I gulp down the rest of the tea. The hermit is working up to something, though I can't tell exactly what. "Where you going with that, preacher?" I ask. I don't mean any disrespect, it just comes out that way. He smiles at my harmless indiscretion.

"Listen," he whispers. "Hear that soft breeze that just came up in the pines?"

I'm not sure if I do or not. It might only be something I hear in my head, like the sound of surf when you put your ear to a seashell.

"Science is going to explain it one way, certainly, but there's a whole other way of looking at it. A whole other way of understanding it. The Iroquois believe the air is peopled with spirits. For instance, that sound of the wind in the pines is the song of a young woman as she floats down a raging river toward a certain death, mingled with the roar of rapids and the strange cry of her lover as he plunges headlong into the waterfalls after her. *Do you hear it?* And this fire—a giant spirit feeding on smaller spirits. The stronger the wind, the bigger the flames. There are spirits everywhere. The northern lights are the reflection of campfires burning in the hereafter. And see those two moons over there? A gift given to peaceful tribes to help them ward off attacks from invading warriors. Reflected on the water, the fires they built at night doubled in number, making it appear to their enemies that they were twice as strong."

I look at the moon and its mirror image on the lake, thinking the hermit might be warming up to a long yarn. But I'm in no hurry to go anywhere, not with this ball of fire raging in my belly. Best to settle in until it cools down some. I look at Annie and see the reflection of firelight in her eyes.

"The air is peopled with spirits, lots of 'em. Good ones who help you out in times of difficulty, and bad ones who cause trouble if you neglect them."

Now she turns to look at me.

"It's always been that way, you know," the hermit explains. "Thing is, there's no difference between ... I mean, it's still happening ... it's *all* happening. But how do I say this? No, it's impossible to explain. All we can ever know are the effects ... *the effects*."

I look back into the fire.

"Can you imagine what it must have been like," the hermit continues, "to be taken from your home and placed in this world with all its wonders and terror, its dangers and mystery? To wander a wilderness utterly indifferent to the fortunes of man, a world that had never known his kind, a hideous and spectacular place of riotous vegetation and rapacious monsters all vying for domination?

"The Creator imagined the world into being from a great island floating in space. He tore a large tree from the ground, opening a passageway to a sea that was covered in clouds. He then called for a woman with child, wrapped her in a ray of light, and sent her below. When the birds and animals of the sea cloud saw Sky Woman descending from above, they worried that there would be nowhere for her to land. So, Loon dove to the bottom of the sea and returned with a clod of earth. Turtle then offered the hard shell of its back as a place to put the earth. As the light came nearer, the birds flew to receive Sky Woman on their wings and carry her safely down. When she stepped on the island, the earth began to grow. Having lost her former world, Island Woman danced a new world into creation on the back of Turtle.

"Soon, she gave birth to twin boys—the spirits of Good and Evil. Good set out to beautify the world, but Evil sought to destroy it. When Island Woman died, Good shaped the sky with his hand and created the Sun from her face. But Evil put darkness in the western sky to cover up the Sun. Good then created the Moon and Stars from his mother's breast, to guard the night sky. Finally, he gave her body to the earth so that life could appear."

I look at the two moons burning brightly—one in the sky, the other on the surface of the lake.

"But can you imagine what it must have been like? For the first people, it must have seemed a savage and magical place, a bewildering exile from the home they had known. But this was the point, you see. It was all too easy. There were no evil spirits to challenge the people and make them brave. Yes, there were consequences if they strayed from the right path, but the consequences were not that great— not like they are now. Maybe they thought they were taken care of and nothing bad would come to them. Maybe they grew complacent and took things for granted—you know how people can be. But imagine the fear, the longing and regret ... haunted by the memory of a home they had *lost*—a place of clear running streams and fertile valleys, forests and plains alive with deer and buffalo, bear and wild horses, where everything had a place, a purpose ...."

The hermit proceeds to describe how the people had danced around the campfire at night, banging drums and singing, telling stories and laughing, keeping all the animals awake, carrying on until they were taken from their home in a basket under the cover of darkness so they wouldn't know where they were going or how to find their way back.

But, honestly, at this point, I have my hands full with the fire. Not only is there the glowing canyon country to deal with, but now there's something else. Waves of light and shadow, passing through the glowing coals, have come to life. I catch glimpses of faces, wan visages, waving arms and wild gestures. Restless spooks fly through the burning coals from one side of the fire to the next, like animals trapped in a cage, looking for a way out. There's something in there, something *alive*. They have faces, I can see them! It's all happening too fast for me to get a handle on, especially with the hermit going on about how the people were told that they could return home only when they had acquired bravery and circumspection.

"Bravery and circumspection," Annie repeats, letting the thought sink in. "Meet the beast on its own ground," she says.

"They were afraid," the hermit continues. "How should their prayers be heard, they wondered. When they felt joy or sorrow, how would their messages reach home?

"They were told that a second self exists for each person—a spirit that lives in the air, who knows the way to the other world and who conveys all prayers and messages exactly as they are spoken. These spirits would answer their calls so that none of their words would be lost. And they would guide each person on the long journey home when their time was ready.

"To test out the system, one of the people walked down to the water's edge and began to speak in a loud voice. After he spoke, he heard his words repeated across the lake by the first messenger, who then passed them along to the next, until the words traveled over the treetops and across the mountains and lakes, growing fainter as they went."

The hermit pauses, glancing at the two moons. Annie's face is ghastly red, streaked with shadows. She's no longer the beautiful wildlife partner I've come to know so well. She's a demon from hell, turning slowly to look at me.

"Do the right things, the people thought. Observe the rituals and ceremonies according to ancient customs. And be careful because there are always unintended consequences to what you do. This was the understanding. Do what you're supposed to, and eventually you can go home.

"Well, story has it that two brothers moved with their families to a river near the outlet of a lake where they practiced the ceremonies as they were told to do. In return, a large white stone magically appeared one day. It was unlike any other they had seen. It was understood that they should hold their councils and ceremonies around this sacred stone, and, if ever they moved their village, the stone would follow. Sure enough, when they moved to a different location on the lake, the stone magically appeared. They moved two more times, eventually to the top of a mountain, and each time the stone followed. They performed their sacred rites around the stone, and it was here that the wisdom of the nation was formed.

"Then, news came that white people had arrived from beyond the sea in the east. It wasn't long before they encountered these new people and misfortune befell them—disease, famine, and the like. The council-fire was extinguished, the people scattered, and there was nowhere for the stone to bring them together. It became like a stranger in its own land, an exile in its own home. Once the faith of the people was broken, the magic was lost. The stone became just another ordinary rock. Today, this piece of white granite, unlike any other in the whole region, remains all that's left of the ancient ways. In these valleys and mountains, along these rivers and lakes. Once a home, now a memory."

The hermit draws a deep breath, cups his hands around his mouth and cries, *"He-o-weh-go-gek!"*

A gust of wind blows across the fire, chasing sparks through the glowing coals. The hermit stands and walks to the edge of the lake.

"He-oweh-go-gek!" he cries again. His voice carries across the lake, echoing in the distance, rippling through the valley into the shadows of the night.

A TELEPHONE RINGS—the mechanical monotone from the phone in the hall. On the other end is a reporter from the Associated Press who wants to do a story on the loon survey, to be syndicated in newspapers around the country. She and a photographer can be in Saranac next week. Would it be possible to get a few shots of loons and their chicks in the field? A nest might be good, too. Preferably with eggs.

Later, I drop Annie off at the bus in a steady rain. She'll be gone a few days, down to Albany to visit the main office and take care of a few personal items.

The rain and wind keep me inside today, which is good because I've fallen behind on the journal. For the better part of the afternoon, I retreat to the study where I catch up on what has happened the past few weeks, using the field forms to record the loon data, consulting articles and books to fill in natural history information, and, of course, relying on my high-octane imagination to see me through the rough spots and tie the whole thing together. In fact, it all goes so well that not only do I catch up to where I am now (sitting here in the study writing these words), but I use the extra time to actually get *ahead* in the journal. It seems like cheating, I know, but it sounds more complicated than it actually is.

NEXT MORNING, storm clouds give way to silver-lined cumuli. Enough blue sky, I figure, to go out and cover a few ponds on my own. I pick two small lakes on the Rockefeller property out by Keese Mill.

Driving down the lane on my way out, I come upon a group of Colby campers, no more than eight or ten years-old, playing croquet on the lawn. I slow the car down, inspecting each contestant until I notice one boy with a large, square head and dark, menacing eyes. *That's him!* That's the reprobate who sabotaged the Impala. I'm certain of it. Next time I see Flashlight, I'll let him know.

When I arrive at the Rockefeller gate, I'm met by the caretaker's wife who happens to be walking her pack of dogs. She tells me I should have called in advance, but that it shouldn't be a problem. And then it sinks in: *this is Rockefeller property.* All 20,000 acres of it. The woman leads me back to her house where she phones ahead for permission. Seems I just missed a chance to meet one of the family patriarchs. She gives me directions to the main house and bids farewell.

At the house, I'm introduced to two of the Rockefeller brood—a pair of nubile nieces. Shy, demure, prone to paroxysms of twitching in and around the leg area. It occurs to me that perhaps the Rockefellers, like the royal family in England, could use a little diversity in the gene pool. You know, mix in a little of my data base. Good wholesome Rocky Mountain ribosomes. I can see the headline now: "Rockefeller Heiress Marries Recidivist Ne'er Do Well—Nelson Riled."

I say good-bye to the girls, fire up the Impala, and start down a sandy two-track, passing a docile herd of white-tailed deer. The terrain is flat and open, with tall grass and stands of birch. The caretaker's wife informed me there was once a golf course here that has since gone to seed. Make for an interesting succession study, I would think. Puts one in the mind of an African savannah back in the day, when old granddad had to watch his step lest he be snatched by some stealthy feline lurking in the bush. Keep an eye out, stay close to the trees. All those thousands of years of evading predators put a bounce in his step, alright. Life on the move, now wired into the circuitry of modern man.

After two miles of two-track, I come upon a classic Adirondack camp on the groomed shores of Cat Pond, complete with a log lean-to and woodstove, picnic table and lantern. I try to imagine what it would be like to grow up in a place like this, with all this space and solitude. Of course, it might lead to a decidedly twisted view of the world, but I'd be willing to take that chance. All in all, it seems like an ideal place to while away the formative years, without a care in the world but what one could concoct on his own.

I put the canoe in at the dock, flushing a merganser with seven chicks in tow, starting them helter-skelter across the water. Progeny. Clutch. Reproductive success. The hummocks at the east end of the pond look like good habitat for a loon nest, but there's nothing to report. No loons, no nest.

Once I'm done with Cat, I load the canoe back onto the Impala and continue on to Cranberry Pond. Along the way, I pass a truck towing a trailer of cut timber. I give it a wide berth, driving off the sandy two-track into the tall grass and a habitat to which the ungulate is most assuredly accustomed. The Impala responds beautifully—proud and noble son of the Serengeti.

Like Cat, Cranberry is rimmed with manicured lawn grass. Close to the water, two white Adirondack chairs gleam in the sunlight, reminding me of Annie and how it's not the same without her. When I was thirteen, I had a job cleaning up a high school football stadium every Saturday morning after the games on Friday night. I'd be the only one there, walking on the cinder track around the field with a garbage bag, rooting around for dimes and quarters and the occasional lost ring. Only a few hours earlier the place had been packed with people—cheerleaders, players and coaches, fans screaming under the stadium lights. Teenage girls in tight jeans in the shadows under the bleachers. Come Saturday morning, though, the place was deserted—hot dog wrappers and popcorn boxes blown against the cyclone fence, flapping in the wind. Forgotten hats and coats in the grass behind the track. And I'd get a lonely feeling in the pit of my stomach. What it might feel like, I supposed, to be the last person left on earth.

Staring at the two empty chairs on the grass, I feel the same queasiness take hold. So I get down to business. The pond is shallow and sandy along the bank. I remove my shoes and walk along the edge in the warm water, pulling the canoe behind me in case I need it. Lush ferns grow knee-high at the edge of the woods. There's deer bedding in the tall grass. A cold brook winds through the trees down to the pond, chattering in the bright sunlight.

On the far side, I stop and sit on the prow of the canoe in the dappled sunlight along the bank. I stay a while in the hypnotic flicker of shadow and light, toes buried in the warm sand beneath the shallow water. Mustering the gumption to get on with it.

Annie is due back day after tomorrow.

CHECKED OUT HEART POND this morning in preparation for the newspaper reporter. Figured I should have everything in order so she can get her photos of loon chicks. Heart seems the logical choice, since it's relatively close and we've already found eggs there.

From the bow seat, facing the stern, I paddle out to the island where we saw the nest. The lake level has risen noticeably—from the recent rain, no doubt. The muddy bank is submerged and some of the island has flooded. Coming around the leeward side I see a loon thirty feet offshore, watching me as I come into view. I check the nest. The eggs haven't hatched yet, though the water level has reached a dangerous level. Any further rise, and the lake could flood the nest.

I get out of there fast, thinking it strange that the loon should be on the water. I was careful to approach the island quietly, and loons typically don't abandon a nest until the last possible moment.

When I get back to Colby, I enter the information in one of the "follow-up" forms that track the progress of nests and chicks we've found in the field. This is one we'll have to keep an eye on.

Heart is out, obviously, for the photo-op. Instead, we'll take the reporter to Little Clear where, last we checked, the adults and two chicks looked to be in good shape.

ANNIE'S BACK IN THE FOLD and not a moment too soon. Today's the day we meet the CO's at Upper Saranac Lake.

Bright-eyed and bushy-tailed at seven in the morning, the two officers look downright giddy at the boat launch near Saranac Inn when we pull up in the Impala. And why not? Theirs is a prized occupation: patrolling mountain lakes, looking for any breach of state law. (Gainful employment being a challenge in these parts.) Bradley and Stryker seem like regular guys, just as content to be casting to pike as to be writing someone a ticket. But make no mistake, these are cops who pack heat. Snowhare told me once they shot and killed his dog for chasing a deer—technically within their legal right (since we don't want any harm coming to our game species, now do we?) but a cold and heartless act just the same. I guess you don't worry too much about that, not when you have the full apparatus of the State behind you.

Pin a badge on a man and watch him metamorphose. It starts in the brain just behind the eye sockets—twinges of confusion whether this is what he ought to be doing. But any pangs of doubt are quickly dispelled by the seductive power of authority. He may even become overzealous out of some vague sense of righteousness, necessitated perhaps by the need to keep his nagging conscience down and out of the way. Enforcement with prejudice. Of course, allegiance to duty comes with a price. In this case, it's the freedom to think and act on his own. He is compelled to behave in ways that he might not otherwise choose for himself. Better to trust your initial instinct, I say, and not wear the badge in the first place.

So the CO's are joking around at the boat ramp next to the Whaler, thumbing through their tackle box for spoons and plugs in anticipation of a leisurely day on Upper Saranac Lake, enjoying the perks of their job which includes the company of whomever they happen to encounter in the exercise of their duty.

Annie and I take our seats in the back of the boat. Bradley fires up the forty-horse, and just like that we're speeding around the northern end of Upper Saranac. In the time it would take us to reach Tommy's Rock in our canoe, we circle Dry Island and Green Island and all the various islets in between. Amazing thing, the combustible engine. Cashing in on all that solar energy harnessed long ago in the tissue of plants and animals. Dirty and noisy, true, but incredibly efficient.

After covering all the islands, we begin a systematic search of the bays, concentrating on the leeward shorelines that look like potential habitat. When the water becomes too shallow for the Whaler, I hop into the lake in waders and investigate on foot—checking hummocks and banks where loons would likely nest. Our eyes and ears are honed to such terrain, our senses tuned. Like predators on the hunt, we know what to look for when it comes to loon habitat. But rather than looking to kill, we aim to protect. Using the same instincts, mind you, but in the service of conservation. And how whacky is that? I can hear Flashlight now, ranting about how everything is ass-backwards.

Sometimes I step into holes, suddenly finding myself chest-deep in the lake. The water pressure immobilizes me for an instant, and it's hard to find footing on the bottom. My arms and hands flail to regain balance, much to the delight of the CO's on the boat. I laugh along with them, shuddering at the thought of what might lie below. What primeval serpent lurking in the sludge of mud and rock and log? What fanged reptilian monster? In the absence of tangible evidence, the imagination is free to roam, ready and willing to fan the flames of hysteria.

Truth is, I went at it pretty hard last night in the cupola, nearly depleting the contents in Door #2 and washing things down with six Falstaffs. Now I'm paying the price. Helped along by good old-fashion paranoia, the residuals of my altered state lead me to places I'd rather not go—not when there's muddy water up to my neck and law enforcement agents looking down at me, laughing at my misfortune, my mobility reduced to a slow-motion struggle like the recurring dream I have of being stuck in the middle of the road, unable to move, with an eighteen-wheeler bearing down on me at high speed. It's as if I'm caught between a pair of sadistic cops and a swarm of electric eels, with no way out. Beads of sweat gather along my forehead. But to panic in this liquid quicksand would be disastrous.

So I think of other situations I've been in to help me relax: the time I was covered in leeches and had to burn them off with a butane lighter, the nest of cockroaches I discovered inside the mattress of my bed in the Keys, the brown recluse that bit me while putting on my pants one morning in Colorado. And as for the hyper-thyroid cops on deck, well, the worst they could do is aerate me with their .38's. So smile, I think to myself, things aren't so bad.

"Nothing to report!" I yell to Annie.

But she's deep in conversation with the CO's. The boat is far enough away that I can't hear what's being said, but all three are smiling and laughing. And what's going on now? Are they hitting on Annie?

I turn and start to walk back, but it's slow going. I feel like a bull elk struggling to keep his harem in place while the cows wander off, much to the delight of the bachelors horning in on the periphery. Distracted by the thought, I slip on something along the bottom of the lake and begin a long, slow-motion fall into the water. Whatever I've stepped on (probably only a tree limb) *comes alive*, twisting and slithering, climbing my leg. I grab wildly for anything to keep me upright, abandoning all pretense of poise, thrashing my way through the water—anything to get the hell out of there without touching the bottom.

When I finally get to the boat and hoist myself over the gunwale, I'm met with howls of laughter. A cavalcade of yowls. It seems Bradley and Stryker have enjoyed themselves at my expense. Even Annie has to smile.

From that point on, I'm in good with the water cops. Bradley gives me a towel to wipe away the mud and lets me take a few casts with his spinning rod. We spend the rest of the afternoon circling the lake, checking the shoreline for nests. The CO's are helpful to a fault, ready and willing to do whatever they can. And while there's no question that a powerboat is an efficient way to look for loons, I'll take a canoe any day. When you introduce a machine into the equation, everything changes. You scare the birds and animals into hiding and lose the sound of waves washing against rocks. You shut yourself off from the natural rhythms of a place.When we return to the boat ramp, Annie and I watch the CO's winch their Whaler onto the trailer. When all is done, we say our good-byes. We could do this again, Bradley offers, on another big lake. Raquette Pond, say. Annie thanks them for their help, letting them know how much time they've saved us.

"Sure beats a llama, huh?" Stryker laughs.

Bradley grins, his even row of white teeth flashing like stilettos. Bradley is not a bad guy, and I bet we could be friends under different circumstances. Stryker, on the other hand, is not very funny.

"I hear they're intelligent creatures," I reply without missing a beat. "Sense of humor, too."

Bradley chuckles, but Stryker isn't quite sure how to take my comment. Either way, we decide it's a good time to leave. No loons to report on Upper Saranac Lake.

We meet Barbara, the freelance reporter, first thing in the morning. Over coffee, she asks us questions about the study, jotting down notes in a small journal. Annie does most of the talking, explaining the basics of the survey while mentioning a few facts about loons—their habitat, reproductive traits, etc. At one point, Barbara asks where I'm from.

"Thunder Bay," I say.

"What state is that in?"

"Ontario."

Annie frowns, but I can tell she doesn't mind. She looks especially fetching this morning with her silky hair falling over her shoulders, and it dawns on me how lucky I am to have her as a partner.

The photographer shows up after coffee and we all drive out to Little Clear. Barbara has a brand-new Mad River canoe strapped to the roof of her Bronco. After we unload the gear and get the canoes on the water, the photographer activates the automatic shutter on his camera and the show begins.

The loons seem only too happy to oblige. A single adult and two chicks swim out to greet us as we approach the first nest, close enough for Mel, the photographer, to get plenty of pictures. Both chicks climb onto the back of the adult for a free ride through the waves—a service afforded them in the early months of maturation. Barbara loves it, sighing when the adult stretches its wings, exposing its white belly.

We take them to the other nest on the lake, where Barbara asks to get a picture of Annie and me with the two eggs. Annie's not thrilled about scaring the adult off the nest, but we comply with the request. "Now point to the eggs," Barbara says, "as if you're just now seeing them for the first time."

I can tell Annie is dismayed by the whole charade, so I ham it up to balance things out, exaggerating my look of surprise. The automatic shutter clicks away, followed by the rhythmic whine of auto-rewind. After three minutes at the nest, Annie decides it's time to leave so the adult can return to the eggs.

Later, back at Colby, I pull Barbara aside and ask her about "freelancing," telling her that I'm a bit of a writer myself.

"It just means you get to choose the stories you want to write," she explains.

Something about this sounds appealing. If I'm asked what I do for a living, I could say "*freelahnce*" with a French accent.

"You gotta have an interesting story," she tells me, "something that'll sell."

"You mean report the cold hard truth," I reply.

"Well, not exactly," she says.

"How do you know when you get a story right?"

"You may never know for sure," she answers. "But you have to make it interesting, that's the key."

"More important than getting it right?"

"Look," she says, eyeing me like a seasoned reporter. "These days, it's all about *image*. Reality is just too messy and confusing for the average person to grasp, especially given the short attention span of everyone. Your message has to be quick, concise, juicy—something that'll grab the attention of people in a way that they can understand and remember. If there's any 'truth' to it [and here she does the bunny-eared, quotation-mark sign with her hands], that's fine. But, honestly, don't let that get in the way of a good story. We're *writers*," she says, taking me by the elbow. "We create the image that shapes the perception that determines the reality. Nothing is 'news' until we say it is, got it? It's the way of the world. Sad to say, but I'll probably do more for loons in this hour of work than you and your partner will do this entire summer. Now if you'll excuse me, I have a few more questions for Annie and then I have to go."

There's something about what she says that makes me uneasy, especially the part about doing more for loons than Annie and me. Even if she's right, it still doesn't sit well. My gut tells me not to trust this writing business. There's something about it that seems deceptive at the core.

Feeling deflated, I leave the reporter with her questions for Annie and step outside. Across the way, Flashlight is raking grass clippings left over from mowing the lawn, which reminds me of the little matter I need to discuss with him regarding the campers. He's raked about a half dozen piles so far, and, judging from the thick mats of grass that still cover the lawn, he has a few more to go.

When he sees me walking toward him, he pauses to wipe the sweat from his glasses.

"Anything new to report from the frontlines of mayhem?" I ask.

It took a while, but he and I have found a comfortable midway point in our discussions of nature and apocalypse. He doesn't mind if I rib him a little, just so long as he knows that I'm interested in what he has to say. I think he's just happy that there's *someone* who will listen.

"An armadillo was spotted in Illinois."

I stare at him blankly, not sure where he's going with this. Undeterred by my bewilderment, he turns and resumes his raking.

"Yep, the genie is out of the bottle," he says, "We've unleashed an experiment of epic proportions. Thanks to us, the planet's species have been relocated and redistributed like never before. We've pulled the rug out from everything, taken all the earth's species from where they've evolved according to local conditions, tossed them up in the air to land where they will, and said: okay, evolution, let's see what you got."

As he's talking, his raking becomes more vigorous to the point that he's digging up some of the living grass, and I feel as though I should intervene. Besides, there's the little matter of the camp kid.

"Why are you raking all these clippings?"

"Why? Because it gets so thick that it chokes out the grass that's actually growing. Then you've got a bunch of brown grass on your hands. Plus, it's a bit of a menace—all this dried-up dead grass."

"Because it's a fire hazard?" I ask.

"I suppose it could be if it ended up in the right place," he replies. "But, no, it's more about the critters."

"Critters?"

"Yeah, they use it to build nests. Can't hardly blame them. Out west, marmots gather dry grass to make their nests in the rocks above timberline. The grass insulates them through the winter. Plus, it provides nourishment during their long hibernation. Same kind of thing happens here, though it's a little out of whack. Like a lot of things these days, the instinct is right but the situation is wrong."

"Oh?"

"Yeah, the squirrels—and it's mainly squirrels we're talking about. They gather the clippings to build nests, only they do it in the wrong places, like inside a chimney or under the hood of a car."

"*Under the hood of a car?*"

"Yeah. They build nests in car engines to keep them out of the rain. And then once they're in there, they start chewing on the wiring and create all kinds of problems."

He stops what he's doing and stares, one eye sliding like a ball rolling across a table on its way to falling off the edge.

"Did you know that jaguars in the Amazon intentionally ingest psychoactive plants to help them locate their prey?"

ANNIE BOUNDS OUT OF THE HOUSE, fresh as a honeysuckle blossom, clipboard and binocs in hand. I join her in the car and together we set out for nearby McKenzie Pond.

Cruising through town, she gives me directions from the topo map folded in her lap (*let's see, follow Bloomingdale out of Saranac and take it all the way to the dirt road after the second bend in the highway*) while twisting a lock of my hair in her fingers.

The road climbs through the hills above town before entering a meadow where distant mountains rise above the trees. The forest glows green and gold in bright sunlight. We turn down a primitive two-track into deep woods, the car splashing through mud puddles. The farther we go, the more the ferns strangle the two-track, scraping the undercarriage, until there's barely even a trail to follow and it's clear we'll have to portage.

I turn off the ignition to the sound of a ticking engine. Together we lift the canoe off the roof and set it in the ferns. Mosquitoes hover in shafts of steamy sunlight. As cool as it is in the shade, it promises to be hot once we're out in the sun.

We pile the gear in the canoe and each take an end—Annie in front, me at the back. But the trail proves treacherous with deadfall and saplings, and it's not long before we decide on a different tack. Annie gathers the cushions and paddles in her arms while I sling the canoe over my head, catching the balance of it on my shoulders.

Following her through the woods, I keep my eyes focused on the ground so I don't stumble and bring the whole operation down on me. An eye on the overhanging branches, too, so as not to bash my forehead against the thwart. It's tough going in these trees, and soon Annie gets ahead of me on the trail. A chevron of sunlight flashes off her hair as she rounds a bend and disappears behind a stand of sumac.

Beads of sweat trickle into my eyes. My heavy breathing is amplified in the aluminum shell of the canoe. Eventually, I see an opening in the trees and the sapphire glitter of McKenzie Pond. At the shore, I flip the canoe over my shoulders and set it on the bank.

We take a moment to rest, looking across the water at Little McKenzie Mountain gleaming in the sun. The pitch of its slope increases as it nears the summit. There are no houses on the lake, no sign of people, only forest. And it's quiet, not a breath of wind.

I slide the bow of the canoe into the water, starting a series of ripples across the calm surface. I accidentally bang a paddle against the gunwale and the sound reverberates across the lake. When we speak, our words carry over the water, dissolving into silence and whatever lies inside of that. And for a moment, I have the strange impression that my *thoughts* are doing the same, set free into the world, starting their own chains of reaction in a vast and dazzling network of interconnected signals, each affecting the rest as it in turn is changed by the others. Be careful what you say. Be careful what you do. There are consequences to everything. Everything matters.

"Miles?"

I turn to see sunlight reflecting off the rippling water, playing upon Annie's face.

"Are you ready?" she says.

We cut across the glassy water, immersed in bright light, peering down at fallen trees resting on the bottom of the lake. A loon appears, a big healthy adult, circling above us in the clear sky. We watch as it glides in, feet forward, and rips a V across the surface. It dives twice and then yodels. The resounding cry echoes off the mountain, carrying over the hills. It's clearly a distress call, a warning. The loon dives again and disappears.

We paddle toward a small island not twenty yards offshore, approaching quietly, looking for any movement along the bank. "On the other side," Annie whispers, making a circle with her finger.

We begin a slow arc around the island when something large slips into the water, starting a ring across the surface. The speckled loon swims along the shallow bottom in front of the canoe. Wings tucked close to its body, the bird moves through the clear water, propelled by its webbed feet. Cruising on a straight course, it swims to a safe distance before surfacing to watch us.

There are two eggs on the nest. We take our measurements and get out of there fast, paddling away from the island toward the center of the lake where we circle around to watch. But the loon is nowhere to be found. We wait, listening and watching. Still no loon.

"Did you *see*?" Annie says, turning to face me. "It was like looking at it under glass, the checkerboard was so clear. I bet that first loon was part of the pair and he yodeled to warn her. And the one on the nest ... so calm and quiet."

Most loons we've encountered throw a fit when we approach the nest, but not this one. Waiting till the last possible moment, it calmly dropped into the water and swam away.

"Maybe it's the tranquility of the place," I say.

Annie reaches with her dripping paddle and begins to work again. "Or maybe it's us," she says.

"You mean word has gotten around? The loons *know* who we are?"

Annie's skin is bronze from the weeks of being outside, her muscles toned. She looks like some mythical Norse goddess of the high country, and I have to remind myself she's only Annie, my partner.

Above the northeast bay, two enormous raptors circle in the blue sky, wings broad and straight. Bigger than either osprey or heron, the birds appear black through the binoculars until one changes its angle of flight, revealing a bright white head in the sunlight. Spiraling on a thermal opposite one another, the two bald eagles drift north toward Little McKenzie, rising higher and higher in a circle that carries them over the mountains.

WE'VE BEEN TO SO MANY LAKES and islands this summer that it feels like we've come to know them intimately, like the body of a lover. Strange as it may sound, it feels like they've gotten to know us in the same way.

In the morning, we paddle along the near shore of Follensby Clear before angling toward one of its many small islands. After dragging the canoe up, we lie beneath a couple of big white pines, watching and listening to the wind in the branches overhead. Annie pulls herself close and rests her head on my chest. I move slightly, carving a soft depression in the dirt with my shoulders, when I recognize the moment from the dream I had weeks ago. The island is flat and the trees well spaced. I raise my head just enough to look across to the far shore. No cottages or docks or boat ramps, only an evergreen shoreline and the blue outline of distant mountains. Just as it was in the dream. I feel her body rise and fall with each breath as she drifts off to sleep, her hair pressed against my cheek. I begin to doze off, too, shifting my weight to make our bodies fit better, watching the gentle sway of pine boughs overhead.

At the edge of sleep, time dissolves like ripples from a stone dropped into a still lake. Thoughts drift aimlessly, tossed on a sea of feelings and memory. The world goes on with all its sound and fury, everything abuzz in frenzy, humans in a perpetual state of agitation across the face of the earth. But it's all taking place somewhere *out there*, too remote to matter. Here on the island, there are only trees and rock and the play of sunlight on water.

Sliding toward sleep, I'm visited by places from my past: the swimming hole with the swing rope where I spent summer days as a kid; a chinook wind blowing through the screen door of our family cabin, curling the pages of magazines piled on a coffee table; the mangrove bay on Key Largo under a full moon, with the sound of a halyard clanging against an aluminum mast. There are no people in these places, no family or friends. It's as if they've all vanished without a trace, leaving only the haunting memory of when they were there and the dull ache of loss.

That night, Annie tells me that Frank will be paying a visit to Colby and it might be a good idea if I get away for a few days. I suspect something is up. Guess I'll get lost a while in St. Regis.

I SIT ALONE on my little island somewhere on Upper St. Regis, stoned out of my gourd, writing in the journal, compelled once again to recall in reverse order the events that have led up to the present moment. Something like this: Annie suggested that I make myself scarce while she consults with Frank about the loon study to which I have lent my services as a consequence of prior transgressions stemming from the failed attempt to recover lost love and an ill-advised academic foray into the theory and practice of particle board—two failed endeavors, I might add, that themselves can be traced to a rumor I heard at a tiki bar in Islamorada that Jessie, the woman of my dreams, had left the Keys and moved back to upstate New York.

All of this despite my recent efforts to quit this life of dissolution and finally, goddammit, make good.

I've pitched the tent in the best defensive position I could find, tucked inside thick brush so that my flanks are covered. As the western sky bleeds from gold to mauve to indigo, I prepare dinner with the precision of a brain surgeon, careful to do everything in proper order: boil water on the cook-stove, add freeze-dried stroganoff, stir, reposition lid, lower flame, wait. Camping alone will do this to you. Decisions related to food and shelter and clothing take on a sense of urgency, if for no other reason than there's not much else to occupy your time. The trick is to focus on menial tasks, so as not to dwell on the bigger questions. Which, of course, I get around to anyway.

Stirring the stroganoff, I wait for a revelation out here in the bosom of God's creation—some divine light to enter my soul and allow me to see the world imbued with the fine essence of eternal glory. But in the end, the lapping waves remain nothing more than lapping waves; the lichen-covered rock, lichen-covered rock; the gnarly shrub, gnarly shrub. In this cold-hearted universe in which we toil and flail, chance alone steers a rudderless ship. There is no purpose to things beyond what our puny imaginations fashion. Even if there is some master plan, some cosmic blueprint out there, it remains beyond our grasp. I am a clod of clay, a dust mote, forced to choose among bad options, utterly alone and misunderstood.

The stroganoff tastes fantastic. I wolf it down, then go about building a fire as if my life depended on it: a dry pine bough at the base, a pile of twigs, and four stout branches stacked in a tepee. I brought the wood from Colby, along with my trusty six-inch clip-point Buck knife.

I build the fire high, as the last gasp of day collapses into a portal of golden light on the horizon—a passageway west to the Great Lakes, Plains, and Rocky Mountains beyond. The undulating ridgeline on the far side of the lake cuts a black silhouette against the indigo sky. A loon wails in the dark. The pine limbs crack and hiss in the flames. I take my place among the spirits of the great north woods.

The Milky Way appears—a fuzzy swath across the night sky. Polaris, the Big Dipper, and Cassiopeia assume their rightful positions. Indifferent to the affairs of man, perhaps, but steady as clockwork. My eyes water from the fire smoke, as the stars and mountains begin to waver. I might as well be looking at a mirage of heat waves over a scorching desert floor. The mysterious ebb and flow of things. Cosmic law of attraction and repulsion.

Eventually, I come around to the inevitable—what I've tried not to think about since arriving here on this island.

Annie was scheduled to meet with Frank this afternoon, and whatever he had to say to her has already been said. By now, she would have fixed herself some dinner—a salad or beans and rice—finished a little paperwork, and maybe ridden the bike to town for a little social interaction. And what's happening at the Waterhole, I wonder. This very moment. I close my eyes and picture the barroom—hanging light over the pool table, phone booth in back, long copper bar .... Wire standing by the cash register, hands in his pockets, eyes darting. Snowhare sitting at the bar, drinking a beer, maybe talking to Spot who laughs at something he says. Down at the end, Yukon whaps the last-call bell with his cane. A few others linger around the pool table, talking low in the dim light. And at the center of everything, like the eye of a hurricane: Annie. It's all happening *right this second*, just fifteen miles away as the crow flies.

I stare into the fire. Lonesomeness creeps in, as I think about what fun everyone must be having. I pine for festive times.

To ease the pain, I redirect my imagination to Lake Colby—its dark shoreline and surrounding forest where I sometimes take a midnight stroll. The different bends in the trail, the dense thicket, the bog beside the train trestle ... all as familiar to me as a close friend. And I get to thinking about my life here: working on the loon survey, living at the compound between the comedic and tragic faces, hanging out at the Waterhole, being with Annie. And it dawns on me, like an arrow shot out of the star-studded sky to strike me between the eyes, it dawns on me that *I belong here*. I belong on the loon count. Hell, I'm good at it. Haven't I learned all those bird songs? Haven't I earned my stripes, proven my worth, carried myself with professionalism in the field? Well, maybe not that last part. But still. This is who I am: wildlife biologist, state tech, *loon ranger*. And this is where I live: Saranac, northern Adirondacks, Canadian Shield.

And all the whackos who live here. The Waterhole gang. Flashlight and his theories. The hermit and his Indian stories. The guy with the pH kit, and the clerk with his vow of silence. All are my *compadres*. Yes, this is where I belong. I want to pile all my gear in the canoe right then and there, find my way back to the portage, paddle like hell in the dark to the car, drive down to town, bust through the swinging doors of the bar and throw my arms out wide and declare my allegiance to the whole crazy lot of them ....

But I'm not going anywhere and I know it. I bank the coals and throw on another limb. To make it official, I say, "You ain't going nowhere and you know it." Loud enough for any spook to hear who might be wandering by, or any loon swimming within earshot of the island.

As it turns out, my little exile on Upper St. Regis wasn't a total loss. All that time alone got me to thinking about things, and for the first time in a long while I hatched a plan about the direction of my life. No more drifting from place to place. No more lone-wolf syndrome. I'd grown tired of being on my own, always picking up and moving, living out of my pack, crashing on sofas of people I didn't know, surviving on hot dogs and beer nuts and whatever else I could scrounge. I was ready for a change. I resolved then and there to throw in with Annie if she'd have me, maybe even give it a try on the home front. Get on the straight and narrow, by god, come hell or high water.

And I felt free, like a weight had been lifted off my shoulders. No longer caged by a life on the run. On the surface, it didn't make sense that I should feel liberated by locking myself into a course of action and becoming tied down to all the cares and responsibilities that went along with it. But there's a point when you can have too many choices, and what ends up happening is that you spend all your time keeping options open without actually pursuing any. A person can't do everything in this world, but they have to do something. At some point, you have to dig your heels in and make a stand. And what I had was worth fighting for. I knew in my heart, there was no difference between my feelings for Annie and our work with loons. I couldn't explain it, exactly, but they were one and the same.

WE ARE DOWN TO THE LAST LAKE on the list. All that's left to do after that is return to the places where we found nests and check on each clutch. We've been at this for nearly three months, methodically covering all the waters assigned to us in Albany, and now the summer is winding down. The sun rises a little later each day, just enough to notice. The nights grow cold. A maple tree on the road to Gabriels has already gone red.

Blue Pond is remote, requiring a portage of over a mile. A glacier lake, it shines turquoise and sapphire in the sunlight. The south shore is rimmed with birch and maple, and there's a small beach at the far end. It's not a big lake, so it doesn't take long to check the shoreline. With nothing else to do today, we pull the canoe up on the beach and sit a while in the sand.

Annie decides to take a swim, and I watch as she walks into the dazzling sunlight on the surface. She's never looked so beautiful—bronzed skin, toned body, golden hair. Her movements are graceful. And it's like a dream, watching her swim in all that glittering sunlight like she's part of the light itself.

When she returns to sit beside me, she shakes her hair to get me wet, letting it fall across her shoulders and down in front. She moves closer. Her corduroy cutoffs feel cool against my skin.

"I talked to Frank," she says. "The man you punched with the turtle glasses, he's pressing charges. He's going to sue the State unless something is done."

She looks at me, checking for a reaction. "The state vouchers are starting to come into the office," she smiles. "Frank wants to know what we're doing with six cans of spray paint."

She traces the muscles on my forearm with the tip of her finger. "He knows about the llama, too. He wants you off the study, Miles. He's arranged for one of the Acid Rangers to help me finish. Roy is coming tomorrow to move into Colby."

Just then a loon flies down and skids to a stop in the middle of the lake. The bird watches from a safe distance, before unleashing a yodel that echoes off the far shore. The song of Blue Pond. *I am here, and this is what I see.* Then it preens itself on the water as if it hasn't a care in the world. Meanwhile, cloud shadows move across the granite flank of Whiteface. To the north, the rolling landscape retreats into a smoky distance—ancient mountains worn smooth by eons of ice and wind. And in the west, clouds build along the horizon like palaces in the sky.

I lie back in the sand and Annie rests her head on my chest, tapping a finger to each beat of my heart. Hands calloused, arms and shoulders strong from a summer of paddling, senses tuned to a life outside in the woods, I might as well be the earth itself. This is the payoff. I place my hand on Annie's head and look into the sky.

And isn't this what life truly is, or what it could be? To follow the day wherever it leads, go freely into the world with all its wonders and mystery. To lie in the grass beside a flower trembling in the wind, follow the drunken flight of a bumblebee, watch a hawk glide high in the heavens.

Nothing lasts, that's for sure. Everything is doomed in the end. And yet there I was, trying to convince Annie with every fiber I could muster that it wasn't so. Love, loons, this feeling on the beach ... somehow, it had to last. I'd see to it, one way or the other. I'd talk to Frank, convince him to keep me on. If that didn't work, I'd wait for her to finish the survey and she could join me and we could get a place together, maybe even in Saranac. In all my life, I never gave a thought to planning out a future, and yet there I was—spilling my guts, going a mile a minute about all the ways I'd make good. In my heart of hearts, I knew this was my last best chance, and I wasn't about to let it go.

"Shhhh," she says, putting a finger to my lips, closing her eyes. Resting her head between my neck and shoulder, she seems weary all of a sudden. She'll give me a key to her place, she says. I can gather my things, take a bus to Albany, and wait for her there.

THE RAIN STARTS THAT NIGHT and doesn't let up for three days. It's a cold rain, the kind where you can see your breath.

Annie's called Roy and convinced him to wait a few days before moving in, since there's nothing to be done in this weather anyway.

The old stone house holds a chill, so I build a fire with the hardwood logs stacked next to the fireplace. The wood has been there all summer, so it's good and dry. I ball up some newspaper, pile on a few twigs and branches, lay two split logs on top, and set the whole thing ablaze.

Once the fire burns a while and the living room heats up, we decide to move all the forms and maps down from the cupola, spreading everything out on the dining room table—a summer's worth of field research distilled into a heap of paper.

Annie begins to organize the forms, while I go to the kitchen to see what we have in the way of food. For the entire summer, we've used only one shelf in the refrigerator and one cabinet to store our edibles, deferring to Flashlight and official visitors to the house. The heck with that, I decide. It's time Annie and I move in and make it our home, no matter that this is the last week we'll be here. I plan out the meals for the next two days, writing out what we need on a pad of paper. Tonight I'll make stir fry with broccoli, carrots, snow peas, and cashews, all piled on a helping of wild rice. Maybe some ginger and thyme for seasoning. A bottle of chardonnay, too. Tomorrow night, I'll grill barbeque chicken with mesquite sauce to go with coleslaw and biscuits.

In the living room, I move the love seat closer to the fire and toss a few pillows on the floor along with a quilt I found upstairs. Standing next to the long dining room table, her hair falling forward to hide her face, Annie studies the papers scattered across the table. She looks good in her pajama bottoms, wool socks, and oversized flannel shirt.

I grab my keys and tell her I need to do some food shopping in town. She curls a lock of hair behind one ear. "Hurry home," she says. I can't tell if she's making fun of my newfound domesticity or if she's just being sweet. But it doesn't matter. I'm happy as a lark to be running an errand, especially something as simple as going to the market to get dinner for two.

The Impala glistens in the rain. Primer gray, black sidewall tires, all the metal lettering ground down to a nub … a thing of beauty. Well worth any consternation it may have caused Frank.

I spark up the old girl and drive into town, passing the firehouse where the two firemen have moved their folding chairs out of the rain and into the garage. They wave as I cruise by, and I return the greeting. By now, everybody knows the gray coupe with the canoe on top. I recognize Ray the welder walking down the street and give him a honk. Inside the deli, the Olympic hopeful stands at the counter, fixing a sandwich for a man holding hands with his young daughter. Coasting by the Waterhole, I catch a glimpse of three patrons seated at the bar. I have half a mind to stop in for one, but I'm on a mission that takes precedence over any charm there might be in the way of idle truancy.

I gather up the goods at the village market, thanking the silent clerk, and return home where I go to work on dinner. Annie joins me in the kitchen, sitting at the kitchen table where she opens the bottle of chardonnay and pours two glasses. I light a candle and we toast to *Gavia immer*. When dinner is ready, I dish out two steaming plates and sit down at the table.

"I'm impressed," she says, putting a hand to her breast in feigned surprise. "A man of many talents."

"You haven't seen the half of it."

"Oh?" Annie watches me closely as she raises the fork to her mouth, pausing before taking a long slow bite.

I can't think of anything to say so I just keep chewing my carrots and peas. I think I know what she's thinking, but I can't be sure. I certainly know what I'm thinking. But I stick to my guns and play it safe.

"And the wine," she says, raising the glass to her lips. "So sweet and mellow." She looks into my eyes, shaking her head ever so slightly in a kind of mock seduction. "It's to be savored, taste by taste," she says. "You have to go slow to let the *essence* come to fruition. It's better that way, don't you think?"

This kind of thing has been going on for a while, and I have to say it's not without its pleasures. It's not that she wants to be coy, it's just that she prefers to go slow and enjoy the ride. And yet she can't resist making fun of it all. As excruciating as it can be, I'm content to let this old-fashioned courtship play out to the end.

After dinner I bring the wine out to the living room, where we lie on the oriental rug in front of the fire. "Let me guess," I say, pulling the quilt over us. "Your place has a white picket fence and flower garden."

Annie doesn't reply right away, and I get the sense she's thinking about something else.

"Tell me what needs to be done on your house," I ask hastily. "I'm pretty handy, you know."

She places her head on my chest, listening to my heartbeat. "Hmm," she sighs. "There's some woodworking on the inside.

A greenhouse would be nice, too. Eventually we'll need a well."

"A well? You don't have running water?"

"No electricity, either."

Pulling her close, I imagine coming home after a day of work, a warm fire in the house as darkness falls, sitting down to dinner and curling up to a good book afterward, going to bed and making love with all the electricity of nothing between us—like I used to do for the thrill of taking a risk, only this time it would be for the right reason.

She moves on top of me until we're pressed together in a tight fit, both our hearts beating hard. I feel her desire and she feels mine. Neither of us gets ahead of the other.

We spend the night easing in and out of sleep. Three times I get up to put more wood on the fire. Each time I return, she squirms to get close so our bodies lock into place. When the flames grow high, I'm able to recognize the features of her face. But if the fire is low, it's not so easy. Sometimes my imagination gets the best of me, and I begin to see things in the shadows just as I did at the hermit's campfire. And as we each go in and out of sleep, it's like we're moving in and out of each other's dreams.

The next day we do pretty much the same. In the morning, I make coffee and scrambled eggs with toast and marmalade. Flashlight is to stop by with my final paycheck and go over what we need to do before leaving. After washing the dishes and tidying up the kitchen, I go through the house and put things in order—returning books to their rightful places in the study, straightening up the cupola, organizing the tools in the basement.

When Flashlight arrives, he gives Annie a list of things to do to close up the house: latch the windows, lock the garage door downstairs, unplug light fixtures, clean out the refrigerator, leave house keys on the kitchen counter. We're the only ones left on the compound, he says, the campers and counselors have all gone home. When he's finished with what he has to tell us, we shake hands and I thank him for all his help this summer. But I can tell there's more he wants to talk about. And I can pretty much guess what it is.

"Have you seen the latest population figures?" he begins. "We are well on our way to having 5 *billion* people on the planet. Did you know that when Europeans first arrived in North America, there were 5 billion passenger pigeons in the U.S. alone? And look what happened to them ...."

"Flashlight," I interrupt. I don't mean to be rude, and, yes, there have been times when I welcomed and perhaps even solicited his apocalyptic bulletins, but all summer he's badgered me with his doom and gloom and, well, there's only so much a man can take. At the very least, I figure I'm entitled to an observation or two.

"What am I supposed to think about all this bad news?" I say. "I mean, if all these disasters are going to happen and it's a done deal, then what's the point? There's roads and cars and buildings everywhere you look ... those things aren't just going to go away over night. What am I supposed to do?"

As if on cue his footloose eyeball begins to wander, and I feel bad that maybe I triggered it. It's as though he's watching someone walk behind me, someone or something that only he can see. Whatever it is, it appears he's tuned me out.

I'm going to miss Flashlight, his bizarre musings and wayward eye. He's part of the charm of this place, one of the characters in a cast of crazies.

For the rest of the day, Annie and I work in the living room. She sits on the floor with all the field notes spread out in front of her while I lie in the love seat, putting the finishing touches on the journal, making a few changes so it reads better. She's been working on the "Exit Form," a worksheet that compiles all the data into a basic statistical analysis: how many lakes covered, how many nests found, where we saw loons, how many chicks hatched, etc. All that remains to do is revisit the lakes where we saw nests and check on the clutches. Annie knows the precise location of all the nests, so it shouldn't take long to complete the task. She could even do it alone, if she had to. In any case, it should only take a few days to finish. She could be back in Albany by the end of the week.

"You're going to have to leave the journal, you know."

I stop writing and look up.

"I know how attached you've become to it."

She joins me in the love seat, and together we listen to the rain falling on the copper roof overhead.

ON THE THIRD DAY, the rain slackens and the storm clouds begin to break apart. The clouds move furiously through the sky, dispersing and collecting, just as they did that day in May when we drove up from Albany.

Roy is due at Colby sometime before dark, and I want to get off the grounds before he arrives. It's bad enough as it is, I don't need to see my replacement get settled in. Annie will spend the day going through more forms and mapping out a strategy for the coming week. We might not talk for a few days, she says.

We say goodbye in the foyer of the front door. The rain starts up again, so I tell her to stay inside and not bother about coming out. I grab my pack and walk out the door, taking one last look behind. Annie's moved to the window, where she smiles behind the runnels of rain pouring down the pane of glass.

In a way, it's a relief to be outside and away from the house. These last few days have been pretty intense, and it's good to be walking in the fresh air. I bid the old spook house farewell and start down the path around the lake, sidestepping a large puddle not far from the fallen tree where I sat the first night trying to blend in with the darkness. Now I bet I could find my way blindfolded through these woods. I start across the train tracks to the sound of falling rain, locking into a rhythm on the wet creosote ties. Feeling carefree and confident, the swagger back in my step.

Any hope I had of the clouds parting is put to rest when I get a good look at the sky over the trees in the northeast. A massive thunderhead gathers above the mountains. The storm isn't moving off at all, only intensifying for another assault.

In town, I check the schedule at the market to see when the bus leaves for Albany. Behind the counter, the reticent clerk looks at me over the top of his reading glasses. That's right, I think to myself, I'm leaving town. But it's not what you think, oh wise one. Nope, now I have my ducks in a row, my life in order, my priorities straight.

"Much obliged," I say to the man, slapping my hand on the counter for good measure. My way of sealing the deal.

He stares back with a blank expression.

I have a few hours to kill before the bus arrives, and for a moment I consider walking back to Colby to be with Annie a while longer. But I decide to leave it be. I'm tired and in need of a break from everything. Besides, there's something about that last image of her, smiling with the rain running down the window, that tells me I ought to leave it at that.

I figure I'll go for a walk instead, no matter that it's raining. My slicker keeps me dry, and besides, I'm a man of the elements now. A seasoned ranger of the high country. I get it in my mind to hike to the top of Baker Mountain where Annie and I spent an afternoon earlier in the summer, but the rumble of thunder convinces me otherwise. So I decide on McKenzie, instead. I walk the back streets through town, but not because I want to stay out of sight. Nope, no more of that. I have a plan now. Direction and prospects. I take the back streets for the one and only reason that I find them more interesting than the main drag.

Eventually I get to the two-track and start down the trail for the lake, slogging through mud, waiting for the clouds to part so I can enjoy one last view of the peak. But the sky grows worse, dark and threatening, and it's clear that it's only a matter of time before all hell breaks loose. I guess I should have known better, nothing is ever the same the second time around. By the time I turn around and walk back to town, the rain is driving hard with flashes of lightning and thunder.

With nothing else to do, I duck into the Waterhole to escape the storm and wait for the bus to arrive, checking to see who might be hanging around. But only Wire is there, standing behind the copper bar. It occurs to me I haven't been in the Hole in quite some time, but it seems word has gotten around about me. From the Acid Rangers, no doubt. Wire has me pegged before I even sit down at the bar.

"On the house," he says, sliding a draft my way.

I find a stool and tip the mug in salute.

He picks up a beer glass and begins to dry it with a dish towel.

"Here's to a good summer," I say.

He dries a second glass and looks out the front window. I glance at the painting with the moose, thinking about Snowhare's long story and his friend who tied a bow line to the antlers, wondering how the story ends. Guess I'll never know. Then it sinks in that this might be the last time I'm ever in the Waterhole. So I study it hard: the pool table and phone booth, the steps leading up to the porch, the box of geraniums and bench seats outside, all the junk hanging from the 12-point, and, of course, the long dimpled copper bar. By the time I'm done with my inventory, I've damned near finished my beer.

"Another?"

"Sure, why not."

He slides a fresh mug my way then returns to drying glasses.

"My work is done here," I say. "Just killing time."

Strange that I may never be here again.

"Guess I won't be forgetting this place anytime soon," I say.

Wire looks up for a moment and nods. But it's clear that if there's going to be any chitchat, yours truly is going to have to do the honors.

"I gotta tell you the truth," I begin. "I wasn't so sure about this town when I first arrived. Thought it was just another backwater. More like a quagmire."

He stops what he's doing and looks at me.

"I liked the bar, don't get me wrong," I say, putting my hands up like he just pulled a gun on me. "I liked it the first night I came in—everybody partying on the houseboat, Snowhare does his loon wail, all the stuff hanging over the back bar ...."

But I run out of steam. It appears I've lost my knack for barroom banter—the price you pay for sticking to the straight and narrow.

Wire pours a shot of rye whiskey and places it in front of me. He seems especially calm today. I've never seen him so methodical.

"Sometimes it gets to be too much, and a man has to forget himself for a while," he says.

"Isn't that the truth?" I reply, raising the shot glass to throw back the whiskey. "Anyway, the town grew on me little by little. And, well, now it feels like home. With you and Spot and Snow and Yukon and all the other characters around here, I feel like I fit right in. Everybody in this town is boiled down to the bare essence of who they are, and no one bothers to pretend otherwise. Everybody's fine with their own particular brand of weirdness."

I take a big gulp of beer, set the mug down on the bar, pick it up again and drain the glass.

The pressure is off, summer is over. It feels like I've been holding my breath for three months and now I can let it out. All the DEC business is behind me, I have found true love, and the bus will be here any minute to whisk me out of town on my way to happily-ever-after. For the first time in a long while, I feel ahead of the game.

"You're looking at a changed man," I say, as Wire brings me another beer. "A redeemed roustabout. A *re*-formed reprobate."

I take a moment to consider the sound of my words.

"You know, I've learned a few things since I've been here. I've learned that you have to trust in things. We're all different and sparks are gonna fly from time to time, but that's okay. There's plenty of room for everybody and every*thing* in this world. It's all part of the grand design. I might not understand how it works half the time, but I gotta have faith that everything happens for a reason. Everything has a purpose, a place."

I make a sweeping circle with my hand, encompassing the entire room: the pool table with bottle rings stained on the green felt, the empty cardboard cases stacked in the corner, the phone booth that smells like piss.

"All of this ..." I say. "A place for everything and everything in its place. Just as it was meant to be. Whatever happens to be is the best. It *has* to be. Think about it, why should there be anything when it seems just as likely that there should be nothing at all? I mean, who are we to judge? An asteroid could hit the earth this very minute and wipe us all out. We could be sucked into a black hole or zapped by gamma rays from deep space. Now that's something a guy can hang his hat on."

I wait for him to respond, but there's no reply.

"Now I'm not sayin' there's a god or anything," I continue, "not like some old guy with a white flowing beard perched in a high chair. Not like that. But if you have the right feeling inside, then it makes you want to do good just for the sake of doing good. Ya know what I mean?"

Now it's coming back, my words flowing like honey. Tongue properly loosened, a warm glow from the whiskey, and just like that I'm feeling gabby.

"Of course, it was Annie that got me straightened out. She showed me how to do right by the animals and birds. Everything is *alive* out there in the woods, all of it *aware* with intention. Not only that, but there's a constant conversation going on. Birds and animals and plants, all jabberin' away as they go about their business. Spirits, too. Spirits are afoot in this world, they're mixed up in everything. All of this is going on around us *all the time*. It's all part of a big mystery where everything is connected, all space and time. All of it energy, and if you know how ...."

I can see I'm losing my audience.

"Anyway, the point is, there's no need to be lonesome in this world. Not with all the birds and animals and trees and clouds. You just have to keep your heart open, stay humble and reverent. *Circumspection*," I say, leaning closer, "that's the key."

Wire goes back to drying glasses. "You know, I never took you for much of a talker, always hanging back on the edges, but now that I look at it, I'd say you have potential."

"Why thank you, Wire," I reply. "I'll take that as a compliment."

Could be we're both getting a little soft in the head. But so what, the occasion calls for it. All those weeks of chomping at the bit to get out of here, and now the moment has arrived and I'm feeling bittersweet. I tip the mug in commemoration, guzzling the backwash at the bottom of the glass.

"Guess I have time for one more."

Wire already has a mug out, ready to pull the spout, when he stops and looks out of the window. I swivel on my barstool in time to see Snowhare's van pull to the curb. He jumps out of the driver's seat with the engine still running and charges through the swinging doors, marches straight up to me and grabs my arm. "Come on," he says, "we're going."

"Whoa, brother," I say, leaning back. "Haven't you heard? This loon ranger is history. Bus leaves in twenty minutes, see? I'm having my last ceremonial beer. Sit down and I'll buy you one."

"No," he says. "We have to go *now*."

There's something in the way he says it that makes me go silent, so I follow him outside and climb into the van. We start out of town when he tells me that he picked up an emergency call on his scanner, from the fishery station at Heart Pond. Some kind of accident on the lake. What kind of accident, I ask, was it Fowler? He can't say. The reception wasn't that good and he could only hear part of the conversation.

… and then it's like the dream again, where I'm caught in slow-motion in the middle of a dark highway, headlights bearing down on me, and I can't get to safety on the other side …

I look at Snow with his hands locked on the wheel, trying to get my head straight, feeling the alcohol buzz give way to the bile rising in my stomach. An ambulance drives toward us in the oncoming lane, passing us at a pretty good speed, but not really so fast either. Red lights flashing, no siren. I follow it in the rearview mirror until it disappears around a bend in the highway.

… like I'm stuck in quicksand, headlights coming fast, and all around the land is dark.

We turn onto the dirt road leading to Heart, splashing through mud puddles, fishtailing through the curves until the parking lot comes into view, clogged with DEC trucks and police cars. Down by the water, I see the white CO truck with the Whaler on its trailer, parked next to the canoe. Fowler seems to be the center of attention, talking to Bradley and a state cop, waving his hands in the air like he's trying to convince them of something ... *and it seems only yesterday I stood here on a warm sultry morning, the black-and-white feathers of a loon folded beneath my fingers, summer at its frenzied best with blooming wildflowers and buzzing insects, trees waving in the breeze like Egyptian fans ...*

When Snowhare stops the van, I bolt from my seat and start across the lot toward Fowler and the state trooper who looks up from his notepad. There are others on the periphery—DEC agents and town cops. They turn away one by one as I come closer, their voices muffled and distorted as if spoken underwater ... feeling smaller with each step I take, everything slowing down (... *the film sputtering in the projector, the voice-over slowing, dropping in pitch at the still point between thunderstorm and sunlight streaming through broken skies—skies that brighten even now along the western horizon, where the Adirondacks give way to the prairie and plains and Rockies beyond ... all in a dream with a soft rain falling, dimpling the lake surface.*)

And then the movie speeds up again as Fowler resumes his harangue.

"I told her not to go out there," he exclaims. " 'This is Fisheries,' I said. 'You don't have the right ....' "

But the trooper is no longer listening, looking at me instead. Fowler stops talking, jolted into silence by his own words. Everyone is staring, the cops and COs and

DEC, waiting for me to say something. Do something. But it's different now. I'm no longer one of them.

"I said 'don't go out there,'" Fowler explains, now pleading his case to me. "But it was like I wasn't there, she never even looked at me. She just paddled out past the islands ...."

Snow takes a step in my direction, scanning the crowd. "Come on," he says, taking my arm. "Let's get outta here."

As I turn to leave, Stryker puts his hand on my shoulder, just firm enough to let me know his meaning. "Be sure to stick around a few days," he says for everyone to hear. "We'll be in touch."

I pat my pant pocket out of habit. I realize I still have my keys, so I get Snow to help me load the battered canoe onto the Impala, then follow him out to the highway.

By the time I get back to town, the rain has stopped and the wind has picked up again. And why not? All went according to plan: the storm rolled in, hit where it was supposed to, and moved off. It seems everything has a role in this little drama and knows its place. Everything, that is, but me.

All I know is that I have to see Annie. I drive straight to the hospital and walk into the emergency room where a nurse sitting behind the counter asks my name. When I hesitate, she says that only family members are allowed in. A cop stands by the swinging doors that lead inside, listening to our conversation. He packs a .38, and I'm just not in the mood to deal. I tell the nurse, stout in her starched uniform, that I'm a friend of Annie's. She shakes her head slightly, glances out the window at the large brownstone across the parking lot, then tells me she can't divulge that information.

It's nearly dark when I turn into Colby and shine the headlights on the two faces that have greeted me all summer long. The embossed masks are distorted by shadows, their expressions exaggerated and grotesque. A chill runs down my spine like a breath of cold air on my neck.

It all makes sense now. The two masks: one a jester's smile, the other a picture of horror. It's simply a matter of seeing things for what they truly are. Most times we're only privy to the little jokes—the in-between jokes that show us the folly of our efforts and make us laugh. How silly, we think, how life makes fools of us all. But sooner or later, it's the big joke that gets the last laugh. We're given no more trouble than we can bear, people say. But this is just more of the same joke.

Not five minutes after I walk in the door, the phone rings upstairs. It's Frank. He's been calling nonstop, he tells me, since he received the news from Ray Brook. Thank god you're there, he says, thank *gawd*. I can see him in his cluttered office, feet up on the desk, and I'm reminded of the day back in May when I sat across the table from Annie in the conference room with the rain pouring down outside. After taking just the right amount of time to express how bad he feels and how unfortunate it is that something like this could happen, especially to someone like Annie, he gets down to the real reason he's called.

"Listen," he says, drawing a breath. "I'm going to need someone to collect the last of the data and bring it in, and you're the best person to do that. You know the research and what needs to be done to finish the job."

I don't have anything against Frank personally, other than he's a hopeless bureaucrat who can cover his ass with the best of them.

I remind him that he's already fired me.

"I know, I know," he says. "Listen, I'll make you a deal. You finish the survey, close up the house at Colby, drive the car down here with all the data, and I'll see to it that you're back in good standing with us. A clean slate."

I can't believe it. He's giving me another chance.

"What about the assault charge?"

"I'll make it go away."

"You can't do that," I say.

"Oh, yes I can."

The whole thing stinks and I know it. But I have nothing to lose and it seems like the easiest way out.

"I know a magistrate who might be interested in all of this," he says.

So I agree to the arrangement and hang up the phone, take a seat on the floor with my back against the rucksack and run through the reasons why I shouldn't get up and do all the things I know I'm going to do anyway. But none of it changes the fact that I should have been with Annie today. I let her down. I couldn't even keep a goddamn job in the woods, for chrissakes. There must be something I can do to make things right again ... *keep moving* ... make everything the way it was ... *run fast enough* ...

And then the power goes out.

Everything's quiet, with only the sound of the wind outside. Objects materialize in the dark, as my eyes slowly adjust. I can see the dim outline of the banister leading down the staircase to the front door. It occurs to me that I'm the only one on the grounds tonight, all the campers and counselors have gone home.

I rise and start for the candle in the cupola when a flash of lightning brightens the inside of the house, casting shadows of windblown trees, before everything goes dark again. The sound of distant thunder comes on slowly, echoing through the mountains.

As I approach the cupola door, I hear a noise coming from inside the room—a shrill repetitive sound like the squeaky wheel of an old-fashioned sewing machine. I turn the knob and push against the door, but something resists from the other side as though someone doesn't want me to enter. The squeaky wheel on the treadle machine turns faster, round and round. I force the door open and step inside when … *I'm attacked by a swarm of albino bats, flying around the room like debris caught in a tornado!*

I reach down and snatch one from my shoe, and realize that they're not bats at all, but rather pieces of paper blown around the room. By opening the door, I created a wind vacuum that swept the field forms off the desk.

I lunge for the window and yank the stick free so it closes with a thud. Then I reach for the door and slam it shut. Sealed off from both the storm and the house, I take a moment to gather my wits. A tree branch scratches at the window outside. That explains the sound of a squeaky wheel. As for all the paper, Annie must have returned the survey forms upstairs.

A flash of lightning freezes everything in place like a still frame on a strip of celluloid—the walls, the paper, the chest of drawers on the desk.

I open the lower drawer and find the half-burned candle and book of matches exactly as I left them. Out of habit, I check the doors of redemption and, to my surprise, find leftovers in all three. In all the bustle of packing up and moving out, I forgot about my stash. It's been weeks since I last dipped into the doors, not since Annie and I became serious. But now, I can't imagine bumping into a better friend—the one *compadre* that has seen me through thick and thin.

I take stock of the inventory. Probably not enough to kill my misery, but certainly enough to make a dent: a few scraps of psilocybin, enough blow for a half line, a pinch of weed at the bottom of the canister. I mix it all together—powder, stems, stalks and caps—tamp it down in the one-hit and bring it to an orange glow. By the time I exhale, I can feel the chemicals circulating through my brain, taking the edge off. Safe in my little cocoon, I strike a second match and take another hit. Then a third.

The dregs of my stash prove stronger than I anticipated. Thinking I'd be lucky to catch any buzz at all, I underestimated how much of a punch they'd pack. In no time at all, I'm high as a kite—higher than I want to be. I grab handfuls of paper off the floor and throw them onto the desk, trying to restore some kind of order, but it only makes matters worse. The pages slip from my hand, lie crumpled on the floor, and suddenly I'm back at the conference table in Albany with protocol and memoranda piling up in front of me. The walls begin to cave, paranoia seeps in at the edges.

I grab the candle and matches and rush into the hallway, bounding down the stairs to the living room when another burst of lightning flashes in the windows, illuminating the grandfather clock and high-back chairs and painted portraits. Griffith, Buckminster, Taylor, and the rest. Patrons of the arts, ruthless barons of capital—watching me from the wall with their murderous schemes of empire.

I round the corner of the staircase just as a low rumble of thunder rattles the windowpanes, hurrying down the crooked hallway until I come to the basement door where I stop to light the candle. Turning the knob slowly, I hold the flame away from the gasp of cold air that rushes into the hallway. Stepping into the darkness, cupping my hand around the burning candle, I start down the stairs. The candlelight shines only as far as the next step, and it's mostly only me that I see in the dark.

Down through the cobwebs into the dank basement, the air becoming thicker and colder with each step. Lightning flickers in the two windows of the garage door like blinking eyes. With the help of the candlelight, I inch my way along the unfinished wall, using the studs and coated wires for balance, until I enter the room of old furniture where the breaker panel is.

Since that first day with Flashlight, I never paid much attention to this room, preferring to ignore it altogether. Now, in the glow of the candlelight, I wend my way around marble side-tables, cabinets, velvet armchairs and leather sofas. All the while, shadows jump when the flame flickers. I cup my hands around the candle, shielding it from the drafty air. The play of shadow and light in the room creates its own effect, and it's tough to see anything clearly.

The breaker box is mounted on the back wall. A half-dozen frayed wires sprout from the top, each crimped at the end. I open the metal door to inspect the fuses. The panel is old and there's no disconnect switch—only two columns of plug fuses, and below that, the two main cartridge fuses. In the dim candlelight, I remove the cartridge fuses one at a time, carefully pulling them free of the tension clip. I check the amp rating and look for any spares that might be close by, running my finger across the dirty top of the metal box, then lowering the candle to the hard-packed dirt floor. Nothing.

I turn and start for the workbench in the garage, thinking I might find some fuses there, when a draft of cold air brushes my neck and *extinguishes the candle.*

The wind moans outside, buffeting the aluminum garage door. Lightning flickers in the basement like the lead-in frames of an old movie, counting down the numbers: *five, four, three, two* ... when a bright flash lights up the entire garage with a thunderous *BOOM!* I turn to see the two-garage windows wink at me, framed perfectly by the open doorway, and for a split second it's as if *I'm looking directly into a face!*

The shock of recognition freezes me in place, until the windows go dim again and I drop the candle, scrambling for the stairs in the dark. I stumble and lose my balance, knocking over a floor lamp before hitting the ground. I scurry across the dirt floor to the bottom step, then climb the stairs on all fours to the top, collapsing on the red carpet in the hallway ... jumping to my feet and running down the crooked hall, rounding the last corner just as lightning flashes in the windows, reflecting off the wooden floor at the bottom of the staircase. I grab the banister and spin myself around, starting up the stairs, ready to grab my pack and get the hell out of there, when I stop dead in my tracks. *There's something at the top of the stairs.* I can't see it, but I can feel it ... *something in the dark watching me.*

I wait on the bottom steps, my heart racing.

To the sound of soft footfalls, it seems, a woman moves away in the direction of the hallway. I climb the stairs and peer into the darkness, seeing only the flecks of electrical impulses from my own eyes. But something keeps me there in the dark, some kind of magnetic attraction.

I keep still, watching.

Overhead is the door to the attic, and it seems I have a choice: give myself up to the darkness once and for all, or step back and soldier on in this hopeless dying world where nothing makes any sense.

I wait, looking for a sign. The slightest sigh or whisper, and I follow her down the hall and don't look back.

But there's nothing, and I'm left wondering if it's all just a figment of my imagination, fueled by the cocktail of psychoactive scraps cooked up in the cupola. Nothing but a mirage gleaned from the three doors of redemption and an excited electromagnetic field. As far as I can see, there is no one in the hall, and I go no further than where I stand.

I pull on the rope that lowers the unfolding stairs, climb up, and gather the cardboard boxes we stowed there in May. I take one of the boxes into Annie's bedroom and close the door behind me, crossing the room to her dresser where I begin packing her clothes, starting with the top drawer and her socks—two sets of woolies and a number of ankle socks balled up in pairs. I make my way through the drawers to her shorts and jeans, tank tops and tee-shirts and long-sleeve flannels.

At the back of the bottom drawer, wedged behind a rag sweater, I find an envelope stuffed with letters and photographs. I hesitate for a moment, uncertain whether she would want me to dig into her personal items. By now the wind has died down and it seems the storm is moving off, even as lightning continues to throb along the horizon in a long flickering strobe.

I sit at the bottom of her bed by the window and open the envelope, using the glow from the lightning to see the words. There's one letter postmarked in California from a friend who wants her to come live with him. He's ready to settle down, he says, and make a home. Raise a family. No more fighting hopeless battles and lost causes.

The rest of the letters are from her grandmother, dated years earlier. Life stuff, mainly, with a few pearls of wisdom tossed in. Love, faith, trust ... that sort of thing. But the handwriting is shaky, and it's difficult to read in the unsteady light.

There are two photos with the letters. One is a black-and-white of Annie when she was a little girl, wearing an oversized cowboy hat, sitting on a pony with a long blond mane. The other is of her riding in a Zodiac, speeding over ocean waves. From her action days, no doubt. She's wearing a black wetsuit, her hair blowing behind her. Her gaze is steady, calm.

I stuff the photos and letters back inside the envelope and toss it into the box with her clothes. Looking around the room for anything I might have missed, I spy the music box on the nightstand.

I know I'm pushing it by staying in her room, surrounded by all her things. I'm taking chances I can't afford to take. Still, I move to the top of the bed and pick up the little wooden box, studying the colorful carousel painted on the top, turning the knob on the bottom until it's wound-tight and the chiming bells begin to play. When it winds itself down, I play it again—the song I know by heart from the ice cream truck that would drive through our neighborhood when I was a kid.

But when all the braves returned,
The heart of Red Wing yearned,
For her warrior, far away,
Had fell bravely in the fray

I play the song three more times as bursts of lightning flash in the distance, capturing the night in still frames like snapshots of memory. The storm has passed, the wind is down. There's only the pitiless death throes of silent lightning.

When I return to the cupola I clear a space on the floor near the window and move the chair against the wall. The room is a mess, papers and maps everywhere. Seated in the chair, back against the wall, I prop the window open and assume my familiar position.

Outside, a crescent moon peeks through the restless clouds. Three days of rain and I'd forgotten all about it. But now it shines pretty-as-you-please, casting a frosty glow over the mountains, like it would have me believe everything is back to normal and tomorrow Annie and I will be on the water again in the canoe, checking on loons, watching them go about their business. Only I know better. I feel as though I've awakened from a dream to find myself in a nightmare, and the harder I try to get back to where I was, the further away I get. It's as if everything that's happened this summer never even existed. No Waterhole. No loons. No Annie.

I slam the back of my head against the wall.

Tough guy. The fighting, the drinking, the running. Big tough guy. *And now here you are.* All these years of honoring the credo and what's there to show for it besides the lead role in a dumbass B drama that nobody gives a damn about anyway. *And why should you care?* A role that's played me every bit as much as I've played it. *What's in it for you, anyway?* All this time too busy gutting it out and going it alone to know any different. And for what, to be sitting in the dark in some backwater spook house ... *it just goes to show* ... alone with nothing ... *run fast enough* ... less than nothing ....

And that's when I hear the loon. A wail rising in the moonlight across the lake, piercing a hole in the darkness. My brother, the loon! Lunatic prophet freak. Fallen warrior caught between worlds. And it's as if I fall through the hole myself, slip through the spaces-in-between into a world unseen ....

I look around the room. Paper is scattered everywhere. I sweep the desk clean with my hand, grabbing loose pages off the floor, organizing them into two piles, one for the maps and field notes and the other for the forms. Buried at the bottom of everything is the black-and-white journal. I'd nearly forgotten about it.

Once I have all the papers in order, I place the two piles side-by-side in a cardboard box. Scanning the room, looking for something else to do, something mindless to buy a little time, I decide to catch up on the journal.

I flip to the first empty page at the back and begin to write, picking up the story the last night Annie and I were in the house. I go at it feverishly, scribbling like a madman. With the door closed, the cupola feels like a cocoon again, sealed off from the world. I'm writing along, fast as I can, when suddenly *the words come alive on the page.* I put the pen down and remind myself that they're only dead letters on paper, nothing but chicken scratch on parchment. But it doesn't help. The words are alive with a power all their own. They're *aware* of me in ways I can barely understand. I'm caught in an enormous web and the more I try to free myself, the more entangled I become until it's clear that the best option is to stop fighting. In the moonlight, fueled by my goodies and guilt and god knows what else, I bring the journal up to date.

Time is getting short and there's nothing more to do. I put the journal away and walk downstairs, open the front door and step into the night—picking up the path through the woods, passing in and out of the moonlight, continuing around the lake to the low trestle spanning the water. I walk the railroad track one tie at a time until I'm all the way across, breathing hard now, telling myself to slow down. At the edge of town, a streetlight hums in the still air. A raccoon disappears into a water drain along the curb.

I follow a backstreet up the hill to the parking lot outside the hospital entrance, remembering the subtle glance of the nurse. Inside, the reception desk is brightly lit, but no one is there. I keep to the grass at the edge of the lot, careful to stay in the shadows, walking around the side of the brownstone building past the spruce trees until I come to three windows at ground level. The windows are the old kind, iron frames and soldered sashes. One is ajar. I slit the screen with my pocketknife, reach in and free the latches. After removing the screen, I open the window far enough to lower myself inside and drop down to the floor.

The room is dark, too dark to see very far. Sliding my hand along the painted cinderblock wall, I make my way around the room until I find a switch plate and snap on the light. The room comes alive with the buzz of fluorescent lights, and it takes a moment for my eyes to adjust. Close by is a long wooden table with a vinyl covering draped over it. Along the far wall, six large cabinets are set in steel housing, each with its own handle.

I start at the top right corner, turn the steel handle and pull. The empty cabinet slides out on tracks. I work my way horizontally along the top until I come to the third cabinet door. This one's different—more weight inside and harder to open. I pull the cabinet forward, unzip the black plastic bag and look inside. White disheveled hair, gray skin, vacant expression ... an old man, dead as can be. I zip him up and continue on.

Annie is bottom center. I barely get the zipper open when I recognize the slope of her neck and the way her hair falls across her shoulder. But what catches my breath is the subtle trace of a smile. Even now, the gypsy grin.

I pick her up, carry her to the table, and lay her on the vinyl covering. Then I unzip the bag all the way and slide it down past her shoulders and arms, around her hips and legs, and over her feet. She wears a cotton hospital gown, nothing else. I open the gown wide enough to see the red bruise on her back. Her skin is cold, but it's Annie alright.

On the shelf above the table is a stack of folded blankets. I take one down and shake it out. Then I shut off the light, get myself ready, and return to the table to lie beside her under the blanket.

A trace of gray fills the window. I figure there's at least an hour or so before hospital personnel arrive for work. I'm not sure what to say, so mostly I'm quiet. Just lie there. I think about what Flashlight told me, how electricity continues to travel through the body even after the heart has stopped beating. So, in a sense, Annie is still here, merely in a state of transition. But it's more than that. I feel her presence.

I put my head next to hers. *What's it like?* I whisper.

Electricity still firing, I wonder what else may be working. I try moving her arm to see how flexible she is. Her hands work, too. The skin is smooth and white and beginning to harden. It's only been ten hours since Heart Pond, and I know it's just a matter of time. Her skin is like clay that's been left out a while, cold and slightly pliable.

But the table is uncomfortable, too narrow for the both of us, so I slide her on top of me until our bodies fit together and she's resting her head on my chest, her ear to my heart. I adjust her hips so it's comfortable, and I don't ever want to leave. I want us to be preserved this way forever, like lovers in Pompeii who died in their sleep when the volcano erupted and buried them in lava, preserving them for all eternity in a loving embrace. The two of us immortalized in stone to be discovered thousands of years later by some weird new species—evolved from a cockroach, no doubt. I hold her close so her hair falls over me, as if all these years of drifting and wandering have been leading up to this one moment. I kiss her once, holding her in my arms, and *now I understand*. It's as if I have journeyed to some forbidden land and returned with a deeper awareness. What I loved is gone, and the world will never be the same. And it's as though I have died, too. If I came here thinking I could recover something that was lost, I leave with a whole new understanding. I am home now, grateful to see her one last time and wish her farewell.

I stay as long as I can, until the first birds of morning fill the room with song before crawling out the window and making my way back to camp. As I'm crossing the trestle, the sun rises over the trees in the east, shooting orange flares across the lake.

Back in the house, I return to the journal and bring it up to date, filling in gaps and smoothing out rough spots. I enter everything I can remember and even some things I don't. When I'm done, I pack the journal in the box and tape the whole thing shut. This goes to Albany. I'm not going to be like those other guys and withhold the data on account of some petty bone to pick. Annie and I did our job. We did it the best that we could, and now it's out of our hands.

After moving the box to the top of the stairs, I walk through the house, searching each room, looking for anything we might have forgotten. I return to the cupola, checking the drawers one last time, making sure I'm not leaving anything behind. I find nothing. But something doesn't feel right, like I'm forgetting something. It gnaws on me as I carry the box down to the driveway and load it in the Impala along with Annie's things and my rucksack. Chalk it up to mental fatigue. Not surprising, given the fact I haven't slept in a few days.

Closing the front door behind me, I hear a familiar sound: the *clunk-clunk-clunk* of the sapsucker rapping his beak on the copper roof. He goes about it like he always has, determined as ever, blinded by an unshakable conviction despite the obvious futility. "I hear you, brother," I say when he pauses. My words sound strange. This is the first I've spoken since the morgue.

The plan is to take the highway north out of town, swing through Gabriels and Upper Saint Regis to check on a few nests, then make my way east to the Northway where I'll turn south for Albany, deliver the boxes to Frank, and be on my way.

I turn right at the entrance and cruise through town, passing the storefronts and deli, peering through the open doorway at the Waterhole to the barstool inside where only yesterday I sat thinking of a life with Annie. I turn off the main drag and wheel through the backstreets, heading north.

The further I get from town, the more I think about what's been gnawing at me, the loose end I can't put my finger on. It has something to do with all the chaos of yesterday. From the moment Snow charged through the swinging doors, everything seems a blur: the drive out to Heart, passing the ambulance, seeing all the vehicles in the parking lot, the long slow walk to the water, Fowler waving his arms as the cop scribbled in his tablet. *It was something he said.* The cop stopped writing and turned to look at me just as Fowler mentioned he saw Annie *out past the islands.* But why would she paddle *past* the islands, away from the nest? There was no trail or other nest there that I remember. It wasn't even the quickest way off the lake in a thunderstorm. And another thing: Fowler had spoken to her before she went out on the lake. He knew what she was there to do. But what was said? Why was he so adamant about warning her? And what was so urgent that she needed to go *then?* We hadn't spoken a word about Heart in the morning. What was so important that she had to paddle out in the middle of a lightning storm? She must have learned something in the hours after I left. But what? And where was she going? *What was she doing on the far side the lake?*

And then it hits me—hits me like a silver bullet between the eyes. And everything comes to a stop. A complete, screeching *STOP.*

I'm five miles out of town when I slam on the brakes, lean back and rip the tape off the cardboard box. Annie must have consulted the journal before going to check on all the mating pairs; she must have read the entries on the lakes where we found nests. Oh, Christ.

Parked along the road with the sun shining brightly, I start at the beginning of the journal and work my way forward, looking for anything on Heart. I find the entry describing the first time we were there and read it through, stopping at one paragraph:

> As we're paddling along the far shore, I notice a small makeshift dam—more like an improvised fish barrier and spillway—constructed at the outlet where a brook drops down into the woods. The construction is rather primitive, just some concrete, an iron frame, and two-by-twelves stacked on top of one another to hold back the water. It occurs to me all someone would have to do is to slide one of the planks free to lower the lake level by a foot or so.

In the ten minutes it takes me to drive the twelve miles to Heart, I think about Annie and the others I'd met this summer—Frank and the COs, Fowler and the Ray Brook bureaucrats, Flashlight and the Acid Rangers .... And as things come clear, I think about me too.

The world is going to hell, alright. It's one thing to talk tall from a safe distance—I can do this as well as anyone—but when it really gets down to it, who's willing to put everything on the line and do something about it? It's much easier just to punch the clock and go home, take the money and walk. Be a good soldier and keep your mouth shut. We slave away in the service of a runaway machine devouring everything in its path, each of us doing our part to trash the planet and drag half of god's creation with us. And no one gives a rat's ass because there's always someone right behind us ready to take our place.

Always someone else to do the job if we don't.

It's a lonely business to give a damn, especially when everyone around you is doing their godawful best to get ahead—too fixated on the pissant task at hand to care about the big picture and where it's all going. Lawyers, bankers, politicians, developers, technocrats ... all just doing their jobs, signing off to business-as-usual, hiding behind protocol, covering their asses when necessary. I can hear them now, all demanding their rights. Greed, conformity, obedience ... these are the values that carry the day, the idols we bow down to. Add a bit of willful ignorance and smug cynicism, and there you have it. Meanwhile, the world goes reasonably and properly to hell. Step by civilized step. Hard to recognize until it comes time to settle accounts. It's like the parboiled frog who doesn't see what's coming because he hasn't noticed how the temperature has gone up little by little, day after day.

And this is why the planet is toast. This is why our days are numbered. The sun will flame out, that's a fact, but we'll do ourselves in long before then. We'll vaporize the world in a radioactive cloud, poison ourselves with petrochemicals from the inside out, go down at the hands of a rogue virus unleashed by some poor slash-and-burn dirt farmer in the Amazon. Hell, there's so many apocalyptic horsemen riding around, it's hard to keep track of them all: famine, war, overpopulation, pollution, acid rain, ozone holes, extinction ... and now we can add Flashlight's global warming to the mix. We have fouled the nest. Big time. Come too far too fast with too many people wanting too many things. It's a done deal. Fait accompli. We've blown our chance at paradise and hardly noticed. *Hardly even cared.*

And here's the kicker: we *know* all this. We *know* that the way we're living can't last, that it's driving us over the cliff. And yet we stay the course, fully aware of the insanity of living a lie. And this is how it's been with me. The rough-and-tumble rebel, too cool to care. Hiding behind a charade of devil-may-care kicks. Oh, I have the talk, alright. As good as anyone. A little rough around the edges, maybe, but deep down the same old sorry-ass drivel.

Back in July, when I was deciding where to take the reporter, I visited Heart Pond and later wrote that the lake level was high. Annie must have read this and figured that with all the recent rain, the levels had gone even higher. She must have thought she needed to check on the nest, that it couldn't wait. And when she got there, she must have realized that the nest was in danger. And now I know where she was going on the far shore. The spillway. She was going for the barrier dam.

I park the car at the edge of the water, free the straps and lift the canoe off the roof. Fowler's pickup is parked on the other side of the lot near the trees. I know he's watching from his house, maybe even placing a call right now.

The canoe and paddle ready to go, I return to the car and grab my pack. The box of forms stays—that belongs to the State of New York. On top of the box is the black-and-white journal. For a second I think about leaving it. After all, Frank said he wanted it at the end of the summer. But it's not his story, and it sure as hell doesn't belong to the State.

I close the door, letting my hand linger a while on the hood of the car. This is the last I'll see of the Impala, my trusty steed. I leave the keys on the seat and walk down to the lake, slide the canoe into the glassy water and set off.

There are dents in the hull from the storm. The gunwales are a bit crooked and the stern is cockeyed, too. But it still floats, that's the key. It still works.

By the time I reach the islands, the COs have arrived in their truck and joined Fowler in the parking lot. The three of them stand beside the boat trailer. They must figure like I do that it would take too long to get the Whaler into the water to make any difference.

Stryker starts down the shoreline, finding his way through the trees. He puts his hand on the butt of his .38, making sure I see.

"Come in *now!*" Fowler's voice booms across the calm lake, amplified by the wall of trees behind him.

"You don't have to yell," I reply. "I can hear you just fine."

"You're trespassing on state property!"

Bradley turns to look at him. "He said you don't have to yell."

"*Well?*" Fowler replies meekly.

I don't think either of them realizes that I can hear their conversation. There's not a breath of wind and their voices carry perfectly over the water. But they both know why I'm there.

Coming around the back side of the far island, I let the canoe drift through the shadows along the shore. A loon watches from the open water, twenty yards away. The other adult sits in the brush next to the nest and a solitary egg. A few feet away, a lone chick bobs in the wake of the canoe.

Annie was right—the lake level is higher than what it was a month ago. It's flooded the nest. Chances are the egg is a lost cause, but I don't care. I start for the far bank, the same place she was going. Paddling away from the island, I reenter the sunlight and come into view again of Fowler and the COs.

Stryker has picked up the pace, stepping quickly along the shore, hopping from rock to rock. The other two watch from the parking lot. "Radke," Fowler says across the water. "Don't do it!"

But it's too late. Too late for a lot of things. Too late for him because I've beaten him to the punch. Too late for me because I know a losing hand when I see one. And it's too late for the whole damn shootin' match because if I've learned anything, it's that you can't get back what is already lost. And that's why I am gone. I am long gone. Another time, another place, and it might have all been different. But none of it matters now.

The spillway is close. All that's left to do is land the canoe and be done with it. But something makes me stop. I can feel my breath getting short, the blood pounding in my ears. The rage rising inside me.

"You could've done something!" I yell back. "You had the chance. You could have done something and you didn't!"

Both of them stare before Bradley turns to Fowler, waiting for his reply.

"I'm not authorized to," he says finally. His voice rings in the air, clear as a bell. "This lake is for game fish, you know that. That takes precedence over non-game, and that includes loons."

"You had a choice, Fowler. You had a choice and you made it. And now here we are."

"I told her not to go out there," he pleads. "I *told* her."

And that's when I realize I'm standing in the canoe, not ten yards from the dam now, everything clear in the sunlight. It's a funny thing, the sun, when you don't see it for days and then suddenly it's there shining brightly, the sky so blue it hurts to look at it.

"What are you trying to prove, anyway?" he says. "What good do you think you're doing?"

"She was the only one of us ...."

"None of this is going to make a bit of difference, and you know it. You're only making it harder on yourself."

Out of the corner of my eye I see Stryker hurrying along the shore, getting closer.

"I know you talked to Frank last night," Fowler says. "I know what he said. This is your last chance, Radke. Do you hear me?"

"'Last chance?'" I stammer. "*Last chance?!*"

It must have been the way I said it because everything stops in place. Bradley and Fowler stand still in the parking lot, waiting. Even Stryker comes to a halt, watching from the rocks.

"*But don't you see?!*"

I look around at the ridge of mountains in the distance, the forested hills, the lake.

"All of this," I say with a big sweep of my hand. "All of this ... *a memory.*"

But how could I make them understand? How could I get them to *see?*

We all loved this place—the mountains and lakes and forests, the animals and birds. You'd think that would be enough, you'd think it would be that simple. But somewhere along the line it all got confused. How complicated and ass-backwards everything had become. And now there we were, caught at a crossroads none of us could fully understand or had the ghost of an idea how to solve. With no way out. As if it were fated long ago by forces reaching back to the beginning of time. All leading up to this one moment, this one place ....

"Make sure Albany gets the box of papers in the back seat of the car," I tell them. "It's for the loons." And that's the last I say.

I paddle over to the impoundment and go to work on the top plank, sliding it upward in the iron grooves. The water starts slowly at first, but with each tug it shoots through the dam to the spillway below, pouring into the brook that runs through the woods and out to the river where eventually it will flow into town. The surge will be more than enough to raise water levels, especially in the narrows where the river runs past the Rusty Nail. Maybe some of the gang will be there. Maybe they'll want to take advantage. I can see them now, doing back flips off the deck.

I pull the plank free and kick it loose, watching as it rushes down the spillway in the surging water. Then I remove a second plank, just for good measure. I leave the canoe on the bank, thinking about the weld job that held up all summer. And with the journal in hand, I swing the rucksack onto my back and disappear into the woods.

James McVey worked as a professor at the University of Colorado for twenty-five years, teaching classes in English and Creative Writing. In 1984, he worked as a wildlife biologist on a loon survey in the Adirondacks.

He is the author of four books, including *The Wild Upriver and Other Stories* (Arbutus Press, 2005) and *The Way Home: Essays on the Outside West* (The University of Utah Press, 2010).

Currently, he is the director of Victory Gardens, a nonprofit organization in Colorado dedicated to building local food systems in mountain communities.

For more information on his life and work, please visit www.jamesmcvey.org.